L.G. BURBANK
PRESENTS
LORDS OF DARKNESS

VOL: II
THE RUTHLESS

Gold Imprint
Medallion Press, Inc.
Florida, USA

Dedication

For all the loving miracles in my life:
Ed, Mary, Wendy, Worth and Leland,
Helen, James and of course, AliStar.

Published 2005 by Medallion Press, Inc.
225 Seabreeze Ave.
Palm Beach, FL 33480

The MEDALLION PRESS LOGO
is a registered tradmark of Medallion Press, Inc.

Printed in the United States of America

Library of Congress Cataloging-in-Publication Data

Burbank, L. G.
  The ruthless / L.G. Burbank.
    p. cm. -- (The lords of darkness series ; v. 2)
  ISBN 1-932815-21-X
  1. Vampires--Fiction. 2. Highlands (Scotland)--Fiction. 3. Egypt--Fiction.
I. Title.
  PS3602.U727R88 2005
  813'.6--dc22
                              2005019796

Acknowledgements:

My humble gratitude is extended to Adam for his brilliance, creativity and soul. This book shines because of you. And always to Sara for lending him to me.

I must also thank the official 'Manservant', JT, who put his own touches on this book. Thumbs up.

Deborah, thanks for keeping it real. For the belly laughs and grand adventures (think NYC).

CJ Hollenbach for Lir, only more human.

To my fellow authors of whom I have the utmost respect and awe for your individual works; Beth Ciotta for the smiles, sunshine and comic relief in this book; Scott Oden for the 'masterful' Hollows in the mines; Jennifer Macaire for WinterKil; Mary Stella for the dolphins and because she just rocks!

Another writer to be mentioned, Reggie (R. Scott Whitley) for his unflagging belief in my writing.

And to all the readers, fans and booksellers who have taken the time to blog with me and who've shown up at booksignings or hosted them. Thanks for allowing me to be someone other than Anne Rice or Bram Stoker. For accepting my own voice and my own tales. You continue to make it all worthwhile. Thanks, BIG time.

"L.G. Burbank is the successor to Anne Rice"
— *H. Klausner, Independent Reviewer*

"*The Lords of Darkness* saga takes you on a remarkable voyage of danger and discovery. It is great writing: primal, engaging, entertaining and fun. You feel yourself very much a part of Mordred's journey as his destiny unfolds. There is so much to learn... and so much to lose, each step of the way. *The Ruthless* thrusts the newly awakened Mordred (and the reader) into a wonderful new world, one well worth returning to. In the second volume of his adventures Mordred's exploits are truly epic... the stuff of myth! I can't wait to see what happens in volume three: *The Heartless* (coming October 2006)!

Move over Angel, Barnabas and Nick Knight! A new vampiric champion with a conscience now walks among us. And he kicks ass! L.G. Burbank has siezed my imagination more firmly than Anne Rice or Bram Stoker ever did. And now I hunger for more..."

— *Thor the Barbarian*
www.thorthebarbarian.com

L.G. BURBANK

PRESENTS

LORDS OF DARKNESS

VOL: II
THE
RUTHLESS

From Transylvania Mordred ascends to the heavenly realm of Valhalla.

From Valhalla Mordred descends to the hellish realm of Death's Kingdom

The Black Sea

TRANSYLVANIA

The Mediterranean Sea

Alexandria

The Adriatic Sea

Rome

Sicily

Late 1400's AD
THE JOURNEY OF
MORDRED SOULIS
FROM ALEXANDRIA
TO DEATH'S KINGDOM

Prologue

crid smoke filled Mordred's nostrils as he edged closer to the enormous wall of flame. He should be burning this close to the inferno. But while he could feel the fierce heat, he was in no danger from it. He was a vampyre.

A blanket of black smoke hovered, clinging to him, filling his eyes with darkness and shadow. The scent of death surrounded him, and nausea threatened when he recognized the smell of burning flesh. He inhaled and then coughed.

Mordred shivered. Something bad had happened here.

Peering through the flames that looked as though they might touch the sky, he saw wooden posts rising from the ground. A huge pile of kindling had been set around the base of the posts, kindling that now provided fuel for the leaping flames. There was not a living thing in sight.

Then he heard the familiar voice. "Mordred," it called to him, the sound almost lost in the great roaring of the inferno.

Mordred looked around to be sure he was alone then focused his mind on the flames. He commanded the fire to part, allowing him to see what it was hiding from him in its brilliance.

Ever so slowly the flames subsided, allowing Mordred to see into them. But the sight that met his eyes was so gruesome and so horrific; he broke his concentration and lost control of the flame. The inferno blazed anew, and in the center of this terrible conflagration, Jakob stood lashed to a pole. The flesh of his face and body had peeled away from the bone. His skull was a charred mass fused to his body by the ropes that bound him. Yet his voice entered Mordred's mind.

Mordred closed his eyes to the image, denying it, as if by doing so he might be able to turn back time and avert the tragedy.

He swallowed hard. He could not lose control of the fire now. He must create a pathway. He forced his breathing to slow and again commanded the flames to part. He then walked to Jakob's side.

His mentor's eyes were open, but Jakob was dead. He had been burned alive with several others. Mordred took in the hideous sight, recognizing the charred but still visible markings of the Templars on one unfortunate victim. The man who had taught so much about what was to come had been burned alive, along with the others of his order. But why? And if he was dead, how, had Mordred heard him?

"Seek your heritage, Mordred, and uncover your past. All is not as you have been told." Jakob's voice again. Confused, Mordred looked back at the burning figure, the fire coming ever closer to him.

"Do not mourn for me, Mordred. I am gone from this place. The quest is up to you alone now. You must not fail."

"Jakob, how can I hear you?"

"I leave this earthly plane, but my spirit will be with you when you need me. Go now, Mordred, you are in grave danger and must awaken."

"I don't understand? Who did this to you, and why?" Mordred wanted answers. He wanted to know who to kill.

But there was no response, only the crackling of the flames and the stench of burning flesh. Unsure as to what to do, Mordred remained gazing on the remains of the man who'd been like a father to him. Anguish filled him and Mordred fell to his knees. Something welled from deep within him, and he released it in an agonized moan.

And so Mordred keened for the dead man, letting his grief and anger explode in a discordant symphony of sounds. It wasn't until he felt his own skin begin to bubble that Mordred realized he's lost control of the flames, and he fled at last.

His vision went dark, and Mordred was left with only the image of Jakob burning alive. It branded itself in his mind and on his heart, and he vowed vengeance on those who had committed the atrocity. Hell would visit those who had destroyed the Templars, and its name was Mordred Soulis.

I

Chapter One

"Jakob!" The scream tore from Mordred's mouth. It was filled with raw anguish. "*Jakob!*"

Opening his eyes, Mordred saw nothing. Blackness surrounded him. A heavy weight, invisible, pushed down on him, suffocating him, stealing the breath from his body. Gasping, Mordred struggled to a sitting position.

He smelled the horrid stench of burning flesh. The scent filled his nostrils. It clogged his lungs and caused him to retch. The violent spasms of dry heaves forced him to groan.

Still he could see nothing but darkness. No movement. No sound but his own heartbeat and desperate breathing ricocheting through his ears. He tried desperately to slow his racing pulse and block the hideous visions haunting his mind. It was impossible. Over and over images formed and dissolved, playing wicked tricks on him, forcing him to bear witness to the nightmare that lurked inside his head.

Pictures of fire and flame and charred bodies had been seared on the backs of his eyelids, forcing him to relive every heinous moment.

Mordred took great gulps of air into his lungs. The scent of death had dissipated somewhat, but still hovered beneath the other smells now filling the air, taunting him.

Where the hell was he?

Voices broke the stillness, shattering the eerie silence.

Soft at first, speaking in unison, the sounds ebbed and flowed like the tides, teasing Mordred's ears. He could not make out the words. Shaking his head, he tried to clear his mind of the dark fog that clung to him. He blinked. Once, twice, and then, the world came into focus.

The blackness of his vision gave way to subtle shades of gray tinged with red. Brightness cast a glow from somewhere in the distance, painting macabre shadows across the walls and ground. Mordred could make out two forms outlined in a strange pulsating light.

The voices came at him again.

Trying to maintain a defensive posture, fearing these were the enemy in his nightmare who had burned the bodies he had seen, Mordred gave a command to his muscles. His body refused to cooperate. Instead, he remained lying on his back.

He felt something pressing against his shoulder and

snapped his head to the right only to stare into the face of a man with dark voids where eyes should be. They weren't human eyes. There was no defined pupil or white area. The entire eye was completely black. *What the hell?*

Panicked, Mordred tried once again to push himself away, but, his legs had yet to surrender to his command. Failing to stand, Mordred inched himself as far away from the cold grasp as he was able, until he hit what felt like a wall. With every ounce of strength he could muster, he flattened his body against the hard surface and tried to get away from the thing staring at him.

The face hovering over him was not human, but more like a skull. The skin was stretched so tight it looked as though the underlying bones might pierce flesh. Shiny and glistening, the thing oozed a thick, clear liquid.

There was no nose, only two small holes where a nose should be.

It was a creature of Mordred's darkest dreams. He tried to inhale deeply, but that action sent his lungs into a coughing spasm, taking with it the strength he was using to remain seated against the wall. *Why was he so weak? And where the hell was he?*

Fighting to gain control over his body, Mordred faced the monster, waiting.

His mind felt as though it was splitting in two from

processing both the thing in front of him and, now, the other noises that flooded his brain. The squeal of a mouse, the flapping of wings, the scratching of claws against stone all competed to be heard. Dripping water, the howling wind, and the crackling of fire sounded at the same time creating a deafening cacophony that sent sharp bolts of pain through his ears.

And then, came the voices . . . Not the two he had discerned moments ago, but hundreds upon thousands of other voices, all fighting to be heard. Whispers, laughter, anger-filled demands and the sounds of sobbing layered one over another driving all else from his mind.

Mordred shut his eyes and screamed. He brought his hands to his ears in hopes of softening the roar of noise. It was no use. The voices were inside his mind. He shook his head back and forth. The movement caused him to wince from the pain behind his eyes.

Perhaps, he would wake from this hell and find himself . . . where? Who was he? Where was he? And what was the thing watching him?

Opening his eyes and dropping his hands, Mordred saw the black orbs of the monster blink and he felt something deep within his aching mind. Soothing and gentle it sifted through his thoughts, calming him despite the gruesome picture it presented.

"Mordred, Mordred, do not fear. All will be well. You are safe here," a soft voice reassured him.

Another face appeared behind the first. This one was entirely human. Mordred couldn't shake the feeling that he should know this man, yet, like a tattered piece of fabric caught in the wind, the wisps of memories eluded him. Here, too, in the depths of this man's golden eyes, he felt something akin to warmth being projected toward him. Mordred could sense no danger. Only a patient curiosity filled the stranger's gaze.

"Mordred, you have come back." The man spoke in a voice filled with wonder. "I was afraid you would never want to return. I feared that perhaps the burden you bear is so great you decided you would simply sleep through the ages."

The other thing with the fathomless black eyes smiled. "For him, there was never a choice to not return, only the timing of it. He is weak and confused. He does not recognize us. We must give him time. He is like a child in his mental state. We must allow his human mind to catch up to his vampyric mind."

Mordred remained silent, watching, waiting. Confusion threatened to swallow him in its black vortex. He could feel it sucking at the edges of his vision. He felt faint and unnaturally weak and he wanted nothing more than to close his eyes and let the darkness return. Yet, something prodded him to absorb the buried images of his past that were slowly being played within his mind.

When he closed his eyes this time he saw both the creature and the man. Then, the image of the man wavered and shifted into the form of a great wolf. The picture distorted again and the man reappeared.

Mordred watched as his mind played tricks on him. The monster-like thing became a dark-skinned man clad in robes and jewels fit for an Egyptian king.

Again, the image of the man trapped in the form of a wolf came back. The beast raced past him toward something floating in the air. He watched the king return to his monster form taking flight in a cavernous chamber . . . and he remembered.

Pieces and bits of his life replaced the panic in his mind, but they did not come in any order. Everything was disjointed and hard to place.

An old man, a kind man, a father figure shimmering with bright light, hovered before his eyes. Jakob! It was the man he had seen burning in his dream. He winced at the horrific scene in his mind as flashes of darkness and light vied for space.

He felt crazed and delirious, like a man caught drifting at sea, lost and without hope. His entire being was melting, and shifting, and then reforming all within the quiet seconds that passed by.

Again, he felt hands on his shoulders. This time he did not pull away. Instead, he allowed the contact and the presence stilled the unrest in his soul. The noise quieted. The images slowed.

Mordred opened his eyes once more. This time recognition flashed.

"Kabil?" Mordred spoke in a voice barely heard above his own breathing. He turned to the other face peering intently at him. "Du . . . gald?"

"He knows us. That's a good start, right?" Dugald asked Kabil.

The other man nodded. "It is a fine start. Let's get you out of your resting place and speak of the things you have seen. In those dreams you have had there will be messages and truths we will need to decipher."

Mordred nodded, noticing he was clothed in a swath of dark fabric reminding him of something. It was a shroud and with the knowing came images of hundreds of dead wrapped tightly in the same black cloth. Mummies.

For a moment, he wondered how it was he knew about the ancient Egyptian burial custom. The wondering caused more knowledge to fill his mind. A dam had broken. Images of himself and Kabil viewing hundreds of mummies beneath a great pyramid flooded him. He was somewhere familiar.

"Where am I?" Mordred asked, still trying to assimilate all the things in his mind. They were coming at a rapid pace. Some clear now, others still shadowy and dark, eluding explanation.

Smiling, Kabil revealed a mouthful of sharp fangs. Mordred fought the urge to recoil. He knew this man from his past. Kabil would bring no harm to him, but his mind struggled with the acceptance.

As if Kabil had read Mordred's thoughts he spoke, "Perhaps you would prefer me in my human form?"

The monster stood back and brought his arms across his chest. He closed his great black eyes and suddenly, right in front of Mordred, his entire being shifted. Now, he was a dark-skinned man, a human by all appearances.

Kabil moved away. The tinkling sound of metal and the slithering of fabric could be heard softly echoing off the walls of the chamber. When the man returned he was clad in a white robe edged in gold. He wore a gold head dress. Gold bracelets and arm bands glittered and winked in the dim light.

"Better?" Kabil asked.

Weakly, Mordred nodded.

"Well, then, let us get you out of there and give your muscles time to stretch and become used to the fact that you are again awake. And, in answer to your earlier question, you are within the bowels of the Great Pyramid."

"I remember." It was still hazy but Mordred knew he had been to this place before.

"You'll be able to piece it all together soon enough. For now, lean on us and try to stand."

Mordred urged his legs to obey his command again and was relieved when he was able to rise, albeit shakily. Hands helped him down from his strange abode. A shiver coursed through him when he looked back. What looked like a coffin had been his resting place.

"Your sarcophagus. Long has it lain beneath the sands waiting for the time of the Prince of Mortals to rise," Kabil spoke slowly, giving Mordred his arm for support.

With the help of both Kabil and Dugald, he was directed to a beautifully carved and gilded chair. There were all sorts of symbols and signs worked into the wood: everything from a serpent twisting around one arm, to a swan's wings creating the back. It was a masterpiece and was clearly fit for the mightiest of kings.

At his hesitation, Kabil urged him forward. "It belongs to you. Take your rightful place among us."

Mordred cocked his head to one side, unsure.

"You are in the second phase of your new existence. This is your throne, Prince of all Mortals. You are the Chosen One."

The name meant something, Mordred knew. Something very important he was sure. Still his thoughts were coming in patches and there were large gaps that needed to be filled.

The soft glow of torchlight filtered in from another chamber, illuminating the space around him while leaving some areas in shadow. The twinkle and shimmer of gold and other precious metals and jewels caught and reflected the light making it shine brighter. Mountains of ancient things, coins, gems and fine furniture littered the cavernous abode.

Running his hands over his face, Mordred tried to wipe away his confusion. He looked first at Kabil and, then at Dugald. "Help me remember. Help me know who I am," he pleaded, grimacing as pain engulfed him once again.

Kabil brought a bony hand to Mordred's own and clasped it. His flesh was sticky but cool. The king smiled. "We will begin. This is your friend, Dugald. He is a were-wolf," Kabil started, keeping his voice low and devoid of any emotion. "And I am Kabil, King of the Narangatti, an ancient race of Vampyres. I am all that remains."

Mordred allowed the ever-present confusion to blanket his mind. "A were-wolf and a vampyre? Who am I that I need such companions?"

Dugald spoke up. "You are the most important of all of us. You are the Chosen One. The one person in this world or any other that can save the human race."

"Vlad," Mordred murmured more to himself than the others.

Releasing Mordred's hand, Kabil moved away into the shadows but his voice echoed off the stones giving him an omnipotent sound, "Yes, you call him Vlad but he is known by thousands of names. This entity is the bringer of the end of the world for mortals. He is your worst enemy and one to be feared. He searches for you and, even now, I've little doubt that he is aware you have awakened. Vlad created you and he will not stop searching for you, taunting you, hoping he can lure you to become his own champion. And when that fails, he will seek to destroy you."

An ominous silence filled the chamber as all present sought to understand the full impact of Kabil's words.

It was Mordred who broke the dark mood. "You sound sure that I will not fall to Vlad's side, but I can feel the pull of the vampyre within me. It is a darkness that threatens to take over. It is a disease I cannot get rid of."

Kabil made a noise of disgust. "You are a half-born vampyre. You are not of pure blood and, even those of us who are, are not the evil you would like to believe. We have been over this before, Mordred. Vampyres simply drink the blood of humans. We prey on mortals and that is the way of things. It is not evil. Evil is something you welcome into the deepest part of your soul. You consciously make the choice to do evil, to be evil. In the natural world there is no evil. There is simply life and death in a never-ending circle. Only among humans does evil lie in wait looking for a crack, a tiny opening by which it will gain a foothold. You are made of stronger stuff, though you have a human's weaknesses.

"Slaves to greed, power and lust, humans are easy prey to all things evil. Vampyres have no need of these things."

"But if Vlad created me how can I hope to resist him?" Mordred asked. It was as if his own brain refused to acknowledge the words Kabil spoke.

Dugald spoke up, "Yes, he found you in the desert. You were dying. You would have died but he made you an offer and you took it. He gave you a new life of sorts and now he seeks to control you."

"He made me into a vampyre to save my life? Why?"

A look passed between Dugald and Kabil that Mordred caught. It was Kabil who spoke. "Those answers are yours alone to discover. In this stage it is important you learn the truth of your existence and in going back to your beginning, you will learn about the distant future and what is to come."

"You speak in riddles," Mordred declared angrily, slamming a fist on the arm of his throne. "I want clear answers."

"The way is fraught with bends and forks in the road. There will be times when you will not see an obvious path, but one obscured by mists and darkness. Trust yourself to know which way to turn. Listen to your inner voice and, at times, listen to the vampyre side of you. Vlad seeks you, but you can resist him if you stay true to your own beliefs."

Dugald scoffed. "I think you've made things worse for Mordred, Kabil." Dugald gazed up at him from his place on the stone steps leading up to the throne. "There is a lot you must learn and a lot we cannot tell you or don't know, but, for the moment, Kabil and I are your friends. We have watched over you as you slept, but the world moved on around you and the danger Vlad presents grows with each passing year."

Mordred looked off into the distance, watching invisible images take form in the shadows. His mind wandered in a thousand different directions. "Yes, now I remember. I am both human and vampyre. Vlad saved me."

A harsh scowling sound came from the shadows. Kabil had drifted away. "He did not save you. He made you into a half-born. You are trapped between two worlds, half human and half vampyre. He is an anomaly, something that was never meant to exist in nature. Men, wicked mortals, conjured him up. He, and they, must be stopped."

Mordred tried to discover where Kabil had gone, but after a few moments of fruitless searching he returned his gaze back to Dugald. "Why do you care what Vlad wants? Why are you helping me?"

Kabil strode back into view carrying a golden chalice studded with red rubies. "Because, I need humans. They are what I feed upon and Vlad, a non-living entity, will exterminate all resources because he has no use for them."

"Nice way of putting it, Kabil." Dugald ribbed.

"It is the truth. Would you prefer I come up with some falsehood about how I love humans? I don't love them. They are the only creatures that consume the planet to such a degree they snuff life out for all others. They overpopulate, they overeat, overbuild. Everything is thrown out of balance because of them."

"So, why help me save humans?" Mordred asked again, trying to understand what exactly Kabil was saying.

The king grabbed the sides of his long, white-gold robes and lifted the hem so he could climb the steps to where Mordred sat. He seated himself in the empty chair to the left of Mordred. Sighing, the king continued, "Because, as I've said before, I need them as a food source and like any other creature, save Vlad, there is a purpose to their existence though at times it is hard to see. All things are connected and if you remove one, you set yourself on a path of destruction. It is not for me to decide their fate, only you."

Kabil handed the ornate vessel to Mordred. Taking the goblet by its stem, Mordred heard liquid swirling inside. His nostrils flared and his eyes widened in disbelief. "You give me blood!"

The king did not flinch at the harsh tone, but merely held his gaze level with Mordred's. "I give you life. This is what you now require, Mordred. What you will require in the future. Drink, and gain strength from the liquid. You've no time to wallow in self-pity or condemnation. There will be others to condemn you soon enough. The world is stirring, as Dugald said. Evil looks for opportunities and there are plenty within the minds of men. Now, drink."

Clenching his jaw, Mordred tried to resist the temptation. He tried to tamp down the rising desire for the crimson fluid, but it moved within him, growing and tearing at his insides like the talons of a bird.

White-hot pain stabbed at his mind and his vision tilted. Everything around him was cast in deep red hues. His hands shook violently, causing him to spill the blood on his clothing. As the liquid seeped past the cloth and onto his skin, Mordred groaned. A sound filled with anguish and horror.

Kabil took the chalice from him. Dugald backed down the steps.

Mordred was thrown back against the chair in involuntary muscle spasms. His limbs twitching, he was flung out of the throne as his body contorted. He could hear the bones in his body stretching, the blood racing through his veins, his heart hammering with life and his lungs gasping for breath as his throat tightened.

He fell to the stone floor, first curling into a ball and then, extending his entire body so far in the opposite direction he felt his spine crack from the arching motion. Back and forth, over and over his body was wracked with spasms.

"Give him the damn blood!" Dugald urged, not able to withstand the sight of Mordred's painful transformation.

Something in Mordred's jaw snapped. He could no longer speak. His teeth grew long and slashed his tongue, filling his mouth with blood. Mordred choked on the fluid, coughing and gagging.

"Help him, Kabil!"

Kabil, sensing the change was taking longer than usual, knelt by Mordred's head and carefully held his trembling upper body as he dipped his finger in the chalice, now resting on the stone floor. He brought his finger to Mordred's lips. "Drink, Mordred. Drink and be free of this pain."

Somewhere in the far recesses of Mordred's mind he heard Kabil's voice. Greedily, he suckled the liquid from the offered finger. It was removed and Mordred felt the cool touch of the edge of the goblet against his lips. The sweet liquid his body craved flowed into his mouth. He drank in long, desperate swallows like a man dying of thirst.

The tremors subsided quickly. Kabil took the goblet

away, but still held Mordred, cradling his head in his lap waiting for the vampyre to recede.

Mordred's vision cleared and his breathing leveled off, deep and even. He could feel himself shifting, organs, bones, muscle moving and sliding back into place. He sat up.

"Just what the hell was that all about?"

Dugald echoed Mordred's concern. "Yes, what happened? He hasn't been that weak to his change since he was first bitten. Kabil, what is wrong with him? He looks as though he has wasted away to nothing and his mind is as frail as his body."

Kabil looked across to where Dugald stood trying to keep his distance from the two vampyres. "He has slept several centuries. Much has changed in the world around him and his human side feels the effects of the passage of time, though his vampyre side will compensate. It will be a few days yet before he is back to the Mordred we knew when last our eyes met."

"I have slept for how long?" Mordred queried, not sure he had heard Kabil correctly. "How can that be?"

A sigh came from Kabil as he brought a hand to Mordred's arm, helping to raise him into a sitting position. "It will be a while before you fully regain your memories. As I have said, you are a half-born vampyre, one who still has a human side. There have been others before you, but they have never survived through their first sleep. Think of your-self as in your infancy. You have just now grown to be a child, one just learning to walk and talk. You are very young in your existence as a vampyre and this requires much from your body. The time you spend above ground will take its toll and at some point you will return to a resting place to slumber, at times, for centuries. That is the side that is slow-ing you down. It is resisting your destiny. You must let it go. Allow the vampyre to come through full force and the con-fusion and pain you are feeling now, will be gone."

As if Kabil had not even spoken, Mordred continued, "but how could I slumber for so long? If I am to fight the great and growing evil in the world, why would I be left to sleep?"

"Your body needed the rest and your mind needed the time to assimilate all that had gone on before and while you were sleeping. It is a certain kind of madness that dwells within you, always keeping you trapped between two worlds. Being caught in that web of being, and not being, has caused you to rest far longer than any would have expected. Several centuries have past since last you were awake."

Immediately, the image of Jakob flashed before his eyes. Before the words fell from his lips, Kabil answered. "Jakob is gone. As are most of the people you knew. You came to me in the eleven hundreds and it is now the end of fourteen-hundred and seventy four."

II

Chapter Two

ather Simon? You are wanted in the cata-combs."

The man seated behind a beautifully polished desk squinted into the darkness, his writing instrument dripping a black dot of ink from its tip to the parchment on which he had been writing.

"You dare to come to me here? This is not a safe place," Father Simon said softly, a trace of fear in his voice. He glanced around the room. It was easy to hide in the shadows that stretched across the marble floor. The room's very design made it possible to eavesdrop from several chambers away. He hated working in this part of the Vatican.

Some would say Father Simon had become paranoid, but they were on the outside, kept at bay by their very ignorance. The ignorant were too afraid to walk the treacherous path to immortality. But not Father Simon. He was so close to unveiling one of life's greatest mysteries he felt his heart racing every waking moment, even when he was performing the mundane chore of inventorying new acquisitions for the Vatican archives.

Sensing he was alone with the young initiate, the father stood. He set his quill on the desk and put the stopper back on the bottle of black ink.

"I assume the Keys are in the Castel?" asked the young priest nervously shuffling from one foot to the other, the motion causing his black robe to undulate like a living thing. The man nodded.

"Then you may go." With that, he hurried out of the room, the sound of his footfalls reverberating off the frescoed walls. Father Simon lingered a moment longer. He blew a soft breath across his inked signature, and satisfied with his work, added the still-drying parchment to a neat stack. He rose from his chair and pushed it back into place against the desk. Cleanliness is next to Godliness, he thought silently as he inhaled deeply.

Father Simon strode purposefully out of the chamber, not following the path of the young man who brought him the request for his presence. Instead, Father Simon walked down a set of winding stairs to the ground floor. Once there, he crossed a large vestibule and took another set of narrow stairs down to a rough, rock-hewn chamber.

A small archway painted with gold was the only indication

there was anything more than the tiny space. Father Simon pushed through the arch, ducking to avoid smacking his head on the low ceiling.

A gust of chilled air forced its way into the underground passageway, bringing with it a low moaning sound. Father Simon shivered, less from the cold and more from anticipation of what was to come. He could almost understand how some believed in the whispered rumor of the hauntings that ran rampant through the halls of the Vatican.

Castel Sant'Angelo was, at the very heart of it, a mausoleum. It had been built to house the remains of Emperor Hadrian and his family. But it was also strategically located in relation to the River Tiber and the city of Rome and had been converted into a fortress. Now, the Castle of the Holy Angel served the Popes and the Vatican. It housed apartments, a treasury and, most importantly, a prison for the Church's heretical enemies.

No longer was it the draft that made the keening sound, but, rather, it was the prisoners. Their voices filled the cracks between the stones, their misery shut out the light, and their guilt snuffed out their lives. A thick blanket of oppression settled within the circular chamber Father Simon entered, but he found himself immune to its sorrows. In the mind of the repentant holy man, they deserved worse. The lot of them should suffer for their crimes against the Church.

Even the sanctioned torture employed to elicit confessions was too mild for those who turned their backs on God.

Father Simon shut his mind to the cries of the condemned. He focused on the task ahead. Meeting the Keys was always a challenge. They were the highest officers in the secret Order of the Red Caps and they expected him to reveal the secret of everlasting life, allowing them to feel the gift and the power, while denying him the power. Father Simon determined he would experience the gift himself when it was time, only giving what was left over to those who thought themselves better than he.

The Church had always danced with visions of eternity. The papers Father Simon had discovered hidden in an unmarked tomb beneath St. Peter's had brought him to this. In the scribble, among the ramblings, was something that drove the priest to madness. From the moment he first carefully unrolled the papyrus with its ancient symbols, he had been consumed with finding the answer to a riddle none had solved.

To live without fear of death. To live forever. What a magnificent gift. He would rise above all others with his new power. From nothing to something, one remembered forever, that was Father Simon's fondest wish and his most extreme desire.

Reaching into the folds of his robes, he withdrew a

small gold cylinder cut in several places on each side. He approached a set of large wooden doors made of solid oak, reinforced with black iron cut into the shape of a finely detailed peacock with its tail in full plume. One half of the bird filled each side of the door.

Father Simon slid the cylinder into a round opening. He heard the soft clicking sounds of the locking mechanism as it fit perfectly into the cuts on the metal key. Pushing the door open, Father Simon heard the protest of hinges squealing with age. They continued to make noise until he closed the door firmly and heard the sound of the lock sliding back into place.

The dim light of several large candles cast a golden glow around the circular room. In the center was a set of stone steps that led to a round platform. There was a marble pedestal of obsidian on which sat several scrolls.

At the edges of the room stood the Keys. They were dressed head to toe in crimson robes trimmed in gold. Red hats sat on their heads and red masks hid their true identities.

"Do you have the answer yet?" a voice called from the shadows.

It was always the same question. Each time he met the Keys, Father Simon went through the same routine. He walked to the raised dais and unrolled the papyri before replying.

"No, I do not have the answer, but I will soon."

"When?" asked another masculine voice, this one always less patient then the rest. A nasal voice that caused the same wincing in his head as the squeaking hinges.

"One cannot rush that which will grant you everlasting life," the father replied calmly. Grimly, he set his jaw and began the show of reading over the scrolls. He pinched some gold shavings between his fingers and threw them into a small silver chalice studded with black stones. Next, he reached for a fine white power and mixed it into the gold flecks.

"The Keys grow impatient. You continue to promise we will have the gift soon, but you fail to tell us how soon. You would not be toying with us, Father Simon?"

He focused on the task at hand, hoping none could see how his hand shook at the well cast arrow of truth. Were these men powerful enough to divine his deepest thoughts? Serenely, he replied, "I would never think to betray the Order of the Red Caps. I am only thy humblest of servants. It is not for me to attain immortality; I am not worthy."

The room filled with the sound of low laughter. Father Simon could only see three robed figures, but it sounded as though there were more, many more.

"You are correct, Father, for you would have no need of this gift. You have pledged yourself to the Church, and you will be the mere vessel of our greatness. Yet, it is an honor bestowed only on you, one who has shown himself to be worthy."

Father Simon bowed his head in acknowledgement and reached for a small golden vial. He uncorked it and let the contents spill into the chalice. Red droplets of liquid mixed with the gold and white powders. Father Simon added a small pinch of a black powder and lifted the chalice. "We are ready to begin," he announced to the waiting audience.

At once the room was filled with a soft monotonal chanting. The chanting was in Latin and repeated in three verses. As the voices grew in volume, Father Simon poured the mixture in the chalice, held over the flame of a candle. The fire changed colors, first to white, then red, gold, and finally deep blue. A puff of black smoke emanated from the flames which grew larger than the candle.

At once both the candle on the dais and those all around him were extinguished and the chamber was plunged into darkness. Through the blackness came a voice, hovering above Father Simon, startling him.

"What is your bidding, Masters?"

Father Simon made the sign of the Cross, for this was unexpected. He'd been conjuring nothing, only going through the motions for many long months, deliberately not following the scrolls' instructions exactly so he could discover the secret of the gift himself. He'd never meant for it to be revealed in this time and place.

"Masters? Who has summoned me, and to what purpose would you seek to imprison me?"

"Who are you?" asked one of the Keys.

"I have many names," came the reply.

"By what name should we call you?"

"The last name I was called was Vlad. And now you have sent me into the form of a human named Vlad, why? What is your bidding?"

The room fell into silence. It appeared Father Simon wasn't the only one surprised by the voice.

"You are the key to immortality?" queried one of the members.

Laughter sounded. Sharp and grating, it beat upon Father Simon's ears as though it had become fists. "I have the gift to give you."

"What must we do to obtain it?"

Again there was laughter. The temperature in the room had dropped to a bone-chilling cold and it was pitch black.

"First," said the mysterious voice, "you will release me to my true form. You will get me out of this body you've put me in so I can reign as I was meant to be. Then, I will bring you the gift."

Father Simon felt beads of nervous perspiration trickle down his back. He had never once considered that his actions would actually conjure a spirit. What if he had brought

Lucifer to life? What if he'd just opened the gates of Hell? Was it worth world destruction to be immortal?

Something slithered across his skin in the dark. It crept beneath his robe, stroking his clammy flesh. "Yes," the thing whispered. "You want the gift more than all the rest, don't you?"

Coughing, Father Simon tried to cover the voice with his own, hoping the others didn't hear it, too. "Please, someone, let us continue this by the light of the candles. I cannot see anything."

"Agreed," said one of the Keys. "Let us light the candles."

There was fear in the voice that spoke, Father Simon realized. Every single person was afraid of whatever else was in the room with them. And they thought he was the one who called it forth.

"Shhhh," the entity purred seductively. "It will be our secret. From this day on you will hear me in your mind, but no one else will know. You will do as I command and I will grant you life everlasting."

There was suddenly a rancid smell in the room. It carried the scent of death with it. But whether it was from the torture rooms in the Castel, carried on the air currents, or it was a new odor, the father was unable to determine.

A flare of light illuminated the room and both the smell and coldness were gone. It was, the father thought, as if the light had banished the entity, as it had cast the darkness away.

"Let us adjourn for this day and, Father Simon, let there not be any more unplanned surprises. You caught us all off guard with your little show tonight, but be warned, it shall not happen again."

Father Simon bowed his head in submission, but wondered if he had any control whatsoever over the thing that had come to them.

He moved off the dais, glad to be away from the place where the magic had been worked. He unlocked the heavy doors and after hearing them lock behind him, nearly sprinted out of the vestibule. He was ready to leave the Castle Sant'Angelo and never look back, but a voice stopped him in mid-stride.

"Father Simon, that was quite an excellent display of your skills. Perhaps we have misjudged you. Perhaps you should be initiated into the order?"

The masked, robed man spoke softly, but his voice echoed off the stones, bringing with it a strange hissing sound. Father Simon remained still, silent, unsure of what to say. He was scared out of his wits by the presence he had somehow conjured. He had felt it inside of him, squeezing his heart, poisoning his veins, speaking in his mind, and it brought him a fear he'd never felt before.

Eyes rimmed with gold, black pupils dilated from the absence of light, stared at the father, and he had the uncanny feeling he was being tempted by the snake from the Garden of Eden. The watcher never blinked, never showed any emotion. The Key simply stood, waiting.

"I . . . am, I . . . well, I'm not sure how to respond. It would be a great honor to be initiated into the ways of the Order," Father Simon stammered, nervously.

"It is the highest honor a man of your beliefs could achieve, second to your death at the hands of the Creator. It is a rare opportunity we extend to you. For the rest of the members, the Order of the Red Caps runs in our ancestry. Membership is passed on to each firstborn son. This is a gift we present to you because you have shown such promise.

"We are well pleased with tonight's activities, even though you surprised us. This Vlad you have brought forth, who holds what we seek, wants to be released from human form. You will go to the East. We've heard rumors of one called the Impaler. A heinous fellow, a heathen in our eyes, but someone who might prove useful if he is, indeed, the vessel by which we can receive the gift."

Father Simon remained silent. He'd heard of the man they called the Impaler. He had no desire to pay him a visit, or travel so far from the bosom of the church.

"I sense reluctance. Why don't you head to the prisons

for your first round of last rites? We have a particularly sinful heretic; some say he fancies himself a Templar. He will not repent, and so he must be put to death. You understand our crusade to remove evil from this world continues on a daily basis? And then, after you have done the deed, you may prepare for your journey to the mountains of Transylvania."

Afraid to show weakness, Father Simon merely nodded, then thought to ask, "A Templar? But I thought the order was destroyed many years ago? In 1309, I think?"

Raising a hand and waving as if swiping at a fly, the Key scoffed. "There are some who believe they are still around, hidden, but watching. Waiting for signs of their rebirth. It is rumored they even have connections to a source which will thrust us all into the darkness forever. Don't you think it was entirely too convenient that most of the members vanished when the French King sent out the order for their execution? Don't you think it odd that their treasure has never been found? To assume a vast and powerful order like the Knights Templar just disappeared from the face of this earth is entirely too impossible. Only fools would think the order gone."

The robed figure walked toward a stone wall and paused. He turned once more to face Father Simon. "Take yourself to the prisons and give the last rites. Then prepare for your journey. We'll need you to perform an exorcism on Vlad the

Impaler in order to release the entity Vlad."

"But, I've never . . ." Father Simon stuttered.

"Trust us, brother, the Keys will provide you with everything you need to succeed. You will be one of us soon enough."

A grating sounded in the vestibule. Father Simon watched as the wall of stone in front of the Key moved slowly, revealing a hidden passageway and a winding staircase. The man stepped into the passage and the walls slid back into place. Father Simon wondered just how many walls in Castel Sant'Angelo worked like this one. He wondered about the walls in the Vatican. Maybe his feelings of being watched were not unfounded. The Keys were everywhere, and knew everything. And now, having been invited to join the order officially, there would be no turning back.

The Order of the Red Caps was made up of powerful people, Father Simon had no doubt. They wore masks and met in secret because they claimed the rest of the world was too innocent in the ways of evil and would not understand their cause. Even Father Simon didn't know who they were. But he did know he was treading on very dangerous ground. If he wanted the ultimate gift for himself, he'd have to be very careful not to alert anyone. No one could be trusted.

The screams and moans sounded more animal than human as Father Simon strode into the prison. There was no light except for the torches burning and smoking against the stone walls. The floor was slick with liquids. Urine, water from outside, and something metallic that the father knew was blood, mingled with the stench of unwashed, impure bodies, and burning flesh.

As Father Simon walked down the long stone hall he cast a glance at the cells which were actually narrow tombs of stone. Only a small opening near the floor protected by metal bars allowed for food and stale, putrid air to enter the tiny room. A prisoner had to crawl on hands and knees to get into his cell and, once in, he was only removed for confession, which involved the use of torture.

Somewhere in the near dark, sobbing rent the air, a sorrowful keening from a female voice. The cries did nothing to Father Simon. He had long ago learned the world was filled with many wretched souls whose ignorance of God's love would bring the world into chaos. It was all the church could do to keep up with the steady influx of betrayers.

Those held in Castel Sant'Angelo were the worst of the sinners. They were usually unrepentant and denied God as their savior or, if they did accept Christ, they did so on their own terms, and, therefore, were considered heretics.

While some would find the light, it was too late. No one left Castel Sant'Angelo. These were the church's most terrible enemies and were proclaimed too dangerous to be released.

They would die here, either by torture in hopes of obtaining a confession and a clear soul, or by being forgotten.

A guard saw the father and motioned to him.

"The one you are looking for is down the next hall. He's been brought back to the holding cell temporarily. After you've finished with him, he'll be executed."

Father Simon nodded and found himself wondering at the piety of the guardians who protected the prison. These were worthy souls, indeed. They understood that a battle was being waged for the heart of humanity and the church was at the very center. Like avenging angels, they did their duty, and for that the church was grateful.

He walked down the seemingly endless corridor and came to an intersection. The prison was a labyrinth of passageways, cells, confession rooms, and chambers of torture. The father shook off the thought he could easily become lost here and never found, and forged ahead, side-stepping a puddle of some foul-smelling fluid, lifting his robes as he went.

Before he rounded the next corner, he knew he had reached his destination. He heard a voice muttering something unintelligible at this distance, but then heard a very distinct curse, in a thick accent. Scottish.

Father Simon nodded to the guard posted outside the wooden doors and the guard immediately opened them for him.

"You may go now. I will administer last rites."

The guard nodded and moved off down the hall.

Father Simon stepped into the cell and nearly gagged at the smell of burnt flesh and singed hair. Blood was everywhere. That the prisoner was still alive was a credit to his demonic faith. Clearly, he was not going to confess his sins.

Another priest stood some distance away, not looking at the heretic. His shoulders were hunched and he was reading from the bible by a flickering candle. Torches blazed from their wall sconces, but still the room was cast in darkness. It was a darkness that wouldn't be sent away by the lighting of candles. No, this was evidence of the evil dwelling within the man's soul.

"I don't want any rites read. I'll go to hell with head held high, if ye don't mind, Father," the naked man chained to the wall said in a hoarse voice. His arm was broken, part of the bone clearly visible, poking through severed flesh. Blood dripped from the wound.

Every finger was extended in an unnatural way, making his hands appear like claws, but his fingernails were missing. The sinner's ribcage was crushed on one side, the entire area covered by massive yellow and purple bruises. His abdomen was swollen, his knee caps had been smashed, and Father Simon thought that if not for the shackles and chains, he would be no more than a limp mass of seared flesh and broken bone.

Although Father Simon had seen the results of confession employed before, this was the first time he was witness to something that made his flesh crawl. There was an empty space between the man's legs where his genitals should have been. It was blackened, leaving no penis, no scrotum, nothing but burned flesh.

"Come, now, Father, why are ye lookin' so pale? Surely this can't be the first time ye've seen yer handiwork? And now ye'll be knowing why I am not about to have you or this other priest blathering on about redemption and saving my soul. Ye've taken everything from me so, the way I figure, I only stand to gain from a meeting with the Devil."

His words shook the father from his thoughts. "Here, now, even the lepers and the whores find forgiveness with Him. You only need renounce your participation with the dark order."

The prisoner peered at him through the slit of one swollen eye. The other eye was missing. "I've said this for the thousandth time; I don't belong to no dark order. I'm a simple man with simple wants and needs and right now, if ye'd be so kind, I'd like to be put out of my misery."

"You want to die?"

"Well, I sure as hell don't want to live now that ye've made me like this. What kind of life would that be? I was a warrior, once. Now, I doubt I'd even be able to lift my sword," The sinner rolled his head and groaned. "Besides, it's not like I'd be doing anyone a favor returning to my homeland to start a family, now would I?"

Father Simon approached the blasphemer. The other priest shuffled over, still keeping some distance from the prisoner.

"Be careful, this one may look harmless, but I was told you and I are the fourth set of priests to hear his confession."

Trying to keep the look of shock from his face, Father Simon snapped his head to face the other clergy. "Fourth? What happened to the others?"

"This barbarian killed them."

Horrified, Father Simon took a step back as the Scottish giant growled.

"Aye, I dispatched them as easily as lambs. Ye'll forgive me if I did not go willingly to yer torture chamber?"

"But, you've killed men of God," Father Simon stammered, his mind trying to wrap itself around the deed.

The prisoner coughed, sending a spray of yellow mucous, blood, and saliva across the room. The other priest promptly took a step back.

Father Simon remained rooted to where he stood. It was as if he were staring into the very eyes of the Devil himself. One who killed priests had to be nothing short of Lucifer's servant. Perhaps with his death the church would be one step closer to winning their holy war on evil.

"You feel no remorse over your deeds?"

The prisoner laughed and then gagged. "I feel no remorse killing those who seek to kill me. An eye for an eye, if ye'll pardon the pun." Winking, the sinner continued, "I do believe in God, but not, apparently, as ye'd wish. I don't think God intended this bastardization of His word. Ye call me a blasphemer, but ye are the one who is blasphemous. Yer fellowship is supposed to minister to those who are in need. Ye are supposed to teach us how to live our lives as He would, not as ye think yer organization views His work. Ye cannot vary the meaning of His words, though ye might want to water them down or adjust them to suit yer needs. Ye are the one who will be visiting the Devil, though I think ye've already met him."

An involuntary shudder crawled through Father Simon. Did this sinner know about his conjuring? Who was he?

"What is your name?" he asked.

When the prisoner did not immediately answer, the other priest said, "His name, according to our records is, Bran Soulis."

"Soulis? But that line died out well over two hundred years ago. Why, we . . . all our records in the archives show that . . . This is impossible."

The giant before him, chained, naked, and barely alive,

appeared to have fainted from his injuries.

Father Simon looked at the other priest. "Have you verified this? There cannot be a Soulis alive."

The man came to and smiled, revealing a mouth full of broken and rotted teeth. "Well, he be here, but for how much longer is the question. And ye may be rid of me, but ye'll not wipe us all from this earth. There will be one who can stand up to your holy terror."

Panicked, Father Simon grabbed a sharp instrument from the wooden table closest to him. It looked somewhat like a dagger, but the father had no idea of its true purpose, nor did he care. He was blinded by an overwhelming need to destroy this blasphemer. This abomination of God. There was no way a Soulis could have survived through the last cleansing, according to the scrolls he'd read, and it was important none think the Vatican had erred.

Lunging at the prisoner, Father Simon stabbed him in the throat. He cared not that blood spilled freely over his white robes, staining them crimson. He cared not that the blood splattered across his face. Over and over he plunged the weapon into the heathen, all the while saying the holy words to banish the devil or his minions. Clearly, this man was tainted by the dark side. He needed to be destroyed.

Horrified, the other priest protested that the prisoner had not been given his last rites and was now condemned to walk in purgatory. Father Simon only vaguely heard his words. It was as if the sound were far away. Something else spoke in his mind. Something louder and more familiar. A cold voice devoid of emotion instructed him there could be no witness to his crime.

As if he'd been born to it, Father Simon grabbed the other priest by his arm and twisted it until he came toward him. When he was trapped within Father Simon's grasp, he plunged the metal object through the man's chest, into his heart. After a brief spasm of muscle, the priest crumpled to the floor in death.

The voice in Father Simon's mind receded, allowing his own thoughts to return. His gaze fell first to the dead prisoner hanging on the wall, then to the body of the father at his feet. He saw the object in his hand and threw it to the ground in horror. What had happened to him? Was he possessed? Whose voice had he heard in his head? Where was the voice now?

Inhaling deeply to still his racing heart, he heard a guard call, "Father? Is everything all right?"

Thinking fast, Father Simon replied in a voice he hoped sounded fearful. "No, the prisoner just attacked the other priest! Please, hurry!"

The door was opened and the guard strode into the room, surveying the scene. He saw the dead prisoner and the bloody corpse of the priest. "Damn him to hell. That sinner took five priests to their graves with him. Don't worry, Father. What you did, you did in self defense and this prisoner was going to die anyway. I'm sure the church will see it that way."

The guard gripped Father Simon's shoulder and steered him from the grisly scene and out of the chamber. "Go, now. Back to your office. I'll fill out the report and send a copy to you for approval."

The father could only nod. His voice was lost in the horrors of his crimes. While it was true the sinner was a confirmed heretic and convicted to die by torture from the church, Father Simon had never, ever, killed anyone. It was shocking, disturbing and at the same time morbidly fascinating. In all his years as a priest, he'd never once regretted his vows of chastity. Yet, now, he found himself, beneath his robes, excited beyond any sexual measure. The feeling, he realized, was the feeling of absolute power and Father Simon relished it.

Somewhere in the back of his mind he heard the sound of laughter. Deep and maniacal.

Chapter Three

cowling, Mordred pushed himself from the throne and stalked across the dusty ground. He was still having trouble with the idea he had been asleep for hundreds of years. And that the Templars, the organization that had helped him, existed no longer.

"Why? What could they possibly have done to merit such a horrible end?" He had asked this question over and over, and still there was no sensible answer.

Dugald peered at him from across the underground pool of water. "I was there the day the French King had the leaders burned at the stake. Even then it made no sense, though the king had certainly run a very good smear campaign."

Sighing, Mordred replied, "I know he had the order proclaimed heretical. They were accused of worshipping the devil and of being a satanic cult, instead of the holy order they really were, but why?"

"I would think that is obvious?" Dugald said, his voice carrying across the blue water. Ripples broke the surface as he swam in the depths. The pool itself sparkled with thousands of sapphires and other blue and gold stones. It was a bath meant for the pharaohs of old.

Images of daily life on the Nile were painted on the sloping walls. Tall columns made to look like palm trees, their entire trunks intricately etched with hieroglyphics, served to give the illusion of being out of doors. On the ceiling a golden sun reached out with long rays extending from the ball of the center, and silver stars filled the blue painted sky.

The Bath House was one of Mordred's favorite rooms. Normally, it was a place of refuge for him. Today, however, Dugald had chosen to follow him and he was not to find the peace of mind he so desperately sought.

"So, why do you say it's obvious the Templars were brought down? What did I miss?" Mordred asked.

"Well, you know there was always a rumor the organization dug beneath the Temple Mount and discovered untold treasures."

Waving his hand, Mordred paced near the edge of the pool. "Yes, yes, I have heard this. I was gifted with items I believe have come from that place."

"Ah, but you never saw the really big items."

"You mean the Ark of the Covenant, the Holy Grail?"

Dugald swam to where Mordred stood. He shook the water out of his hair, reminding Mordred of the large canine he could become.

"It isn't just all that, Mordred. There are literally hundreds of people searching for the Grail alone. On top of the fact many thought the leaders of the Templar organization had more wealth than the Roman Catholic Church. You were aware they received a pope's blessing, and a few years after they officially came into being, every family who had a son they thought worthy sent them to the Templars. That required a certain amount of money donated to the cause. Over time, they just got too big and it made the Church uncomfortable. The King of France wasn't the first to look at them with something other than fondness."

Mordred's ear picked up the scurrying sound of the scarabs, the beetles sacred to the ancient Egyptians. He turned his sight to a dark corner of the chamber and watched as hundreds of the beetles moved like tiny soldiers, scouring the ground looking for food. In his mind's eye he saw the image of men, faceless, standing in a circle around a raised dais. He shuddered, a massive trembling nearly bringing him to his knees. Mordred held himself up by leaning on a nearby column.

"Mordred, what is it?" Dugald asked, concern marring his features.

"Vlad," came the faraway reply. Suddenly, Mordred felt as though all his energy was being sucked from him. A cold wind swirled, searching for cracks in his soul.

"You can feel him?"

Mordred closed his eyes, willing the visions spinning in his head to reveal more detail. "No, he is not close, but somehow I can see flashes of something . . . People, in robes, chanting. Darkness, and then the glow of candles. Shreds of a whole image I can't understand."

Dugald stopped swimming and walked through the water to the edge of the pool. "It is the church. They have called him forth again. You and he are linked in some strange way and though he cannot find you here, you are able to see him. His rising means he knows you have awakened."

Mordred rubbed a hand over his unshaved face. He frowned, confused. His thoughts were formless, lurking in a dark fog that had come over him.

Dugald watched the strangeness infect his companion. Warily, he climbed the steps of the pool, water streaming from his naked form.

Mordred stared into the shadows. The flames of the torches flickered to almost nothing before blazing high, lighting the room like the rays of the desert sun. The fire danced from all corners, weaving, swaying, snapping, and crackling. Mordred heard the voice of the flames.

Before he knew what he was doing, he thrust his hands in front of him, palms up, and whispered a word that appeared in his mind. The flames shot from everywhere in the chamber toward Mordred in streaks of yellow, red, orange, white, and blue.

Like snakes, they curled around Mordred's form, igniting his robes. The scent of burning hair and flesh filled the chamber. Whispered laughter echoed in his head, yet Mordred remained in a trance-like state, unmindful of the powerful heat and searing pain eating at his skin. The inferno grew in size as it devoured Mordred.

Snapping out of his shock, Dugald raced toward Mordred and shoved him. Mordred fell into the water, the force of the lunge bringing Dugald with him. He landed heavily on the vampyre with a loud splash, knocking the wind from them both.

Flailing and sputtering angrily, Mordred surfaced. He shot a fierce glare at Dugald who came up for air only moments later.

"What the hell did you do that for?" he demanded.

"You don't remember? Christ, Mordred, you were on fire. All the fire in the chamber attacked you."

Mordred tried to bring his heavy breathing under control as the shock of what had just happened washed over him in waves. Shaken, he hauled himself out of the pool.

"I see the man is still a pup," Kabil said from behind them. The King of the Naragatti was in his human form, white robes floating over the ground as he walked toward the pool.

Dugald glanced at Kabil. "What just happened?"

Kabil smiled. "It appears Mordred will need some re-training in how to control his powers."

"His powers?"

"I have the power to call forth flames, among other things."

"Really now?" Dugald scoffed. "Doesn't Vlad have these same powers? Just what else do you and Vlad share that we should know about?"

"This is *my* problem," Mordred snapped, stalking toward a large sarcophagus. He stopped and peeled his wet clothes from his body. "I don't even know why you're still here."

"I'm here because I'm your friend. I'm here because you need me. You're just too damn proud to admit it," Dugald replied as if wounded.

Mordred ignored the tone. He was too wrapped up in his own web of darkness. "I have no friends and I do not need a werewolf to help me with anything. I am alone and that's the way it must be. I don't know why you stayed. I don't need you."

It was Kabil who broke the deadlock. "Both of you are mere pups, one more than the other. This is not child's play.

Dugald is with you for his own reasons, not the least having to do with a debt he owes you."

"I have told him, he paid that debt the last time I was awake."

"Then perhaps he will leave when the time is right. For now, though, you both will be traveling through the same countries and there is safety in numbers against Vlad and those who seek to control him."

Mordred sighed and continued peeling the charred strips of cloth from his body. He winced when he tugged at the clothing on his back. It appeared the fire had gathered strength there and pieces of fabric disintegrated on touch. "Bloody hell, why do I feel pain?"

"You will always feel some pain, pup. You are, after all, part human."

Mordred stared at the blistered skin of his hands and forearms. He knew it would heal in time, but the confusion over what had just occurred was something he couldn't sort out. "What happened with the fire, Kabil? How come I couldn't control it?"

Kabil drifted around the room, setting two gold goblets on the lid of the stone sarcophagus. "You're still weak from your sleep. Something in the images you saw in your mind triggered the flames. You called them to you. Something you saw brought them to life and they obeyed your silent

L. G. BURBANK

command, but you didn't control them. They took advantage of you, and they will do so again if you are not fully aware of the power you wield.

"Fire is the most primal of the elements. It is the most unpredictable and the one most likely to feed off of you if you show it even a minor weakness. From fire comes life and death, light and dark. Be mindful and masterful each time you summon the flames."

Turning his back to the king and Dugald, Mordred drew his long, tangled mass of wet hair from his back and shoulders. Hearing a gasp from Dugald, Mordred stopped.

"Mordred? When did you get that mark on your back?" Dugald asked, softly.

"What?" Kabil and Mordred asked in unison.

Kabil walked over to Mordred.

"Well?" Mordred asked. "I don't have any marks on my back except for the scars from battle. What are you talking about? What the hell is it?"

"I'm not sure," Kabil responded in a voice filled with awe. "In the dim recesses of my mind, I recall seeing this mark, but long ago, at the very beginning of the world. At the dawn of creation, this was etched upon the earth, and now it is burned into your skin."

"Burned, but how?" Mordred asked, trying to keep the rising panic from his voice. "I don't remember anything and if this is a mark from a burn, wouldn't I have felt it?"

Dugald answered. "It was the flames just now. They did it. They are trying to tell you something."

"Yes, but what? What is it they mean to do now that they have marked you?" Kabil asked, more to himself than the others. He reached out a bony hand, many gold bracelets and armbands sending a shower of noise across the room. Lightly, he traced the path of the symbol.

"I can see it!" Mordred shouted in surprise. "When you touch it, I can see it clearly. I know this symbol, but I don't know it. Its meaning lies at the edges of my memory."

"Well, that clears things up," Dugald said acidly. "I understand everything. Kabil, can you make any sense of it?"

"I can feel it pulsing, riding on Mordred's flesh. The mark has fused itself to him, like a parasite, and it breathes his energy, his thoughts and feelings."

"It is harmful? What's its purpose?"

Kabil continued tracing the design, allowing Mordred to view the image in his mind. "I'm not sure. It vibrates with ancient magic, but as to its source I am bewildered." He glanced toward the flames in the chamber. Everything appeared as it should.

Mordred moved away from Kabil and tried to peer over his shoulder. "Is this Vlad's work? Some mark of the Devil put upon me?"

"Now you talk like a human fool. The power behind this creation is far older than Vlad. It is of the fire itself. This entire world, all that we are in our simplest form is what this image represents. We are composed of the primal elements of fire, air, water and earth."

"My human side maybe," Mordred interrupted. "But certainly not my vampyre side. I was not born a vampyre, but tainted by an abomination that should never have been, therefore half of me is not truly a creation at all."

Kabil waved a hand impatiently. "You think too much, and not at all. You are life. No matter the condition of that life."

"But I died. I wasn't brought into the world like you, I died. I shouldn't be here."

"If that was true then you wouldn't be. There are far greater powers at work than even I understand. I am not sure of the symbol's intent, or why the flames marked you, but in time, like all things, it will be revealed."

"So, what do we do now?" Dugald was still in the pool, motionless.

"Both of you need to begin your journey. There is no time to waste. You are correct that Vlad has been summoned by mankind, again. He is loose and ready to begin his crusade to destroy the human race which means you must get to Lir and the others to gain the power needed to stop him."

"You are not coming with us?" Dugald rose from the pool once more and reached for a white swath of cloth, wrapping it around himself.

Kabil walked slowly over the goblets and picked them up. He handed one to Mordred and lifted the other to his lips, drinking slowly in long swallows. "No, I will not be coming with you on this part of the journey, but never fear, you will see me again. For now, Mordred, you must drink. You must feed and prepare your body and mind for whatever lies ahead. Vlad is out there, waiting, and as you have grown, so has he. He will use everything in his power to either control you, or stop you. Trust no one."

"Where do I begin?" Mordred asked, grimacing at the crimson liquid held captive in the cup. He knew by smell it was blood. Whose blood was not something he wanted to know. He lifted the cup and drank.

"You need to go to the heart of where this all began. Men brought Vlad forth, the same men connected with the church. Go to Rome," Kabil said. "There you must find out where Vlad's true source of power lies and how to defeat him. Then head east to the Carpathian Mountains. I feel a strong presence of evil there. Be wary of the Turks; they are on the move again."

Setting the empty goblet down, Mordred gazed at the king. "And where do I go after that? Will I find Lir in the

Carpathians?"

"No." Kabil shook his head. "Lir will come to you. He does not reside on the earthly plane at all times."

Mordred dressed in another black robe and sat on a carved sphinx by the edge of the pool. "What do you mean Lir does not always reside on an earthly plane?"

"You are still a pup, only believing in what you can see. Open your vampyre eyes this time. You will witness things your human self would never allow you to comprehend before," Kabil replied.

Scoffing, Mordred picked up a small stone and threw it toward the water, watching as it skipped and bounced across the surface. He saw his life moving like the stone, bouncing aimlessly, plunging and then rising before finally sinking. Dramatic highs were followed by unfathomable lows. How could he ever stand up to his destiny?

"I will go alone. I will not take anyone with me," Mordred said softly.

Kabil sighed. "You do not have a choice. It is Dugald who helped you the first time, and he will do so again. Be prepared to meet new companions that will defy your human understanding. They are very real, Mordred, but in order for them to help you, you must accept what they are. Refusing to see your enemies could very well cause you to fail in this quest. Eyes open at all times, pup."

✠ ✠ ✠

"Let us begin once more," Kabil said while standing on the top of an overhanging rock. "And let us hope you have not forgotten all you have been taught by the Templars, and by me. We do not have time to start at the beginning."

Shrugging, Mordred stared up at the vampyre king, "Well, if I remember everything else like I remembered how to control fire, then we are in some serious trouble."

Kabil was in his true form. His shoulders were hunched, his entire body dwarfed by enormous scaly wings that created a hissing sound when they rubbed against each other. The king was naked except for a small bit of white cloth which covered his lower body to his thighs, keeping his genitals hidden.

A clear liquid oozed off Kabil's skin, reflecting the dim glow of the torches located around the vaulted chamber. His face was that of a creature from a nightmare. His head was bald. The entire space of his eyes was filled with black. There was not a single dot of white.

Perhaps the most disturbing aspect of his features was not the absence of a nose, save for two tiny needle prick-sized nostrils, but the fangs that protruded from his thin lips. Not only were the canines elongated and sharpened to a point, but every tooth in his mouth was just as deadly, giving him a gruesome smile. The number of teeth also stretched Kabil's mouth to amazing lengths, and copious amounts of saliva dripped unhindered.

"When you have finished staring at me, we can begin, pup."

"What is it you want me to do?"

"Fly."

Feeling his eyebrows raise, Mordred continued looking at Kabil. The king stepped from the ledge, but instead of falling to the ground, his wings beat once, twice and then he was soaring above Mordred through the cool air of the chamber.

"We've done this once before, Mordred. Last time you were not as successful, so let me spare you the pain and humiliation of failing by guiding you. And this time you will listen. Now, think of yourself as floating on air. Embrace the possibility and in your mind watch as you levitate."

At first, Mordred remained firmly rooted to the ground. He felt the heavy weight of his body and the comfortable feeling of the sand and stone beneath his feet. He thought of lifting off the ground, of soaring through the air, but nothing happened.

Slowing his breathing, he tried to still the roaring noises in his mind. The sound of dripping water was deafening, the scurrying of beetles and rodents scratched his head.

The rustling of wings, both feathered and scaled, howled like the wind.

"Focus, Mordred."

Kabil spoke in Mordred's mind.

Mordred closed his eyes and thought about being weightless. He started with his bare feet and continued up his lower legs to his thighs, waist, upper body, and finally to his head.

He felt himself rising from the ground, moving ever so slowly upward. He kept his eyes tightly shut, afraid that if he opened them and actually witnessed himself flying above the ground, he would snap out of his mental state and slam into the floor.

Kabil had warned him that although he would heal from nearly any injury, he would still suffer the pain of the wound and could very well remain incapacitated for many days. Mordred dimly recalled the first time Kabil tried to teach him to fly, and could still see the image of himself lying broken on the sand, unable to move, while the King of the Naragatti drank his blood.

A shiver raced through him but he clenched his teeth and returned his concentration to the task at hand.

"Pup, you'll have to open your eyes if you want to have any control whatsoever over your ability to fly," Kabil said sarcastically.

Mordred allowed his eyes to open a crack. He could barely make out the floor far below. *Christ! I'm flying!*

Feeling braver after the first few moments aloft didn't send him hurtling to the ground in a panic, Mordred opened his eyes. He was alarmed to realize he had flown over Kabil.

"Now, you need to control your movements, pup. What you have done is bring yourself upward, but that is simply levitation and there are a lot of creatures that can do that. You need to remember what it is to really fly, in any direction. Dive downward, now!" Kabil commanded.

The king's voice shattered Mordred's control and in the blink of an eye, he found himself falling head first. Desperately he tried to pull out of the dive, but his body would not obey. He felt the cool air racing past him.

Fear slithered out of its hiding place within him, filling every pore in his body, overriding Mordred's control. There were only seconds left before he smashed into the ground. Before he felt the impact, his entire body was jerked backward, but not under his own powers.

Sharp talons ripped into the fabric of his robes and an angry voice sounded in his head. *"We do not have time for this, Mordred. Let go of the fear and embrace the vampyre within. Do it, or the next time I will let you fall."*

Mordred felt himself being hauled all the way to the top

of the chamber and before he had time to react, Kabil let him go. Again, he fell forward, the ground racing up to meet him, but this time, as he was about to feel the broken pieces of stone impale him, he rose backward, stopping his fall.

This time it was under his own power. Having made the breakthrough, Mordred relaxed. He allowed as much of the vampyre out as he felt he could, while still controlling the side of him he still considered a beast. He not only rose, but flew through the air, soaring, dipping, and diving. Upside down, backward and forward he moved, laughing and delighting in his own power.

It was as if he had suddenly remembered how to sword-fight, something that came instinctually, and soon he was moving without even thinking about it.

A soft, rasping laughter sounded in his ears.

"Very good, Mordred. You have remembered. You are ready to go now." The Vampyre king smiled, revealing his razor sharp teeth. "It is time for you to begin the next leg of your journey."

IV

Chapter Four

ordred and Dugald said their goodbyes to Kabil. While no tears were shed, Mordred couldn't help but feel reluctant to leave. Under the Great Pyramid he was safe. Vlad couldn't harm him and neither could anyone else who might want to destroy him. But he knew his destiny was not to remain hidden. Nay, it was to become a beacon to which all things evil would be drawn.

Surprisingly, when the pair reached the exit, Mordred's black horse, his Beast of Burden, was waiting for him. The animal looked none the worse for his journey.

"How the heck did he get here? Shouldn't he be long dead?" Mordred asked Dugald as they approached the horse. The stallion nickered softly at Mordred's arrival and butted its massive head into his shoulder, nearly knocking him off balance.

"I have no idea, but he looks happy to see you," Dugald

replied.

"Well, it's only been a few hundred years, right, Sleipner?" Mordred scratched the space between the horse's ears, listening to the sounds of appreciation coming from the beast. "Guess he's immortal, too?"

"Sleipner? You named him?"

"More like he named himself. It's the only name that came to me. Sleipner was Odin's horse in Norse fables."

A voice sounded in Mordred's mind that was not his own. *"I am not exactly immortal. I live to serve you, my master. My life is yours and you decide how long I shall live in this world."*

Mordred shook his head and squinted one eye as he stared at the animal standing in front of him. He looked at Dugald. "Did you hear that?"

"Hear what?"

Mordred returned his gaze to the horse and focused on one large brown eye staring back at him.

"How is it I can hear you now, but I couldn't before?" he asked in his mind.

The stallion snorted. *"You were too young then. You grew while you slept and gained understanding in many things, some even you are not aware of yet. You can hear me because I serve you. I am your Beast of Burden. I will bear all things for you."*

Mordred stepped away from the beast and shook his head. The horse mimicked his movements. He narrowed his eyes and, amazingly, so did the great black horse.

"Well, I guess you'll bear me for now."

The horse's head moved in what Mordred would swear was a nod of understanding, and as Mordred considered how he was going to mount the animal and get all his gear up, the horse lowered itself to the ground. Mordred threw a leg over and was seated. The pack across his back holding his Blood Sword and other items shifted, but remained secure. Once he was situated, Mordred pressed his thighs to the animal's sides.

The horse rose.

Mordred looked for Dugald and saw a golden-colored shape move from the shadows. The wolf approached slowly, waiting for the horse to acclimate to its scent.

The stallion's nostrils flared and he stomped his front hooves, but Mordred spoke aloud, "This is Dugald in his animal form. You have seen him as a man, but he is a shifter and for traveling it is faster and easier for him to move as a wolf. He will stay ahead of us and alert us to danger."

Dugald approached the horse and extended his furred muzzle. The horse extended his nose until the two almost touched. Each inhaled the other's scent.

Mordred knew it was important for the horse to recognize Dugald as a wolf as it could prove deadly to mistake another for his companion. So he waited patiently until each knew the other.

"It's time we depart the desert and move north," he said at length. "We'll look for a boat to ferry us to Sicily, then rest before moving on to Italy."

The horse moved without Mordred having to give it a signal.

Darkness settled on the desert and Mordred became increasingly agitated and wary. Kabil had told him the night would bring the most danger as the creatures that lurked in the shadows were often not of this world's making, but some otherworld imbued with powers of evil.

And Vlad would know he had left his sanctuary. Vlad would know Mordred was moving and would send his minions to locate and destroy him.

A deep blue velvet sky absorbed all light; clouds blotted out the full moon, leaving their corner of the world shrouded in black. Even the sounds of the night were muffled. The horse's hoof beats were softened to whispers on the drifting sand. Mordred heard countless desert animals scurrying about, taking advantage of the night.

Scales slithering across the ground alerted him to a snake scouting for prey. The frantically beating heart of a tiny mouse meant the snake was closer than the mouse would like.

As Mordred moved across the strange landscape, he glanced at the enormous dune rising in front of him. At the summit, he made out several shapes, each with a set of bright yellow eyes. Even without the moon's glow, the creatures' coats shimmered ghostly white.

Dugald came racing back from a recent foray, shifting from his wolf form into human as he ran. He stopped abruptly, drawing in great gulps of air.

"There are strange creatures up ahead. I could see five in all. Ugly things with white fur and long teeth. They are watching you," Dugald reported through ragged breaths.

"I know what they are. They are the Ammut, Anubis' beasts of judgment. I met them the first time I was here when I saved the horse." Mordred patted the animal reassuringly. He sent a thought in his mind.

"Do not fear. We will keep them from you."

"They have not come for me, but for you," the horse replied.

Mordred was caught off guard. "How many are there?" he asked Dugald.

"I counted five I could see."

Mordred gazed around the hostile landscape. "Is there another route?"

It was Dugald's turn to be surprised. "You want to run from them? Who are they?"

Irritated, Mordred chewed the inside of his cheek. "We

wouldn't be running from them. We'd be saving our hides. These are not things from this world, but demons from the underworld. Anubis is the God of the Dead and the creatures will rip out your heart if they find you unworthy."

"But, Mordred, you're immortal. They can do nothing to harm you."

"What about you, and the horse? How do I know I'm immortal against things that aren't of this world? Vlad can destroy me because he is not of the earth but something from an otherworld, so why would it not follow other monsters from hell can bring me down? No, I don't intend to stick around to find out." Mordred spat into the sand.

He heard the Beast of Burden again in his mind. *"You cannot avoid them. They have your scent and they will find you no matter where you go. You cannot leave Egypt without facing them."*

True to the horse's thoughts, Mordred looked up to see the Ammut had come closer. There was no escape. Had he been alone, he knew he could probably fly to safety, but he had two companions he couldn't leave behind. He uttered a curse under his breath and watched the Ammut circle his party.

They were fierce looking things from a dark nightmare. Things Mordred once would never have believed existed. Warning growls echoed across the dunes as the beasts paced back and forth, closing the net they wove, coming ever closer.

Mordred slid from his horse's back. He stood with legs braced apart, fists clenching and unclenching.

"What do you want of me?" Mordred asked.

The wind rose, stirring the sand into swirling masses of dust. Dugald had shifted to wolf form and stood snarling like a large dog at the end of a tether, waiting for his master's signal to attack the enemy. With fur standing on end, Dugald looked nearly twice his size.

The Ammut resembled a cross between a lion and the strange dog-like creature called a hyena that Mordred had seen when he'd made his first journey from Egypt. They were ugly by design. They continued to pace, drawing close enough for Dugald to snap at one, but not make contact. The creature did not appear the least bit affected by the huge, salivating canine.

"We come from Anubis. It is time for your judgment," purred one of the Ammut in Mordred's mind. He could not tell which one spoke.

"You'll have to get through me first," Dugald snarled in response, uttering the warning in both Mordred's mind and the Ammut's.

"You are of no consequence to us. We have been told only to bring the undead for judgment. If you try to stop us, you will be destroyed."

"*The wolf speaks the truth,*" the Beast of Burden said. "*We will do all in our power to stop you.*" The horse snorted and stamped its hooves.

"*So be it. We have orders from Anubis, and he will not be denied. Let us begin.*"

The Ammut attacked in unison, five against three. Not so terrible if they had been five men, but five mystical creatures presented a different set of odds entirely, and not in the trio's favor.

"*Dugald, go and take the horse with you!*"

"*And leave you here for them to pick apart? Never!*" Dugald howled back in Mordred's mind.

"*I will not leave you. I am your Beast of Burden and I bear all you must bear,*" the horse said.

"*Damn you both to hell! They will kill you and probably kill me, too, but I would die better knowing you were away from here.*"

"*We cannot leave you. Not now,*" Dugald replied flatly.

One of the Ammut was upon Dugald. They rolled on the ground in a ball of sand, fur, and claws. The scent of newly drawn blood came to Mordred's nostrils and he felt something dark and deep within break loose.

Sleipner rose on back legs and struck out with forelegs and sharp hooves, knocking one Ammut to the ground.

At that moment something strange happened. Mordred watched each of the Ammut shudder from the force of the blow, even though only one had suffered the impact. For a split second he noticed all the creatures appeared to be affected. Sensing the vulnerability, Mordred's mind moved in swift understanding.

It was as if each of the creatures was a mirage. There was one main beast Mordred would have to fight, and if he killed the beast he had a suspicion he would take down all the others.

Quickly, as the other three Ammut readied themselves to attack, he searched for anything that would mark one as the leader. They came at him with their deadly teeth bared and sharp claws exposed. While he doubted they meant to kill him, merely incapacitating him was not an acceptable option.

He reached with both hands and pulled the Blood Sword from the scabbard strapped to his back. It vibrated and glowed. With no time to spare, Mordred swung. All the Ammut fell back out of range, and while he drew the sword back they leapt as one.

Mordred heard Dugald yelp, but could not look away to see if he still fought. The scent of blood flooded his nostrils, maddening him.

He felt the vampyre stir, clawing at his insides as the beasts of judgment clawed at his exterior form. He felt the skin of his arm peel away as if it were nothing more than cloth. With it came his blood. Another rip and tear and Mordred found himself bowled over onto his back. He threw his sword aside and brought his hands to the throat of the animal that stood over him, threatening to break his neck.

Mordred knew the exact moment he lost control of his human side. The self-preservation of the vampyre trampled his will. His body rippled with newfound strength and his jaw stretched, snapping and popping as it reformed to fit his long incisors and canines.

Everything within his field of vision reddened. The bones in his hands cracked as long fingernails became claws. He raked the sides of the beast above him and snapped at the animal's neck. Snarling, the Ammut backed away and readied itself for another charge. Three against one, they moved in swiftly, each aiming for a different part of the vampyre.

One sunk its teeth deep into Mordred's calf and he screamed in pain. He kicked out, forcing the animal to release its grip and sent it crashing to the sand. Another went for his shoulder, but Mordred slammed into it and had the pleasure of hearing it whine as it bit its own lip from the force. It stumbled backward and shook its head.

Then he saw it. In one of the animal's eyes he watched the yellow color turn to gold and for a split second become black before returning to yellow. Mordred allowed the beast to attack him headon, and while he held the snapping jaws away from his face, he stared into the eyes and watched them shift once again.

This was the leader. He needed to get back on his feet and retrieve his sword. If he could kill this one, he was sure he would rid himself of the others.

With all his strength he pushed the animal back, launching it into the air. Scooting across the ground; he grabbed his sword, and after tripping over the tattered remains of his black robes, he stood shakily and brought the sword high, ready to strike. But the other Ammut had backed off.

They were still too close for comfort, and Mordred wondered if they weren't readying themselves for another attack. He had lost sight of the leader. Then from behind he heard a deep voice, cultured, speaking in a language Mordred could not immediately identify.

Whirling, he took note that both Dugald and the horse were still standing, although both bore wounds. Then he saw the speaker.

A lone figure, taller even than Mordred, stood regally erect and clad in a long swath of gold fabric that left his chest, legs and arms bare.

Astounded, Mordred saw the man did not have a human head, but that of a jackal, black as night with golden eyes. And it was the eyes Mordred found himself riveted to.

Anubis

"I am well pleased with your strength. I had not expected you to fight this well so soon after your awakening," the man-beast said.

"Who are you?" Mordred demanded, still holding his Blood Sword poised.

"Come now, Mordred, you know my name."

Mordred felt himself returning to human form, and with the change, the pain of his injuries returned. He gritted his teeth and swiped a hank of black hair from his eyes, noticing the blood he smeared from an open wound on his arm.

"Speak your name."

"My name is Anubis. I am King of the Dead."

✠ ✠ ✠

Mordred was having trouble assimilating the fact that he was being born by a litter through stone halls decorated with paintings of the Egyptian after-life, while Anubis assured him the pain of his injuries would pass once he was judged worthy.

"Worthy of what?" Mordred asked, feeling his mind fill with a silver fog, dimming his ability to think.

"To continue this course. If you are to be the Chosen One, then you must be deemed worthy." Anubis walked just in front of the litter. Once more, Mordred was struck by his regal bearing.

Mordred's mind wandered into the fields of disbelief. He had blacked out after hearing Anubis announce himself, most likely from his human side feeling the effects of the wounds he'd sustained in the battle against the Ammut. When he had come back to consciousness, he found himself being carried on a soft platform by several human-looking men. They did not speak and moved in unison in a manner that suggested they were not individuals, but part of a collective entity.

He tried to gather his wits about him, but each time his human side rebelled against the notion he was somewhere in the Egyptian underworld having a conversation with the King of the Dead. "It would be easier for you if you would simply accept your surroundings." Anubis turned toward him and Mordred saw his lips curved into a smile. "The longer you deny it, the more pain and detachment you will feel. Did Kabil teach you nothing?"

"You know of Kabil?"

"Of course. How would the King of the Undead not know of the King of the Narangatti? We have known each other for a long time. It is he who summoned me for your judgment."

Immediately, Mordred felt betrayed. Kabil had set this all up? His mind reeled with all kinds of ugly thoughts.

As if reading his mind, the king offered, "Mordred, Kabil did nothing wrong and soon you will come to understand that. All he has done has been in an effort to help you. To get you to stand on your own."

"Wait." Mordred tried to sit up, grimaced, and fell back. "I have a few questions."

He watched as the paintings changed and the pair moved around a corner into another long hallway.

"I thought you would have some. Go ahead. If it is within my power to answer them, I will do so," Anubis said over his shoulder.

"First, why is it I feel so much pain? I'm immortal. Shouldn't I be healing?"

"When you do battle with other immortals, not only Vlad, you will feel the injuries more acutely. Even though the Ammut you saw were of my making, they were under the power of a god. You will feel this pain until your judgment day, and you will bear the scars of this step in your journey for your lifetime, however long that may be."

They came to a halt. Anubis opened a set of large doors and Mordred watched as he was carried through and his litter was gently set on the floor.

It was not what Mordred would have expected as a house for the King of the Underworld. Instead of blackness and roaring flames, he saw shimmering gold, brilliant turquoise, and white. There were reds and browns and silvers in the paintings on the walls and in the floor, but nowhere did he see black, except on the two obsidian jackals that served as the arms and base of a large gold throne on a dais of white stone.

"Not the dreary place you had expected, Mordred?" Anubis said with humor in his tone.

"Not exactly," came Mordred's grudging reply.

"Well, who said the underworld has to be dreary? That's a product of human imagining. You mentioned you had one more question for me before I depart?"

Mordred was lifted from the litter and placed on a low platform cushioned with pillows and silks, satins, and other fabrics.

After the silent men helped Mordred to a sitting position, they exited the chamber, leaving him alone with Anubis. Oddly, he felt no fear.

"Why am I here? I am dead, yes, but I am still, in a sense, living. Why would my soul be judged now?"

Anubis walked slowly up the steps to his throne, muscles glistening in the light of many torches. "You are being judged based on the merit of your destiny. There are none who can afford to have the Chosen One be found unworthy."

Mordred was confused. "What do you care? You don't have a stake in the future of humankind."

"I beg to differ. There are many, many souls to be won and lost as long as there is still a human race. I am neither goodness, nor evil, but merely a judge. Therefore, if there are no humans, there would be no use for me and I find that unacceptable. I like my existence."

"But who believes in you any more?"

Anubis laughed. The sound echoed off the walls and reverberated inside Mordred's head. "You would be surprised who still worships the old ways. And you would be surprised how many faces and names there are for the same god, but that is a lesson for another day. Suffice it to say I am not willing to see the human race exterminated, therefore the one ancient prophecy speaks of must be judged worthy."

Mordred became annoyed. In some ways Anubis was no different from Kabil. There was a haughty arrogance in his answers, and some of them were merely riddles which Mordred didn't have the strength to solve at the moment.

"What has happened to my friends?"

"They are safe in your world. They will not know the passage of time and when you return—if you return—it will be as though you never left."

Alarmed by the word 'if' Mordred asked for clarification. "What exactly do you mean *if* I return? I must return to continue my journey. Kabil has instructed me to find the next king of Vampyres."

Anubis waved a hand before bringing a goblet to his lips, draining the contents in a single swallow. "Yes, well, in order for you to continue, you are to be judged worthy, and if you are found to be wanting, you will remain here, forever. Look around you, Mordred, it is not a bad place. You could rule by my side as a prince, something I have never offered before."

"No, I . . ." Mordred shook his head as the sound of buzzing filled his ears. "No, I don't want to stay here. I must continue what has been set before me."

"Really? Are you so sure? Are you positive that you will not one day let the dark side of you take complete control and become nothing more than a monster, like my Ammut? How do you know you will not simply become an eater of souls? How do I know you should be set free to wander the world unchecked . . . unless you pass the ultimate test?"

Angered, Mordred pushed himself up to a sitting position. He winced from the sudden pain that ripped through him, but he moved past it. "When do I begin this test?"

"Now," Anubis said. Mordred heard him clap his hands and the chamber went dark.

Mordred heard the sound of many feet padding softly across the ground. They scurried around the chamber and as his vision adjusted, Mordred could make out shadows in human form. At least they appeared to be walking upright, giving the impression they were human.

Suddenly, the smell hit him like a thick wall of hunger, engulfing him, surrounding and taunting him. It was the metallic scent of blood. Large amounts of blood. The vampyre began its ascent and its battle for control.

He tried desperately to quell his rising need. A desire, fierce, hot, and wild, rode him as he stood. He felt his body contort and knew the change was upon him.

No! his mind screamed in protest. He had no idea what was in the room and he was not about to unleash the beast inside. He wrestled with his demon, falling to the floor in a puddle of limp flesh and melting bone.

Already the vampyre was surging forward in its efforts to be rid of the human. His bones were cracking and splitting as they extended. His jaw opened and closed reflexively, popping and snapping as tendons stretched and split. His mouth distorted to accept the huge, razor sharp teeth.

It was no use. Mordred fought with as much strength as he could muster, but in the end he realized his human side was no match for the power of the vampyre within. His hands clenched and he growled, a garbled sound to his own ears, as the nails grew and shot forward into curved claws, capable of stripping flesh to bone with one strike.

His mind was now held captive by the rampaging beast. The smell of blood was driving him mad. Thick and heavy on the humid air, it was palpable on his tongue. Mordred licked his lips and rose. His hands scraped the floor when he moved and he heard the sound of his nails as they scratched the stones.

His head rose. His vision, red and dim, grew brighter with every beat of his heart. He saw many different people standing about the room. *Why are they just standing there? Don't they know what I am? Don't they know what I can do to them?*

The hunger demanded appeasement and drove him forward. Blood was everywhere. It was spilled on the stones, the steps, the walls. Human blood. The thing he craved.

A gut-wrenching spasm nearly sent him to the floor. He was being driven mad with the denial of what his body demanded. He only need drink from one goblet, his human side whispered, defeated. He need not strike a human, or kill one. Find the goblets.

Like a zombie he moved forward, but when he found the goblets on a table near the throne, they were empty. Desperate, he licked the insides and then, in a fury, he turned over the table, sending the contents crashing to the floor.

The blood lust was upon him in a way he had never felt before. He must drink.

Still, the people remained with him in the chamber. Like sacrificial offerings, they did not move, or speak, or utter any protest at being near such a monster. But Mordred heard each of them as loudly as if they had been shouting. Their pulses thundered in his ears, and their heartbeats played a divine melody that his hunger matched.

With one hand he reached out and grabbed an individual around the neck, pulling the unfortunate to him. He pushed his head to one side exposing the blood-filled artery that lay beneath the surface. It throbbed under Mordred's touch, calling to him.

He brought his head down. About to gorge himself on blood, he caught the scent of something else. It wasn't fear, exactly, but something he could not place. He stopped and took a second look at the victim.

It was a woman, and she was gagged. She stared at him with horror-filled eyes, but she did not resist. And he knew he could not take her life. She was innocent. The sweet smell of purity scented the air around him, causing him even greater pain.

The vampyre wanted to satiate its hunger, but the human fought to protect what was untainted.

The pain in his gut made him roar his frustration. He shoved the woman aside and moved on to the next victim. Again, he found a woman and again, he smelled her innocence.

Not virginal, but she had committed no great sin. She was a being, deserving a better end than what Mordred was ready to inflict.

Irritated beyond all measure and quickly losing control of his human side, Mordred rushed at another victim. This one was a man, but he, too, nearly blinded Mordred with his piety. Again, Mordred was denied the chance to feed. His humanity would not allow the vampyre to feast on the blood of innocents.

He fell to his knees, willing the pain to go away, yet it grew stronger. He brought his wrist to his mouth and bit down, feeling the warm sticky fluid fill his mouth. But his relief was only temporary; the hunger came back more strongly.

Mordred feared he was about to cause a blood bath. Rising, he once more circled the room, desperate to find something, someone to drink from. He told himself he would control the amount of blood and leave the person alive. He didn't care if he created a revenant, an undead being trapped between life and death.

Something wicked flickered around the room. A shimmering blackness created a hole in the chamber where no light could pass, and Mordred, like moth to flame, drew near. He saw a man standing before him and he knew this one was different from the rest. This one showed no fear, and in the moment Mordred touched him, he knew the man had no soul.

Evil spewed from the man's pores in a thick putrid scent

and Mordred drew away. The man smiled, hatred filling his eyes. In one quick move Mordred snapped the man's neck, plunging his fangs into the soft, pliant flesh.

He suckled at the wound, drawing the crimson into his mouth while lowering the body to the floor. The man's pulse had stopped, his blood poured into Mordred's mouth and, over and over, the vampyre swallowed in great gulps, taking as much as he could as fast as he could.

His mind filled with images, dark and cruel. A child, a waif on the street being beaten to death. A woman, screaming as he tore the clothing from her body and forced himself on her. An old man with his hands raised, pleading for his life as this man laughed and slammed blow after blow into him.

More pictures flooded Mordred's mind as he drank the dark, tainted blood. He lost count of how many had been killed. Yes, this was an evil man. And the evil passed through to Mordred. After a few moments glutting himself on the blood, he felt light-headed and sick. He pulled back.

In the blink of an eye, the torches in the chamber blazed back to life. Anubis was seated on his throne as if he had been there the entire time. Robed men entered the room and ushered out the bound and gagged women and men. Another pair of servants arrived and took the body away.

Mordred remained on his knees and bowed his head.

He felt no sorrow at the passing of the victim. No sadness. Only sickness.

"What you feel is the bad blood Kabil warned you about, and you would do well to heed his advice and not drink too much of it at one time. It will taint you in time if you are not careful, and you have a long time to be on this earth."

"I think I'm going to be sick," Mordred managed through clenched teeth as his vampyre-self, satiated, receded. He felt two pairs of hands lift him gently from the floor and he was brought to the platform he had rested on earlier. He slumped, feeling as though all his energy had been stolen.

"It will pass," Anubis said softly. "And you have passed."

The fog descended once more in his mind, but he was aware he no longer felt the pain of his earlier injuries. Amazed, he closed his eyes and listened to Anubis's soothing voice.

"By choosing the evil from the innocent, though your vampyre-self demanded to feed, you have shown yourself worthy of the cause set before you. We, the Egyptian gods and goddesses, will wait for the day you summon us to aid you in your quest, and we will be honored to do so. You truly are the Chosen One."

As Mordred's eyelids flickered open, he thought he saw an entire room full of robed figures standing watch over him. Each of them had human bodies, and each had an animal head. He thought he saw a hawk, a lion, a hippopotamus, and a black cat. Even an ibis, and a crocodile. It was a puzzling assortment of creatures, and Mordred could make no sense of it. In a few moments, he succumbed to the darkness of a healing sleep.

V

Chapter Five

hat the hell . . .?" Mordred spat sand. His mouth and throat were dry. Not a drop of saliva. It was as if every ounce of moisture had been sucked out of him. Swirling his tongue around his teeth and gums was fruitless.

Opening his eyes, he cursed as a bright spear of light stabbed his vision. "Bloody hell!"

Mordred rolled over onto his side and slowly peered from beneath half-open lids. He saw Dugald lying next to him on the sand. They were beneath a palm tree, but a gentle breeze moved the fronds, causing shards of sunlight to disappear and reappear. "What the . . . ?"

"I'm thinking the same thing you're thinking," Dugald said as he faced Mordred. "One minute we are in a battle to the death with those Ammut things, and the next, we wake up here. I feel like we've completely lost control of time."

"Dugald, what's the last thing you remember?"

Groaning, Dugald replied, "I remember having two of those things one me at the same time. I was fighting them off, but they had long teeth and claws and they were fighting with such precision. Nothing I was doing caused any damage. Instead, I was getting slashed and gouged. I remember seeing you and one of those Ammut was on top of you. You had your hands around its throat. That's all."

"You don't remember anything after that?"

"No. And you?"

Mordred chewed his cheek in thought. "I was fighting the beasts, too, and then I noticed something strange. It was as if they were all fighting exactly the same and when we hit one, the others shuddered like they, too, felt the pain. I looked for a leader and then nothing."

Dugald rose to a sitting position and surveyed their surroundings. He brought his hand to his brow. "Well, we're both unable to recall the past day or so, if indeed that is all the time we're missing. What next? And where did your horse go?"

Mordred stood up. His body felt as though he'd been trampled by an entire herd of horses. "I have no idea. Maybe the Ammut got him? That's what they wanted when I found him."

"But why would they want a horse? It doesn't make sense. Don't they judge human souls?"

Nodding, Mordred turned in a full circle. They were surrounded by sand dunes. He had no idea where they were, or what direction they should head in to get to the sea. The fact they were not where they last remembered was the least of their worries.

"Sleipner isn't an ordinary horse. I think there's something else."

"Like what?" Dugald asked, rising to stand beside Mordred.

"I can talk to him."

Dugald's brows shot up. "Really?"

"Yes. He is a Beast of Burden. He explained to me that he will bear all my burdens. I'm not sure I understand exactly what that means. He's not immortal. Somehow his life is linked to mine. I'm sure that's why the Ammut wanted him. Maybe they somehow keep magic in balance. I don't know, I'm confused. I don't know what happened to us. In my mind I see the shadow of a form and I hear some words, but nothing comes in to focus."

"You think we lost our memory because of something other than the fight with the Ammut?"

Mordred bent down to pick up his pack, and something slid out from under his black robes. He caught it with his hand, and realized it was a necklace.

Crouching, Mordred examined the object on the gold chain. It was a flattened gold disc; upon closer inspection, he saw the fine detail. A familiar image.

It was a scarab beetle with wings extended, curving upward to complete a circle. It was the symbol for the cycle of life and death. The scarab, to the Egyptians, meant eternal life.

He didn't have the necklace when he left Kabil. And he didn't have it last night when the Ammut attacked, which meant that at some point during the missing hours, Mordred had acquired the necklace . . . But, how?

The wind stirred like a restless animal, rising in force.

"Dust storm coming," Dugald announced as he brought his pack to his shoulder.

"Let's get out of this valley and try to get our bearings before things get too bad. Once we have an idea of where we are, we can dig in and wait out the storm."

Dugald nodded and waited for Mordred to choose the direction. Slowly, they trudged up the hill to their right. As they moved higher, Mordred heard the wind grow in fury. Suddenly, it wasn't the wind at all, but a deep voice wrapping itself around him. The tone caused vibrations to race through his body as if the sound came from within instead of without.

"Your heart and soul have been measured. You have passed my judgment. Mordred Soulis, you have been found worthy to enter the next stage of your quest."

Mordred turned to see if Dugald had heard the voice, but Dugald just stared at him, waiting for Mordred to speak.

The storm was fierce. It raged for several hours, coating everything with dust. Mordred and Dugald used their robes to cover their eyes, mouth, and nose. They simply laid down in the sand with their backs to the wind, and waited out the storm.

Darkness descended in a whirlwind of great billowing spirals of sand engulfing the landscape. The roar of the storm was nearly deafening. Neither Mordred nor Dugald tried to speak, but were lost in their own thoughts. Each was trying to find a clue to what had happened earlier.

Eventually, the wind subsided and the late afternoon sun released its last rays onto the desert landscape. Both men rose and brushed the sand from their clothes and shook out the contents of their packs, emptying everything of the fine grains.

Mordred looked up and was surprised to see a familiar shape drifting across the dunes toward them, moving with amazing speed. It was Sleipner.

The stallion came to a stop a few feet in front of Mordred. It shook its head and made huffing sounds of greeting.

"Nice of you to return," Dugald said with sarcasm.

The animal ignored Dugald, turned its great head and

fixed one brown eye on Mordred. *"I came back as soon as I was able. I searched ahead for any signs of trouble. When the Ammut took you and Dugald was unconscious, I thought it would be best to make sure you would be safe upon your return."*

"My return? Where did I go?"

"You don't remember? Why, Anubis himself brought you to the Underworld. It was your soul he wanted to measure, and when you did not go willingly, he took you."

"I have been in the Underworld?"

The stallion raised his head. *"That is why you cannot remember anything, and neither can Dugald. I know the way we must travel to reach the sea. Are you are ready to resume your journey?"*

Mordred was about to reply when something caught his eye. From the black hair on the horse's back and head appeared a saddle complete with stirrups, a bridle and reins.

"Well, well, well, look who's been keeping secrets," Dugald said, just as surprised as Mordred. "Guess he really does have some magic."

"Let's move out," Mordred called over his shoulder, and he mounted the horse. Turning back to Dugald, he said, "He also happened to check the route so he knows how to get us to the water."

Puzzled over the entire turn of events, Mordred sat quietly in the strange saddle. Dugald remained in human form and plodded through the sand behind horse and rider. They crested a dune and began the descent that would bring them out of the desert to the edge of the sea.

Finding a boat to cross the blue-green waters of the Mediterranean Sea that was willing to take a large stallion along proved to be difficult. The only ship the trio was able to hire would only take them as far as Sicily via the Ionian Sea. Once they reached the island, they would need to secure transportation to cross to the mainland of Italy.

Finally, a merchant trading goods from Africa by way of Egypt met Mordred on the dock of the Alexandria Harbor. The dark-skinned captain pointed to his vessel and smiled, revealing several yellowed teeth, although there were more empty spaces than teeth.

The man laughed when Mordred's gaze found the boat, or rather what was left of it. The craft didn't look as if it would stay afloat on the relatively calm harbor, much less on the open waters.

It was riddled with gaping holes that the captain assured Mordred were all above sea level.

"So, we have a deal?" the man asked, holding out his hand for payment. "I will meet you here tonight and we sail for Crete. Okay?"

While Mordred's ability to speak all languages had

been with him since he had become a half-born vampyre, it still amazed him. He replied in fluent Egyptian, "Not Crete, Sicily, and, yes, tonight my companions and I will meet you here."

He opened his pouch of coins and dug until he found the right amount. The old captain took one and bit down on it before nodding and smiling. "Yes, we go to Malta."

"Sicily," Mordred growled.

The captain deposited the coins in his own pouch and without acknowledging the destination, promptly turned and left Mordred standing alone on the dock, wondering if he had made a big mistake.

When night fell over Alexandria, Mordred led both his stallion and Dugald back to the dock. It didn't surprise Mordred a bit that the captain was not present. In fact, Mordred wondered if they would ever see him again, now that he had been paid.

Soon, however, he heard heavy footfalls heading their way. Then the night erupted to a sound like that of cats mating. Only with keen hearing could an individual distinguish a human sound through the cacophony of off-key notes. Several small shadows scurried underfoot, seeking the darkness that had suddenly been interrupted by two men and a large horse.

Mordred heard Dugald gasp, either from surprise or extreme dislike. It was the latter that caused Dugald's outburst. Mordred momentarily settled his gaze on his companion. One eyebrow remained arched while he crossed his arms and waited for the explanation.

"So, I don't like rats."

"You don't like rats? C'mon, Dugald they don't exactly pose a threat to you at the moment. The way you jumped, I thought some monster had slithered out from under the dock."

Dugald moved a few paces toward the center of the ramshackle planking that had clearly seen better days. "Yeah, well, who's to say those rodents aren't pieces of some bigger whole and that somewhere in the shadows they're coming together?"

Mordred let out a soft laugh and strode forward to greet the captain coming toward them. "You've clearly been around me too long if you think we have to fear rats now."

The silhouette that had Mordred's attention was making its way slowly and erratically across the wood dock. It grabbed the flimsy railing for support, slamming into the posts.

At least twice it appeared he was going down, tangled in the tattered remnants of a long coat, yet each time, at the last possible moment, he righted himself. A drunken giggle broke the quiet of the night.

Mordred grimaced. He'd been hoping against hope that the figure approaching was not their captain. It was. And he was so inebriated he could barely stand. He fell forward and grabbed the edges of Mordred's coat, trying desperately to stop himself from landing face first on the boardwalk.

Trying to avoid strangulation, Mordred uncurled the man's clawed hands and shoved him away. A wall of vaporous liquor poured from the captain's mouth, making Mordred's eyes tear.

"This is the person who will get us safely to Sicily?" Dugald asked quietly, trying to keep the mirth from his voice.

"Maybe he has a first mate?" Mordred suggested.

The captain belched loudly before losing his balance once more. He tumbled to the dock in a pile of rags and remained there.

"Well, don't just stand there. Let's get him on his boat and be away from here. The sooner we get to Sicily the sooner our real journey can begin," Mordred growled when Dugald doubled over with laughter.

A fine mist swirled around them as they carried the captain to his boat. A thin sliver of moon peered from its lofty perch in the black velvet sky.

Mordred led the horse up the ramp and onto the deck of the vessel while Dugald threw the captain in a heap by the large wooden wheel. They each stowed their packs and for a moment stood in the darkness, silent, watching the night. There was no sign of any otherworldly creatures afoot, save for the ones on the boat.

"Think we can figure out how to sail this thing?" Dugald asked. Somewhere in the distance a desert jackal barked and howled, and soon its voice was joined by another.

A light wind snapped at the sails.

Mordred stared up at the masts and then back at the boat. "I think we're a vampyre and a were-wolf and a Beast of Burden and we're sorely out of our element. But we have no choice. It can't be that hard."

Suddenly, from out of the shadows came a figure, tall and thin. "Might I be of some assistance this night?"

Mordred's head snapped around as he realized he'd just been caught off guard. That, in itself, was alarming. Something told him not to be too hasty about accepting an offer from a stranger who still kept himself hidden in the mist and the night.

Yet before he could respond, Dugald, acting like the big, dumb beast Mordred often thought he was, bounded over the side of the boat and was already slapping a hearty hand on the man's back. It nearly sent him into the water.

"Divine intervention if I do say so myself, eh, Mordred?"

Scowling, Mordred was about to listen to his inner voice and refuse the offer, but before he could give voice to

The Fane Saracles

his thought, Dugald was already escorting the stranger on board. With white, thinning hair and a long face, he reminded Mordred of a feral beast trapped in the skin of a human.

And still something told him all was not as it appeared.

"Who are you? And how is it you come to be wandering the docks at such a late hour?" Mordred asked harshly.

The man did not seem to take offense at the less-than-friendly welcome. Instead, he brushed his hands down the front of his coarse black shirt and cleared his throat. His voice, when he spoke, was soft and musical. Pleasant, it did not match the face to which it belonged. And then there were the eyes. Even in the near dark, clear blue orbs swirled with purple. Magic eyes, Mordred thought. No mortal could have such eyes.

"I am Saracles, and I was on the docks looking for work in hopes I could obtain passage home," the stranger stated innocently enough.

"What is it you aren't telling me?"

"That I am handy with all manner of water craft and I can get you where you wish to go, if you'll allow me the opportunity."

Mordred peered at Saracles, still captivated by the unusual color of his eyes. Beyond hair and facial features, there was not much more he could distinguish. Saracles wore a long, loose-fitting shirt a size too big for his frame. His legs, though thin, appeared muscled and were clad in snug black breeches, ending in tall leather boots.

Every inch of skin not on his head or face was covered in black fabric. Strangely, even his hands were hidden.

"How much will it cost us?" Mordred barked, moving around the vessel trying to make sense of the equipment.

Saracles smiled, and it was as if the moon had suddenly become full and cast its silvery light across the water. It was blinding and mesmerizing all the same. "Why, far less than you would be thinking, of that I'm sure."

Mordred repeated his question. "How much?"

Dugald, who had been rummaging through their packs for anything that might prove useful, walked quietly over to Saracles.

"I'm not wanting your money, mortal," the man said with a trace of bitterness. "I've not been on this earth as long as I have only to desire fool's gold."

Mordred cursed under his breath and stalked over to Saracles. His great black cloak swung out behind him and the wind played with the edges. The effect was of great dark wings.

Saracles took a step back. His eyes were wide, not with fright, but something else.

Mordred resisted the urge to wrap his hands around the man's throat and throttle him. Clearly mischief was afoot and Mordred was in no mood for riddles.

"What the devil are you and how have you come to be here? If you don't give me a satisfactory answer within the next breath, I'll throw you off this vessel."

He watched as Saracles's eyes narrowed. "You are not a mortal. You are something else. Something both filled with darkness and light."

The sails snapped overhead, stopping the conversation for a moment as all eyes looked to the sky.

Saracles spoke first, "There is a storm coming soon. If you have need to be away from here then we must talk later and work now. We've little time to get the boat out of the harbor."

Wisely, Mordred thought better of delaying their departure. While he still felt some misgivings, he could not discern any danger. If the thing was wicked, its foulness must be hidden deep within.

✠ ✠ ✠

The strange crew worked under the direction of the newcomer. Saracles proved to be knowledgeable about sailing and had gotten them safely out of the harbor. Now they plied the Mediterranean, heading toward Sicily.

The captain managed to rouse himself from his drunken

stupor halfway through the journey, and added his expertise to the task of getting them to their destination.

"So, Saracles, where do you come from?" Mordred asked him after they were under sail.

"I am not from a place you would know. Not from this plane. I come from a middle ground. A place you cannot see when you are here."

Mordred sighed and tried again, "Okay, then, what are you?"

"Ah, it's not worth time to trick you, Mordred Soulis, is it?" Saracles had learned his name from Dugald, who, for some bizarre reason, could not keep his mouth shut around the stranger. To Mordred, the man resembled the Fey, creatures from the Celtic lands. Mysterious and charming all at once, but if a person spent too much time in their company, or were over-awed by their appearance, they might never be seen again, dwelling in the Faery realm forever.

The brilliant blue eyes with swirling rings of purple were enough to proclaim the being from another dimension. And his smile, when he did smile, reflected a far more youthful spirit trapped in the casing of an old, decaying body.

Mordred remained quiet and waited to hear more. With nothing to do but sit in the damn boat, he had plenty of time.

Saracles continued.

"I am a Fane. I move through this world, and my own, in my true form, but have been cursed by the Hollow King. He has something that belongs to me. Now, I am forced to live in the body of an old man. Only my tattoos remind me of what I once was."

At Mordred's questioning look, Saracles pulled one glove off and pushed up the sleeve of his black shirt to reveal his forearm. He held it away from his body, allowing a touch of moonlight to cast a glow on his skin. Mordred watched, amazed, as the light brought forth intricate curling patterns on his arm that seemed to pulse with life. They were not scales, but rather more like feathers, flattened against the man's skin and the same strange blue color as his eyes.

"Fanes can appear in many bird forms. You cannot distinguish us from them unless we wish you to know our secret. By the light of the sun we take to the sky, away from the prying eyes of humans. Always, we are watching from above."

"Watching for what?" Mordred asked, his gaze still fixed on the man's arm.

"We are the disciples of the Warders. They are the Guardians of the gates."

Mordred shook his head, confusion clearly evident on his face. "Warders? Guardians? What gates?"

The Fane paused a moment, then bent his head and began again in a conspiratorial whisper. "Warders are the ones who keep the planes pure. There are some who keep watch over what you think of as heaven or paradise. There are Warders who must guard the very gates of your own hell. They protect the planes."

"But recently there was a disturbance. Something dark and evil that should have gone below this plane into your hell has broken through to this one. Now, not only is the presence upsetting your world, but it left a gaping hole the Warders are struggling to repair, leaving this plane vulnerable to even more horrible and malevolent beings."

When Mordred remained silent, Saracles continued. "At first the Warders had thought perhaps it was simply the existence of the Chosen One, you. But they also know your coming could only mean one thing. The battle between Above and Below is brewing. And it appears the war will take place here. There will be much blood shed. All creation is at risk, mortal and immortal."

"But," Mordred began, "I was told I was only fighting to save humanity, mortals. No one has told me immortals are at risk."

While Saracles proved very forthcoming about his identity, it was hard for Mordred to comprehend. Ever since becoming a half-born vampyre, his world had been flipped upside down in more ways than one. Light became dark and black became white. Things he only believed to lurk in the pages of storybooks or fireside tales of bards, had become real.

Beyond Kabil and Dugald, he had met the Ammut, and the Undead King, Anubis. There was also his Beast of Burden, the great black horse that could not only communicate his thoughts to Mordred, but could grow a saddle and armor plating from its skin.

There were undead revenants, those Mordred had fought before he had fallen asleep centuries ago. They were the minions of Vlad and would search for him no matter where he fled. And there was Vlad himself. The darkest creature, from the deepest nightmare. A thing that should never have been, brought forth from the greed of men wishing to achieve immortality.

So, what then of immortals if they, too, could be endangered?

Saracles smiled. "At first, we thought perhaps the darkness that was welcomed to this place would only seek to destroy humans. One species among many was not a cause for concern. As your time has gone on, it seems the thing is interested in chaos and destruction and seeks to destroy all things, those both mortal and magical.

"I was sent here to see what you were doing. To learn if you were making progress."

"A spy?" Mordred asked, incredulous. "I am now hunted

by both good and evil?"

"Not hunted, watched. And the Warders are less good and evil than impartial. They act as judges and gatekeepers in the realms far beyond your understanding. Everything hangs in the balance now. All things. And you, dear Mordred, are our only hope. But you are not alone entirely. As the blackness moves to take more light, there are many who will be ready to aid you."

"I was told I am the sole hero of this tale."

Saracles cocked his head and Mordred had the distinct impression he was indeed a bird. In fact, the more Mordred thought about the manners and form of the creature, it all made sense. Too much sense. "How am I to know I can trust you?"

"I cannot answer that. I am only looking for a way to get back my true form. You see, for every Fane who loses his bird form, there are fewer soldiers on the front lines of the battlefield. The Warders have great power, but they rely on their troops to bring them information and warnings. They cannot often leave their posts. It takes immense skill to keep the gates solid to be sure something that belongs in one place doesn't enter another."

Mordred felt as though his head was splitting in two. His mind was slogging through a sea of mud. Shapeless thoughts and feelings hurtled past him as he stood staring at Saracles. "You mentioned the Hollow King. How is it he took your true form, and what is he?"

Saracles smiled, but it didn't reach his eyes. It seemed more like a grimace. "Hollows used to be an unorganized lot of monsters. They are soulless things. Simple beings. They do not function much beyond wandering the night looking for dead bodies to consume. They are the lowest of the low, if you will. No real intelligence, no real speech. In that form they posed no threat to anyone. They were simply like rats feeding off carrion, and they went unnoticed through this world, living in shadows and cemeteries, places where humans rarely spent time and, therefore, rarely encountered them."

"Like ghouls?" Mordred had heard about the creatures that haunted the places of the dead.

The Fane tilted his head again. "Yes, but Hollows are very rare. They exist, as far as we know, only in a few places. They dislike contact with other species and there is not much known about them except what we have observed first hand. Strangely, these Hollows seem to have evolved to some degree. This band in Sicily has developed into something we must take notice of. They have a language, and even a hierarchy, and for the first time there is one who has made himself a king and he appears to be able to reason and scheme. Hollows belong to the darkness, so no good can come of this.

"The Hollow King watched me transform when I was unaware. One night, while waiting for the sun to rise, and with it the moment I could change back to my bird form, he summoned a horde of his fiends to attack me. In that attack, in which I barely escaped with my life, the king was able to pluck a feather from my tail. Until I retrieve that feather, I am useless to both the Warders and my own kind."

Saracles hung his head in defeat. Mordred sat quietly for a moment, allowing the movement of the vessel to rock him. Having accepted the existence of the bizarre alternative world, he did not doubt the story, but he found he had little sympathy for someone else's struggles.

He was supposed to be moving forward on his own quest. How could he possibly concern himself with someone else's problem? Didn't Kabil warn him to continue his journey with all haste? Didn't he say Vlad was amassing strength, waiting for another chance to strike?

He watched as the mysterious blue-purple eyes fixed on his. And then he understood. "You knew who I was when you met us on the docks."

Saracles nodded. "Yes, I knew. Other Fanes knew of your existence quite some time ago, but you disappeared and I could not locate you until now."

Sighing, and feeling overwhelmed, Mordred said, "I am newly made and required some rest. I was asleep for a long time."

"Yes, but now you have risen and I need your help. The Warders cannot afford to lose even one Fane in their efforts to keep the balance on all the planes. I must be brought back to my full self, or even more things may come here from places too terrible to imagine."

The sound of the captain's voice singing a song as he plied the sea, reached Mordred's ear. It was a strange world indeed where he could be sitting on a boat sailing deep waters and appear human, yet the person sitting next to him was half-bird, half-man, the man at the bow of the ship a were-wolf, and opposite was yet another unbelievable beast. It was as if he was trapped in his own dream. Or nightmare.

"Will you help me, Mordred Soulis?" asked the Fane, never taking his blue-purple eyes from Mordred's.

"I do not know yet. You are aware I have my own troubles. I fear every day I do not begin is another day the evil becomes stronger."

"You speak of the one called Vlad?"

Mordred was surprised Saracles knew of Vlad, but he quickly explained. "There is much the Fanes know about your mission. Though we do not call this entity by the same name, he is the one who has upset the balance. We know mankind brought him forth. If you help us, I promise we will assist you in any way we are able. Make no mistake, you will need all the help you can get to save this world."

"I'm not even sure this world is worth saving," Mordred said in a hushed voice more to himself than the Fane.

Dugald strolled over to where the two were talking. His face was grim. "I think we have trouble coming."

Mordred immediately surveyed their progress across the open water. The night sky was dotted with stars, but low clouds, dark and ominous, rolled overhead in patches. "Do you mean the weather?"

"No, something less savory. I've been watching the water at the bow and every now and again I see a shadow appear near the surface, but before I can make out what it is, it disappears."

"The shadow is not from the clouds overhead?" Saracles asked. "There are plenty."

"No," Dugald stated flatly. "Something is tracking us. Waiting to make a move."

Mordred nodded and strode over to the captain who had a firm grip on the boat's large wheel. "How long have you been sailing these waters?"

"Why, since I was a babe," came the reply, as the captain continued to stare straight ahead.

"What strange stories have you heard?"

"Stories?" The man bore a grin that sent a warning chill through Mordred. Something wasn't right. The captain had kept to himself the entire journey. He'd not been found drunk since the first night, but neither did he offer any companionship. Instead he was more often than not standing with his legs braced apart at the ship's wheel. His long, stringy blond hair, blew in the wind while he sang old sailing songs. He was not affected by the motion of the boat and did not display any sort of emotion beyond diligence to his current task.

As Mordred continued to survey him, he realized the captain looked more a skeleton. His skin was stretched tight over his facial bones. His thin lips curved into a smile when he noticed Mordred's gaze.

"Come now, you aren't afraid of the Captain, are ye? Why, I'm the only man who will sail these seas under cover of night. Too many others believe the gruesome stories about what lurks beneath the waves. Not me. I'm safe from it."

Mordred snapped alert at the mention of the thing in the water. "What is it? What is waiting for us?"

The captain threw his head back and laughed, a maniacal sound that bounced across the water and surrounded them with its echo. "Only Death, my man. Only Death, and you should not be afraid. Welcome it. Embrace the darkness."

It was Mordred's turn to smile but there was no hint of humor in his voice. "I already have, you fool."

Reaching toward the man's neck, he grabbed hold of

what he thought was flesh, surprised when his hands went through the form, grabbing nothing but air.

"Mordred! We've got some company!" Dugald's panicked voice called out as Mordred felt the entire vessel shudder from the force of something large slamming into the hull. The creak and groan of splintering wood filled the air.

Mordred ran to the side of the boat and peered down into the black depths. He could make out no defined shape, but the water all around the vessel was bubbling and boiling as if being heated by some otherworldly source.

Suddenly an enormous shaft of darkness rose above the surface of the water and slammed down on the deck, nearly sending Mordred over the railing. The thing flipped and slapped as if searching for something. It was a tentacle, a massive slippery arm from something hidden beneath the boat.

"Saracles, if you ever truly wanted to help me, now would be the time!" Mordred shouted over the sounds of the waves crashing and the boat being smashed apart. "Get to the wheel. Get that demon off this damn vessel and sail it!"

"Dugald! Over here. Help me get rid of this thing." Morded yelled while pulling his sword from the scabbard at his side. He couldn't be sure if what was attacking the boat was a worldly being, or something darker, and swiftly elected not to use his Blood Sword. He had been warned by Jakob, the Master Templar, that the Blood Sword could only be used on the undead.

Bringing the curved blade over his head with both hands, Mordred brought it down with as much strength as he could. The tentacle was thicker than a man's waist, and he feared he would have to chop at it repeatedly.

As soon as the blade touched the ghastly appendage, the entire boat rocked again from another blow to the hull. If they did not dispatch the monster soon, the vessel would be lost.

Falling backward, Mordred recovered as soon has he hit the deck. Jumping to his feet, he struck again while Dugald attacked from the other side.

Then a second tentacle appeared and the boat was stalled, helpless in the grip of the beast. Mordred had no idea how close they were to land and, while he wasn't afraid for himself, he was worried that Dugald, his horse, and the Fane would not survive.

Laughter swirled around Mordred as he worked desperately to save the group. The Captain merely stood, staring at them, his eyes vacant, mouth open. His entire being shifted from a thin, aging man, to the skeleton Mordred had glimpsed earlier.

"You paid the ferryman for a one-way trip to Hell. You cannot win against the Kraken."

"We'll see about that," Mordred bellowed over the

The Kraken

deafening sounds of the monster's attack. He brought the hilt of his sword up and smashed it into the captain's upper body, sending him backward. Before he hit the deck, however, he simply split apart and dissolved into dust and was carried away on the wind.

Mordred returned to the task of slashing at tentacles, three now. The deck was slick with sea water, and the motion of the ship caused by the enormous creature below made the going slow and treacherous.

Dugald and Mordred worked feverishly, desperately trying to slice through the thick, oily arms, but as soon as they chopped one away, another came over the side of the boat searching, with harsh sucking sounds, for victims to drag overboard and drown.

The boat rocked dangerously as the beast wrapped more and more limbs around the hull. It would, within a matter of minutes, either sink under the weight of the tentacles, or merely break apart from the Kraken's crushing grasp.

"Can you swim?" Mordred shouted to Dugald. He closed his mouth just in time to avoid swallowing the thick, sticky black fluid that spewed from a severed limb.

Without looking up, Dugald replied, "Not very well. In the Bath House I could only because I was able to touch the bottom. Here . . ."

"What about as a werewolf?"

"Well, I've never tried."

"Now might be a good time to start." Mordred tried to clear his mind, searching for a link to his Beast of Burden, No sooner did he glance over at the large black stallion tethered in the center of the boat, then the horse said in his mind, *"I can swim, but I do not know exactly how far the nearest land mass is. We might be too far out at sea."*

"We'll have to hope for the best. There's no way we can keep fighting this thing," Mordred replied.

"Saracles! Can you swim?"

"I'm a bird, not a fish," came the answer Mordred dreaded. He had two men that would be hard pressed to keep their heads above water, and a horse that might be able to stay afloat if they were close to land.

Jumping out of the way of another massive tentacle, Mordred looked out to sea, wiping wet hair from his eyes with a forearm. He still clutched the hilt of his sword in the vain hope he could strike a final blow that would decimate the monster.

He peered through the spray of the salt water, and prayed for something that looked like a land mass. There was nothing but a blanket of blackness, and the fear that the captain had not taken them on the requested course, but had left them somewhere far away from civilization.

Fear choked Mordred's lungs, threatening to drive the

breath from his body. As it had been in the desert when they were attacked by the Ammut, he was confident of his own survival, but now others depended on him as well.

He tried to will a solution to their predicament, but none came forth and he returned to the futile hacking and slashing of the Kraken's tentacles. This couldn't be the end. He could not fail to save them all, could he? He was a vampyre, or at least half so. Wasn't there something he could do?

Then he spotted the rowboat, barely big enough to fit them all, but there all the same, swinging on the ropes holding it to the vessel.

"Dugald!" he shouted. "Go cut the boat loose and get Saracles, yourself, and Sleipner off the boat. It's going down."

As if to prove him correct, the craft shuddered and part of the side closest to them splintered.

Dugald stopped chopping at the beast and ran to the hanging rowboat.

"Saracles, help Dugald. Get my horse off this boat, now!"

"What of you?"

"I am of no consequence at the moment. Just get moving!"

Mordred watched the Fane race to Dugald. Within a moment they had the dinghy loose and Dugald lowered it as best he could as it slammed against the vessel's side. Saracles went for the horse.

Turning back to face the many limbs of the sea monster,

Mordred stared hard at the tiny lantern of flame that had been left on deck. It was so small and insignificant he wondered if he would be able to bring life from it in the quantity he desired.

He had to hold himself up by grasping the wheel as the Kraken began dragging the front of the boat under the waves.

Mordred whispered in his mind the words that would speak to the flame. Concentrating, he pictured the brand he had received from the element beneath the pyramid. He praised the flame, acknowledging its power even in this tiny form. He commanded it to grow and to move away from the lantern. Extending his arms in front of him, Mordred opened his hands and spread his fingers. He watched as the fire expanded. It shot across the deck in several long arcs of gold and red and encircled Mordred.

Spinning, he directed the flame above him. He felt his skin bubbling from the heat, but needed to give himself to the fire if he was to distract the Kraken long enough for the others to escape.

Searing waves of steam constricted Mordred's throat. His breathing became labored and he struggled to remain conscious.

In his mind he saw the flames shoot forward toward the sea beast. He heard the loud hissing and popping as fire met its enemy water. Then he smelled the horrific stench of something being roasted alive.

A strange, rumble, followed by an angry roar, pierced the air. The boat slid further beneath the water, but the Kraken's attention was now on trying to exterminate the source of the flames.

Dugald, Saracles, and the horse jumped overboard. Dugald climbed into the dinghy, then helped the Fane. They waited for the horse to swim near, and together they made their way away from the deadly tentacles of the Kraken.

The scene as they moved away was macabre. Mordred was totally engulfed in flames, a human torch. They watched in horror as the Kraken brought a number of its tentacles together to grab and perhaps crush him.

The air was filled with the sound of crashing waves, the cracking of wood, and the smell of burning flesh.

VI

Chapter Six

ordred spent his last moments before being crushed to oblivion sending the fire away from himself and trying to shift into a patch of mist. He was struggling to concentrate, but his mind kept returning to the grim fact that every bone in his body was breaking.

His ribs went first, snapping and sending shards of bone through his lungs. Breathing became almost impossible, and Mordred was only able to inhale in very shallow gasps.

All the blood in his body was being sucked to his skin, and a strange coldness filled his being. Flashes of light and dark entered Mordred's mind as pain warred with defeat, life with death.

He knew he would rise again, but knowing he would be shattered and broken was unpleasant to contemplate. Time was of the essence. He felt he could fight Vlad this time around and even win, but not if he lost the element of surprise. Already other beasts were being alerted to his presence. If he had to spend time recuperating he feared all would be lost.

Unable to shift into the light mist, Mordred tried to concentrate on the form of a fish. He wasn't sure that would even be possible. Could he breathe underwater? For an instant, he wished he had paid more attention when he'd gone through training, first with Jakob and then Kabil.

Beneath his feet the boat shattered and broke apart, scattering across the waves with no more substance than a child's toy. Within moments, Mordred felt himself dragged beneath the black, roiling sea.

Noise disappeared along with his sense of reality. Mordred knew he was lost. He could not shift to anything that would help him. Whether it was from his failure to concentrate, or simply an inability to become a form beneath the water, he did not know.

The failure was deafening. His heart slowed, pounding out its last few precious beats. His pulse, too, became shallow as his lungs were denied the oxygen they so desperately needed.

The pain wracking his body dulled him to the point that he no longer cared. His only fear was that he would end up literally in the belly of the beast if he didn't somehow stay conscious enough to escape the tentacles.

Even now he was unable to see the rest of the monster and wondered how far down he would be dragged. What would happen to his body if he went too deep? How long would it take him to recover?

Mordred had long since stopped struggling, recognizing that doing so only made the Kraken tighten its grip. Amazingly, even in the throes of death, a thought broke through the haze in his mind. Maybe he could fool the monster into thinking he was dead. Maybe it would lose interest and release him. Then he could swim to the surface and hopefully find his way to the others.

He prayed Dugald, Sleipner, and his new companion, Saracles, had managed to escape the destruction. Mordred didn't want to think about continuing the journey alone. He found it funny, as his mind wandered, that once he wanted to be alone more than anything in the world. Now, however, he didn't want to be without his companions.

He commanded his body to remain alert, despite the fact he was several stages into drowning, when an odd, high-pitched sound reached his ears. It was like a whistle, bouncing around him. Then he heard another, and another, until a chorus of shrill chatter, chirps and clicks surrounded him in the strange watery darkness.

His vision dimmed, just as he saw a group of gray shapes moving nearer. Mordred felt the Kraken release him as the squealing continued. He felt himself nudged gently upward. He couldn't fight this new entity. Whether they would prove to be friend or foe he did not know.

✟ ✟ ✟

"Mordred!"

The sound of joyous laughter was the first thing Mordred recognized coming out of the blackness. It was Dugald.

Cracking open an eye, Mordred found himself staring at the sky. Then his view was blocked by a great black muzzle, and his own nostrils picked up the smell of oats. Warm breath brushed his face as Sleipner snuffled and huffed, nudging him.

Mordred laughed, then gasped. His entire ribcage felt as though it had been crushed. Then the memory of his experience came crashing back.

He tried to turn his head away from the beast's pestering, but couldn't.

"Don't even think about moving. You've broken just about every bone in your body." The strange face of Saracles appeared. He was smiling and acted as though it was nothing of consequence that the vampyre was immobile. "Dugald told me it might be some days before you can resume the journey, but the good news is we've arrived on Sicily."

"How?" Mordred whispered.

"Oh, that's a pretty amazing story in itself," Dugald replied, squatting down near Mordred. "We were in the boat. The horse was swimming and we had the reins, but we had no idea where we were headed. All we wanted was to get away from that monster."

"And we had no idea what happened to you," Saracles added.

"Yes," Dugald continued. "It looked pretty hopeless, and then from out of nowhere came these strange creatures."

"Dolphins," Saracles offered.

"Dolphins, yes. They were chattering and chirping and they circled the boat. They wouldn't let us continue rowing in the direction we were headed, and forced us to go back toward the Kraken."

"And you know we didn't want to go back there," Saracles said. "But, the dolphins kept leaping over the boat squealing in such high voices we knew we had no choice."

"When we passed the place where we'd last seen the vessel, there was no evidence of it or any sign of you. But they kept us moving and we reached shore some time later," Dugald explained. "Just as soon as we beached the boat, another group of dolphins joined the first and you were being floated between two of them. It was really quite amazing. If not for those creatures, we'd surely be dead or lost at sea.

We're one lucky bunch."

"Yes, I feel ever so lucky now that I can't move," Mordred grumbled. "So, we are where we were meant to be?"

"Yes. Exactly where we should be. It's a miracle, really," Saracles finished.

"I've already made a wooden sled from some of the wreckage that drifted in. I think with Sleipner's help we can move to higher, safer ground," Dugald added as he moved out of Mordred's range of vision.

A warm wind drifted over the shore, bringing with it the scent of danger. Mordred shivered, but not from the temperature. He could not be found by Vlad or his minions, crippled on the beach of a strange land.

"We need to move to shelter," Mordred said, looking first at Dugald, then Saracles. "We're not safe here and something is watching us. I don't want to be caught out in this condition."

"It's the Hollows," Saracles said with an edge of bitterness. "It is their rottenness, their death scent that you smell. They know everything that happens on this island, and they will know you are here."

"You know this place? Can you get us to safety?"

"There isn't enough time. When you can smell the Hollows it means they are already here."

"So, what chance do we have? I am completely useless

at the moment."

"We will need to do the only thing we can, which under normal circumstances I would never suggest, but we have no choice."

Mordred closed his eyes and sighed, not sure he wanted to hear the option. "And that is?"

"We have to strike a bargain. There must be something they want that you could obtain for them, and in return we can get my feather back."

"What?" Mordred was incredulous and angry at the suggestion that he was being offered up as a helpless sacrifice. "How dare you even think to use me as the bargaining chip?!"

"Easy, vampyre. What I was thinking was to prolong your life. In your current predicament, how can you be sure they don't know of a way to dispatch you that guarantees you don't rise again? After all, they're the best dead things I've ever come across. Hollows are centuries old, but over time they've become more curious about the living. So, I was thinking we could ask that they bring you to the Hollow King, and if they allow you to heal, you'll do their bidding. We'll be sure to let them know we aren't staying. Hollows tend to get a little territorial."

Mordred sneered, not at all happy with what Saracles' proposal. "This had better work, or you won't have to worry about getting your one feather back because I'll pluck every other one from your scrawny body myself."

Saracles rose and moved out of Mordred's sight clearly disturbed by his threatening tone.

He heard a conversation taking place some distance away. While he was unable to make out exact words, he recognized the heated tones. It infuriated Mordred that they were obviously talking about him as if he weren't there.

"Hey, I'm still here. If you have something to say, share it with me," he demanded angrily, trying to rise. His bones felt as though they were nothing more than limp rags and pain shot through him, reminding him that for the moment he was helpless indeed and at the mercy of the two men standing nearby.

Dugald and Saracles returned, both agitated. Mordred didn't have to read their minds to know they were afraid of the coming meeting with the Hollows.

"I think Saracles has a good plan," Dugald said at Mordred's questioning look.

Mordred watched Saracles. The Fane was nervous and shifted on his feet. "Yes, well, I think we've come ashore in the territory belonging to Xanthius, the Hollow King himself. The soldiers coming to meet us will be his men. This is divine providence, certainly, because we don't have to pit one group against another to get to the king. Xanthius is very powerful on the island, but with an increase in the number of dead on the Italian mainland, he is forced to wage a war against the encroaching population of newcomers. He's very vain for a member of the undead, so be mindful of that. If we do this right we should make it through just fine. With Xanthius behind us, we'll not be harmed. We just need to convince him that we're worthy of *being* left unharmed."

"Is Xanthius the one who holds your feather? Does he know its worth?" Mordred asked.

"I can't be sure who has it now, but I know he had his men do the dirty work. They waited until I was undergoing the change, attacked, and then plucked it. So they knew what I was."

"But why did they want your feather? What purpose does it serve them?"

"My guess is they thought the feather itself was magical, and by keeping me bound to this plane I would be forced to summon the Warders."

Confused, Mordred frowned. "But, why do they want a meeting with the Warders?"

"I think they would like to be permitted to enter other planes. They are dead but refuse to accept their fate, and so they linger here, unable to move forward. Unable to go Above or Below."

"And by holding you bound to this plane, the Hollows think the Warders will come for you and they can make a trade," Mordred finished for Saracles.

Before Saracles could respond, Dugald spoke up. "We'd best get ready. The stench is getting stronger."

The orange orb of the sun was sinking beneath the azure waters, casting the group in shades of deep purple and blue. Only a band of pale pink remained on the horizon, but before long that, too, disappeared.

Thousands of tiny points of light twinkled in a clear sky. The air was warm and heavy with the scent of sea and sand. It would have been an otherwise beautiful night if not marred by the growing smell of decayed flesh.

The sound of waves lapping at the shore was soon muffled by guttural voices and the clashing of metal.

"Quiet down, you stupid idiots. How the hell do you think we can patrol if you keep up that racket?"

"Patrol? What are we patrolling for? It's not like there's anything else on this damn island but us Hollows and those stupid humans."

"Yeah, Grimlock, Gnash is right. What are we patrolling for?"

"Aw, you idiots, shut up and listen. The king's gotten word there's something new in town, and this something might actually help him put down the Ghouls from the mainland once and for all. But, we got to be the first Hollows to get to this something."

"What something?" came a voice more like a growl.

The sound of metal scraping against metal ricocheted across the clearing. Grimlock scowled, bringing the strips of torn flesh on his face together, cloaking him in decomposed skin. He brought his gnarled hand to his face and pushed the flaps from his sunken red eyes, glowering at his companions.

"Stop that noise and come on. I smell something foul on the air tonight, and it ain't us." Grimlock continued to push through the shrubbery blocking the beach from sight.

He didn't have to turn around to know his contingent of Hollows was following, he could hear them. The more they tried not to make noise, the more noise they made. Grimlock rolled his eyes.

"Well, well, well." The leader of the Hollows changed his voice so it was not simply a muddled bunch of groans and growls. While his words were still heavy with a guttural accent, he could be understood. He sneered when he saw the group of strangers. "What have we here? A werewolf, a horse, a Fane and, oh yes, a vampyre, too. Is today my lucky day or what?"

Dugald's upper lip curled in a snarl as he processed the words. "Depends on how you define luck." He pulled two short swords from their sheaths on his hips and brought them up so they were visible to all.

The lead Hollow stepped closer. "Now, now, there's no need for you to be so testy. Why, we come in peace."

Saracles made a choking sound. "When have Hollows ever come in peace?"

"Aw, you still upset because you lost your wings, little bird-man?"

Mordred, propped up against a rock, spoke with difficulty though he tried to mask the pain. "What do you want of us?"

"Oh, it's not what Grimlock wants of you that matters, it's what the king wants. He's asked to see you and it's our job to bring you to him right away. Come along then."

Dugald stood his ground, nostrils flaring, trying to smell anything but the scent of decomposed bodies. Just to look at the creatures made him ill. They were all in various forms of decay. Some were still covered with gray flesh, others missed large chunks of skin, which revealed inner organs that also bore the look of death. The worst were those whose bones protruded through patches of torn flesh. Dried blood and yellow pus oozed from gaping wounds. Hollows were not for the squeamish.

Even stranger still was the fact that many of the creatures wore pieces of ancient Roman armor. Helms, shields, breastplates, and leg guards covered their thin frames.

Unholy warriors to be sure, Mordred thought.

"We're not going anywhere until you tell us exactly what your purpose is," Dugald stated in a voice that gave evidence of his rising anger.

"It's not for us lowly ones to tell you. We only know what the king wants and we only do what the king wants." Grimlock smiled, revealing missing teeth which allowed large globules of black saliva to drip from his rotted lips.

That made Dugald back up.

Mordred spoke. "It's okay, Dugald. We'll go meet their king. But, Grimlock, we do have a small problem. I have recently . . ."

Grimlock waved a bony hand. "Yes, we know all about your fight with the Kraken. That's why we are here. You are injured. We know it will take you some time to heal and until then you will be at our mercy."

"Well, then, let's be off," Mordred suggested, fearing even he would lose his stomach if the smells grew worse.

As the Hollows moved in to assist, Dugald waved them off. "We'll take care of him ourselves."

Dugald and Saracles carefully moved Mordred to the rough planking. Once he was situated, they tied a rope around Sleipner and attached it to the makeshift litter. Soon, Mordred felt himself moving over the ground. He saw nothing but the sky, and was actually quite comfortable not being able to see the grotesque faces of the Hollows.

"Is it far?" Mordred asked.

He heard Grimlock's gruff reply. "No, not far at all. The king has come down from the mountains to greet you. He is most anxious to strike a deal with you."

Soon the band of Hollows fanned out to surround Mordred, Dugald, and Saracles. With Grimlock in the lead, they left the beach for the interior of the island, clattering and banging all the way.

✢ ✢ ✢

"Your Highness, we present to you, er . . ." Grimlock turned to face Mordred, who had been moved to a sitting position with his back resting against a fallen column of finely carved white marble. The Hollow wore an expression of anticipation on what was left of his face.

The king rose from his throne, which Mordred assumed was made out of bones, many of them human. He was larger, taller than the others, and had managed to preserve most of his skin.

"Greetings, visitors. By what names shall I call you?"

Mordred was on guard for trickery, having been told by Saracles not to trust the Hollows, but he had not expected politeness. "I am Mordred," he said as the king moved toward

Xanthius the Hollow King

him. "And these are my companions, Dugald and Saracles."

"And let us not forget your Beast of Burden." The king made a small bow to the horse before returning his gaze to Mordred. Red pupils floated within yellow orbs. "I am Xanthius, the Hollow King, and you will be my guests."

"For how long?" Mordred asked, uneasy. There was something the king wasn't saying.

"I have a favor I need to ask of you . . . well, okay," the king laughed at himself, "a task you must complete, and then I'll allow you to continue on your journey."

"What if we do not agree on the task you require of us?"

"Then you'll never leave. You see, Mordred, I know all about you. More than you might know of yourself. I know you are, at this very moment, injured, and you cannot harm me. I know that without blood you will remain in your broken state for some time, perhaps forever. So, really, you have no choice but to acquiesce to my demands. In return, I will allow you the blood your body craves, and you will be set free."

"We are your prisoners?" Dugald ground out through clenched teeth.

"In a manner of speaking. I'd like to say we are partners in a common cause."

"And what would that cause be?" Mordred asked.

"Well, we have uninvited guests on this island. Other

creatures from the mainland seek to set up their own group here, on my land. I can't have that. There is an enormous overcrowding problem in the graveyards and cemeteries on the mainland, and we Hollows will not tolerate that here. We were here first."

Mordred, feeling like a useless pile of flesh and broken bones, wanted to know more. He had a sinking feeling he'd just stumbled into a war ready to erupt.

"I've always lived by the creed, 'may the strong survive'. If you are indeed the rightful ruler of the dead here, then you should have enough troops to prevent a takeover, right?"

Xanthius gazed down at Mordred. "Therein lies the problem. I've been here for as long as there have been Hollows, but this is an island, and a lesser amount of dead here. We live in peace and cause no harm to any. Yet, the mainland is different. There are always wars and plagues and new undead coming, which means no matter how large my army, an attack from the mainland would surely outnumber me."

"Why do you think I can help?"

"I need you to convert another group of dead. It would swell my ranks and then no one would dare come to Sicily."

Mordred's brows knitted. "You just told me there is only a finite source of Hollows on this island. How is there another group here?"

"Well, they aren't Hollows, yet. They are in limbo,

waiting to be released from their own hell, and you are the man who can do that. Then, they will be so grateful for all you have done, you need only mention that you want them to swear their allegiance to me and we'll all be on our merry way. Oh, but where are my manners? Grimlock? Fetch a goblet of blood for our new friend, Mordred."

Grimlock stepped out of Mordred's field of vision and swiftly reappeared. In his hands he held a rusted goblet. Mordred's nostrils flared at the scent of blood that lay thick over the death smell. His entire body ached for just one taste. He wondered only briefly how it was that these ghostly beings could produce fresh blood, and then decided he didn't want to know.

"Yes, see, do as I say and I will give you all the blood you need to heal yourself. Don't do as I say and I'll leave you here to rot in this sorry state.

Chewing the inside of his jaw, Mordred nodded.

"Mordred, what are you thinking?" Dugald asked. "We don't need to align ourselves with these creatures."

Xanthius laughed, which caused the whole of the Hollow gang crowded around them to laugh. "Silly wolf, look around you. Where could you possibly go that I couldn't find you? You are on an island. You need my help."

"Under one condition," Mordred said softly.

"I don't think you are in any spot to be naming the terms

of our deal, vampyre," Xanthius bit out, all earlier civility vanishing. His eyes flashed red fire.

"This is a gentlemen's agreement, correct? You want me to do something for you. Something that will help you. Is it not fair that I be rewarded if I succeed in this task?"

"Your reward will be my permission to leave this island."

"Now, Xanthius, you know eventually I will heal. And at that time, do you really want to upset me? I'm asking for something very simple."

Crossing his arms, the Hollow King peered down at Mordred. "Fine, what is it you want?"

"I want the Fane's feather back."

When Xanthius paused, Mordred continued, "It is of no use to you. Saracles can no more summon the Warders to you than you can leave this island. Let it go. Give it back to its owner and be done with it."

It was Grimlock who spoke rubbing his hands together. "But, your highness, if you give up the feather the Warders will never agree to let us leave this plane. You must not give back the feather. They will come for this one eventually."

"Don't you get it, you undead dimwit, I'm of no consequence to the Warders. They're dealing with far more important things than to worry over what has become of one of their soldiers," Saracles snapped.

"So say you," Grimlock goaded.

"Enough," Xanthius said, "You act like children. I will agree to give back the feather if you can convince those trapped in the mines to pledge fealty to me as the rightful King of the Hollows of Sicily."

With that, Xanthius stalked off, Grimlock following like a shadow. The rest of the Hollows shuffled away as well, realizing the main attraction was over. Dugald bent down to whisper in Mordred's ear. "We could escape, you know."

"To where, Dugald, and look at me. I am in no condition to travel, or fight for that matter."

"But why bargain with evil?"

"There's no reason to believe these beings are evil."

"If they weren't evil the Warders would let them leave this plane." Saracles said, "Because they are still here means they have a dark side."

"Perhaps," Mordred agreed. "On the other hand, they could simply have become maligned over the centuries. If there's one thing I've learned so far, it's that appearances can be deceiving. For now, we cooperate. Hopefully, I can help them and they will honor their end of the bargain. If not, we'll come up with a plan B. Now, hand me that goblet."

Dugald gasped. "You aren't actually going to drink that, are you? How do you know it's not poisoned or something?"

"I don't, but right now I could care less if this is pigs' blood. Any blood will do the trick." Mordred paused. "I never thought I'd hear myself say that."

Dugald peered into the goblet and made a sound. "Well, this isn't going to make you too happy."

Mordred grasped the goblet and brought it to his lips. In one swallow, he drank the contents, what little there was of it.

Even so, his body immediately reacted. The pain circulating through his limbs lessened, and he felt his breath coming easier as his ribs began to mend. Clearly, the Hollows were planning on delaying his recovery until he did what they wanted. Not knowing what else lurked in the shadows of this strange place, Mordred did not feel comfortable searching for another source of blood.

Sighing, he realized that though he was older in his vampyre years, he was no wiser when it came to his new lot in life. Hollows, creatures once only belonging to tales told around late night campfires, were alive and well and living alongside humans in the new world he'd been thrust into.

The sound of thrashing and grumbling alerted Mordred to the presence of Grimlock and a few other Hollows. "The king wants us to make you comfortable in our humble abode. We're to take you past the crypts and into the temple ruins."

Without further commentary, and despite protests from Dugald, the Hollows hoisted the planks Mordred rested on, and marched him past a field full of ancient graves, some marked by simple stones, others, though worn from the passage of time, bearing the intricate carvings and graceful columns of royalty.

Above the smell of the Hollows, and the dead beneath the earth, Mordred could make out the scents of oranges and lemons, olives and grapes. He was lowered and brought into a small temple. Several columns had fallen and there were large cracks snaking their way across the marble floor and up the walls.

Mordred was placed on the ground.

"This is where you will stay until the king summons you again. If the wolf needs to hunt, we advise he go no further than the olive grove. Beyond that lies the land that the mainlanders have claimed, and they will not be so friendly." Grimlock grunted.

Dugald snorted. "You call this 'friendly'?"

Mordred put a stop to further complaints by kicking Dugald in the calf. "We thank you, Grimlock."

The Hollow shuffled out of the temple, followed by the rest of his kind. Once they reached the endless field of tombs, the group shimmered in the moonlight, ethereal and ghostlike, before being swallowed up by the unhallowed ground.

"I don't like this," Dugald said in a whisper. "It smells foul."

"Everything smells foul around here," Saracles replied, voice thick with sarcasm.

Dugald rounded on the Fane and Mordred. "Am I the only one thinking making a deal with the dead isn't smart?"

"Dugald, I'm dead, well actually undead. And before you offer any more of your brilliant deductions, let me tell you one more time . . . We don't have a choice," Mordred stated calmly. His body was still reconstructing itself and he was in no mood to explain why they would have to deal with the Hollows.

"But, Mordred, how do we know that after you've convinced these 'others' to join forces with this crew, if you can even do that, the king will honor his word? These are Hollows you're dealing with. They aren't human . . . They're sub-human."

Saracles took a seat on the floor, back resting against a fallen column. "I am truly sorry. I thought perhaps it would be simple getting my feather back. The Hollows, they didn't seem too terribly bright and, well, I figured you would be the person who could make them give it back to me."

"Make them?" Mordred inquired, "as in 'do battle with'?"

Hanging his head, Saracles nodded.

"So my reputation as a blood-thirsty killer precedes me, does it? I hack first and ask questions later, if there's anyone alive to ask, right? That was my former life."

"But you're a vampyre. You drink blood. And before that you were a mercenary."

"Saracles, there is much you claim to know of me, but you have revealed that you understand nothing of who I am. I left my mercenary life behind me the day I died in the desert. And I did die. Now, I will not surrender to that side of me that whispers always of bloodshed and murder. If I did, even you would not be immune to my lust. I must always keep that part of myself contained. Do not seek to release it."

"But, if we could just get you more blood, you'd heal faster and then we could be off and away from here," Dugald persisted.

"Away to where? We don't even know where we are, and if we choose to cross into Italy, we are likely to face whatever is causing trouble with the Hollows, the Mainlanders, according to Xanthius. And who knows what trouble they will bring to us."

"And what about me?" Saracles spoke up while eyeing Dugald. "Sure, you both leave and I just rot here for the rest of my unnatural life?"

"Hey, I don't mean to be rude, but honestly, it isn't our fight, right, Mordred?"

"Might I remind you that you weren't technically my fight either, Dugald? I could have left you to die beneath that timber."

"Maybe, but that was different. I brought you to the Book of the Undead and I've helped get you out of trouble."

Mordred scowled. "More like you've brought me to more trouble than I would have had on my own. And, Dugald, wasn't it you who brought Saracles aboard our boat without even knowing who or what he was?"

"Well, yeah, but . . ."

Mordred raised a hand but only managed to lift it to just above his chest before letting it fall limply back to his side. "Enough. The point is, you invited this particular trouble, and now you want to dismiss it? Where is your honor, Dugald?"

Dugald's head snapped up as if he'd been slapped. "My honor? You have no right to question my honor. I have done nothing but help you any way I could to repay you for saving my life. Hell, I waited for hundreds of years while you slept. And not once have you ever bothered to thank me. My honor? I'm just trying to get out of here with the least amount of casualties. Forgive me for thinking of someone other than myself."

Before Mordred could reply, Dugald stormed out of the temple. By the light of the moon, he saw the man's silhouette shift and change, becoming that of the wolf. And then he was gone.

VII

Chapter Seven

An entire day passed without word from Dugald, and though Mordred was loath to admit it, he was beginning to worry. Maybe the werewolf simply needed some time to lick his wounds, or perhaps he'd gotten himself into trouble . . . again. And, still, Mordred was in no condition to help anyone.

When dusk touched the horizon once more, Mordred was brought another goblet of mere drops of blood, which he drank like a man dying of thirst. Even the small amounts enabled his body to continue healing. He could now sit upright without help.

Mordred focused his mind on repairing his body. With Dugald missing, he needed to recover faster than he could with the amount of blood the Hollows gave him.

"I'd go out and search for him, but without my wings, I can't help. The Hollows patrol everywhere these days,"

Saracles said.

"It's not your fault," Mordred countered, staring for the umpteenth time at the artwork painted on the walls.

Saracles stood and paced the temple. "It is my fault. If I hadn't sought you out, you would never have been attacked by the Kraken, and maybe you would never have come here."

"You are forgetting that we made a bargain with that nasty captain before we even met you. If you hadn't been aboard the boat, I'm sure we would have ended up nowhere near here."

"Fat lot of good that did you. You're forgetting about the Kraken."

"No, I'm not, but the Kraken had nothing to do with you. What I don't get though, Saracles, is why you couldn't just summon one of the Warders to come and get your feather back."

"It doesn't work like that. We Fanes pledge our lives to the Warders. We know that they rarely, if ever, leave their posts, and, it would be wrong of me to request intervention for myself. If one Warder fails for even the blink of an eye, who knows what might try to reach this plane. It could be devastating."

"I think more than one has already failed," Mordred scoffed.

No!" Saracles stopped in his tracks and turned to face Mordred, his strangely colored eyes wide with fright. "Don't say that. Don't even think that. Even thoughts can be used against those of us trying to preserve this world."

"Don't you understand how powerful Vlad is? As I grow, so does he. If I don't get to him soon, he will be far more powerful than any of us. And here I sit, useless."

"You cannot speak so negatively. If you think you will fail, then it will be so. Mordred, you must believe in yourself and all those who are here to help. You must believe that you are the one to put a balance back in the world."

"Balance?" Mordred ground out, "It's more like I'm to do battle with something far darker than you can even imagine. It wants to suck the life from every human soul on this planet and perhaps every non-human soul as well. How could it have been brought forth? How did humans manage to bring it through the gates you claim to be watched over so well? I think your Warders have definitely slipped up."

Mordred closed his eyes. Just thinking of Vlad made him feel weaker than he already was.

Saracles had a forlorn look in his eyes. "I deeply regret taking you from your duty. It is far more important than what I wanted of you."

"Look, we're here and we might as well see if we can get your damn feather back."

"Maybe I am not meant to have it back. Maybe it is my destiny to simply never feel the currents flowing through my wings," Saracles said softly.

"Now look who's thinking of failure." Mordred found it odd that only moments ago it was he who spoke of giving up, and now he was busy trying to keep the Fane from doing so.

"That doesn't mean you have to accept it. Look at me. You think I was happy about becoming a vampyre? I didn't want to die, that is true. But, had I known what I was to become, I would never have agreed. So, I can sit around and wallow in my own self-pity as you've clearly pointed out, or I can suit up and fight the battle I am supposedly meant to fight. But who's to say I have to accept any of this?"

Saracles lifted his head. "I've made such a mess of things."

"No more than me."

There wasn't anything left to say, from Mordred's point of view. He could well understand what it was like to have something precious taken away, but deep down inside he also knew lamenting one's fate did nothing to change it. He watched as the Fane wandered out into the night.

A heavy sigh escaped Mordred's lips. He was so tired. It was strange. His vampyre-self supposedly would not need the rest his human side craved each day. He should be able to go many nights without needing sleep, but tonight his human side was making it known it wanted nothing more than to close its eyes and allow his mind to simply vanish from this world for a few short hours.

It was beyond depressing to know he would spend many lifetimes watching the moon make its journey across the sky, chased by the fiery globe that was the sun. An endless march of time witnessed by him for years to come. There would be many moments like this, when he would be alone with his thoughts. Alone with the voices in his head questioning his strengths, and his purpose. Wondering if he indeed would live up to the notion that he was a champion.

And moments when the voices buried deeper still tried try to convince him he belonged to the darkness and that he would one day succumb to his true self. These insidious thoughts told him that while he might prolong the outcome, maybe for centuries, in the end the darkness would call to him in a voice too seductive to ignore.

Mordred also found himself wondering if the people he joined with would still be with him in the future. Would they stand beside him and experience the victory, or would they, too, fall prey to their weaknesses? Who could he trust? And who would he call 'friend' in a world full of invisible foes?

Still caught in the gloomy web of his thoughts, Mordred heard the sound of someone approaching. He hoped it would be Dugald, but the figure who entered the temple was King Xanthius.

"You and I are not so different," the king began. Without

an invitation he sat his decayed body down on a fallen column across from Mordred. The moonlight cast half his face in shadow while the other was brought to horrific life. His eyes were sunken deep into his skull and while he had retained most of his flesh there were large sections of skin missing on his face.

Mordred's own eyesight, sharper at night than in daylight, studied the spectral image. He could see where worms had woven their way into the man's body. Ribs showed through areas where the skin had fallen off.

And, of course, the putrid stench of death was ever present. Mordred kept his mind off the smell.

"How is it you think we share something beyond the fact we both violate the laws of the living?"

The king smiled. A blast of fetid air filled the temple when he laughed. "Yes, it is true we are both creatures that should have remained dead, but it is more than that. You and I are misunderstood. The Hollows have always been misunderstood."

Mordred gazed hard into the red eyes of the king. "It is with good reason I am maligned. As a vampyre I have little control over my desire for blood. You would scare the armor off a full-grown warrior if he were to meet you in the midnight hour. I can well understand the fear others have of both of us."

"But is that a reason to destroy us? To take the life of something simply because you do not understand it? Would that be the way of your human race?" Xanthius asked, a sadness creeping into his voice.

Mordred felt a wave of loneliness roll off the king, and it struck his own. It was what they shared. "Sadly, that does seem to be the way of my former race. As a human, I was encouraged to participate in the slaughter of thousands simply because their beliefs were different from those who commanded wealth and vast armies. Even if I had not been turned, I would still bear the blood of innocents on my hands from the time before now."

Xanthius looked out at the moon and sighed. "So, there really is no hope for us?"

"I'm not sure I understand. What is it you hope for?"

The king turned back to Mordred. His face wore an expression of utter defeat. "I suppose what all of us hope for. To live. To feel the sun on my skin. To have skin. To not watch humans and other creatures recoil in fear of me simply because I cannot control the way I look. We Hollows have never harmed another living thing. We have existed peacefully, although unhappily, for centuries on this island, from the time of the first Romans. And now, because humankind cannot control itself, we are forced to go to war. To develop factions and troops and think of ways to kill our own. Do you know the truth of our race?"

Mordred shook his head. He assumed Hollows were a form of ghoul, the kind of creature that arose from the body of a dead human.

Xanthius continued. "We are the children of hundreds of Romans. We were deemed imperfect. We were born into this world as humans, but were killed unmercifully because we exhibited a weakness or deformity. We became Hollows, the shells of human souls that were never allowed to grow up. Cast aside in infancy, we were doomed to live on this island in the Valley of Demons, where the humans would tell gruesome tales about us in an effort to scare the living away. Now we wander aimlessly, looking for away out of this nightmare, one we did not create."

Mordred closed his eyes. He could well imagine the horror of what Xanthius spoke because he had watched the Crusaders kill thousands of children over the course of their journey. He wondered if there were Hollows back in the desert, but he had been too young in his vampyre life to see them.

"This is why you took Saracles's feather? This is why you want a meeting with the Warders? Because you are not the evil we have been made to think of you?"

"Yes," Xanthius responded. "We belong to the light, yet we have been denied it. Why should we suffer for the sins of those who cast us aside? Why are we painted black when we have done nothing to deserve the title of darkness?"

"But why did you threaten us when we arrived, and why have you not given me enough blood to fully recover?" Mordred asked.

Again Xanthius sighed. "I am centuries old, Mordred. Far older than you can imagine, yet I rule here by a thread. There are some Hollows who, over time, have not taken to the idea that we should be confined to this island for all eternity. They seek to join the new dead and overthrow my kingdom, and I fear they will doom all of us to the darkness, should they succeed. I can not show weakness in front of these men."

"It is not weak to want to prevent war," Mordred snapped, more to himself as the image of a man, a king from his past, flashed across his mind. Conrad, the man who sent him to his death and ultimately to this new life. Cursing under his breath, Mordred continued. "What you seek to do, bring a resolution without bloodshed, should be seen as the only course of action."

"Ah, but it has taken too long and the Warders are no closer to coming here to hear me than they were ages ago, and yet we are closer than ever to a battle that will, if allowed to continue, take human lives and those of every other creature on this island. Like the living, the dead do not fight fair by any means, and there are legions of soulless soldiers from the mainland who will know far more than we ever could about how to wage a war."

Thinking about the history Mordred had learned as a warrior of the mighty Roman forces of long ago, he knew Xanthius was right. If there was to be a battle against the mainlanders, it would not go in the Hollows' favor. They would be forced to fight, thereby condemning them to darkness when they did not rightfully belong to that side.

"How do you think I can help you?"

"You are a vampyre. You are a powerful creature. Even the Hollows are afraid of you regaining your full strength."

"I am only half a vampyre. I'm not even fully capable of all the things a true vampyre can do."

"I just need someone who can give the illusion of being vicious. If you can convince the Carlini family from the mainland that the Hollows have made a deal with legions of your kind, we can make them leave us alone for good. And, we have the soldiers in the mines, too."

Confused, Mordred looked to the king for further explanation. "They are Hollows also, left behind from a great battle long ago. They were the enemy of Rome, and were sentenced to being buried alive in the mines. To this date we have not been able to communicate with them, but we know they are there. We can feel their presence."

"Where are the mines?"

"Not far from here is the land where they begin, but we have never been able to find the entrance. The Romans sealed it off long ago, ensuring the Athenian soldiers would be trapped forever."

Silence fell between the two. As strange as it had sounded when Xanthius had first spoken, there was truth to the fact that he and Mordred shared similar thoughts. Xanthius, a soulless being never allowed to have a life, was destined to exist in an altered state living out a lonely existence on this island by an act of careless humans. The king wanted nothing more than to experience life. Mordred could well understand the simplicity of that wish.

He watched as the king rose and walked slowly out of the temple with a shuffling gate.

"I would have been a king, Mordred. Had I been allowed to live, I would have been a mighty leader. Not one who preached bloodshed and war, but one who believed in a peaceful coexistence with other nations. Imagine what mankind's history would be now, if only I had lived my life."

Xanthius did not look back at Mordred. His shoulders slumped in defeat; he walked down the steps and out into the moonlight.

"I will help you," Mordred whispered.

The only sign that the Hollow King had heard was a

slight nod of his head before he shimmered and disappeared into the burial ground of the restless dead.

Grimlock arrived just as the first rays of sunlight touched the earth. He carried the familiar goblet. Grumbling, he handed it to Mordred.

"Xanthius said you are to have a full one this time." The Hollow peered warily at Mordred, watching as he drained the contents in a few deep swallows.

"What are you waiting for?" Mordred asked.

"To see what happens. You are supposed to be a mighty vampyre, but I see no difference in you. Why should we fear you? You are nothing more than a strange man," Grimlock said and turned to leave the temple.

"Would you be happy if I were nothing more than a man?"

The Hollow did not turn around, but the pause before he answered was telling. "No, I would not be happy. You are supposed to help us. You can't help us if you are not a vampyre. We should surrender."

The last words were said very low as if the man were speaking to himself. Mordred watched as he shimmered under the dawn's first light, and in that moment, when the sun touched Grimlock, Mordred wasn't certain if it was simply a trick of light, but he saw Grimlock made whole.

Knowing the Hollows would not be back until dusk,

Mordred had plenty of time to plan. Something about Grimlock made him wary. He did not trust the man, human or not. And he was too quick to assume that Mordred wasn't a vampyre.

The blood was flooding Mordred's body, easing all the remaining pain and bringing with it a renewed strength and energy he hadn't felt since arriving on the island. His mind felt lucid as images of his past merged with his present in his glutted and satisfied state. He felt like a snake who, after devouring its meal, wanted nothing more than to lie still and allow its body to digest the food.

He went over his predicament in his mind. He had a bird missing a feather, whom he had promised to help. And now he had an entire island of ghosts looking to him to help avert a battle over final resting grounds. Would he ever get to his own quest?

For the first time since coming to Sicily, Mordred stood. He stretched his muscles, feeling the euphoria of the simple movements. It was good to be back to his normal self. He moved out of the temple and was heading down a small path overgrown with vines and shrubbery when, from the opposite direction, came Saracles at a run. Before Mordred had a chance to call out a warning the Fane hit him head-on, nearly knocking him to the ground.

"Christ!" Mordred growled as he grabbed hold of

Saracles by the shoulder to prevent him from falling.

"Sorry, so sorry, Mordred, but I have news of Dugald and it isn't good. He's been trapped and taken hostage by the mainlanders that have crossed over to the island," Saracles sputtered nervously while taking large gulps of breath.

Clenching his teeth, Mordred dusted the Fane's shoulders. "How do you know this?"

"I was searching for him after I left you. I had a feeling he left in such a mood that he wouldn't listen to the warning from the Hollows about not going too far. But I am surprised at how close the invaders have come. They are over that next rise, within a day of here."

Dawn had just arrived, which meant it would be hours before the Hollows would be up and about. Mordred couldn't wait for their assistance, and he couldn't he help release the others in the mines since he had no idea where to begin. He would have to hope that the mainland undead were also below ground during the day. Then, perhaps, he could simply bring Dugald back.

Stupid wolf! Mordred thought to himself. The beast was entirely too touchy about wanting to be thanked for saving his hide, and Mordred wasn't at all ready to admit he needed Dugald, or anyone for that matter. The less he cared about others, the better it would be for everyone.

But for now, he certainly couldn't leave the werewolf in

the hands of the enemy. And he'd made a promise to Xanthius. They would need every available body, the living dead, a shape-shifter, and a Fane, to pull off what he had planned.

"So, what do we do?" Saracles asked following Mordred's prolonged silence.

"We do nothing. I will ride over to the camp and bring Dugald back."

"And then?"

"I help the Hollows and I get your feather back, and maybe I can continue on my own journey."

Saracles's eyes widened. "Wait, did you just say you're going to help the Hollows? But they're evil. You can't help them. Let them go to battle with the others."

"For one connected to those claiming to be powerful, you don't know a whole lot. The Hollows aren't evil. They've been unjustly condemned."

"You can't upset the balance of souls, Mordred. The Warders determine the placement of all creatures, living, dead, and undead. They have decided the Hollows belong to neither the light nor the dark," Saracles protested.

Mordred shook his head. "I can't upset the balance of souls? I think that balance was skewed the minute someone resurrected Vlad, and I think it was further botched up the day I was remade. Your Warders are slipping, and if they have a problem with what I am about to do, then let them come here and tell me themselves."

"But the Hollows, they aren't . . ."

"How would you know? Were you here when this all began? Can you even allow yourself to believe these beings aren't evil? Look, they could have surely killed me in my weakened state and they chose not to."

"Because they need you."

"No," Mordred continued. "It was something more than that. They realize killing would add to the condemnation they have received from the Warders. Do you, or your Warders, have any evidence that the Hollows are a menace to any other living thing?"

That stopped Saracles. Mordred could almost hear the wheels turning as the Fane tried to come up with a plausible argument.

"Look, it's pretty simple. I help the Hollows, we avert a mass war with multiple potential casualties, and you get your damn feather back. Everyone is happy."

Saracles shook his head. "Not the Warders."

"I don't give a damn about them. I care about getting Dugald back and getting off this blasted island. You need to remain here. If I'm not back before dusk tell Xanthius where I went. I don't want him thinking I abandoned him."

Mordred brushed past Saracles, nearly knocking the Fane over with the force of his stride. He brought his hands to his lips and whistled. From nearby came an answering call and within moments the big black stallion appeared.

The Beast of Burden snorted a greeting as Mordred patted the animal's neck.

"How do you fare, Beast?" he asked in his mind.

"Better than you and your friend. The Hollows don't want anything of me so I am left alone."

"Speaking of my friend, I need to find out where he's being held. The mainlanders have captured him."

"I knew he was headed for trouble when he stormed out of the temple."

"Yes, and now we must rescue him."

Mordred mounted the horse, smoothly adjusting his black robes. With only pressure from his thighs, the horse and rider moved off in the direction of the next valley. Having no idea what he would find or exactly how he would get Dugald free, Mordred spent the ride in silence.

Halfway between the Valley of the Demons where the Hollows resided, and the place where Saracles had said Dugald was being held, Mordred began to hear voices. They started out very faint at first, but as he continued across a plateau they rose in volume. It was as if many people were calling out to him.

Mordred halted the horse and gazed across the rolling

hills. He detected movement. The voices were not coming from the living. Then he remembered the mines. He must be hearing the dead soldiers trapped far beneath the earth.

There were too many and they were all calling out to him at once in a cacophony that threatened to drown out his own thoughts. He resisted the temptation to put his hands over his ears to soften the noise.

It was time to concentrate and once and for all make some sense of the voices. He had heard the dead speak before, but as now, their messages were muddled because they all seemed to be speaking at the same time. Mordred had yet to learn how to sort out one from the many.

He dismounted from the horse and walked across the grass-covered ground, trying to discern an increase in volume, or a decrease, depending on where he moved.

When he approached a strange configuration of trees, whose trunks had grown together, the noise level rose. Mordred's every sense told him this was the entrance to the mines the Hollows had never found.

It was no wonder the spot had gone unnoticed. The ground was overgrown with tall grasses and shrubs that rattled with dryness in the light breeze. There was nothing to suggest that this had once been a prosperous mining area.

Squatting on his haunches, Mordred touched the brown earth and was startled to feel it trembling. There was a vibration coming from the ground that invaded his entire being.

"I cannot hear you when you all speak together," Mordred called out.

At first there was no response. The noise kept coming. They were male voices, all of them moaning and groaning in a macabre song lamenting their demise. Mordred repeated the statement again.

The voices quieted and then silenced completely. The ground still vibrated, but nothing could be heard except the wind rustling through the parched leaves of the trees overhead.

"Who is it that hears us?" came a gruff voice. As always, it took a moment for Mordred to understand the language they spoke. It was Greek. "Who hears us?"

"I am Mordred Soulis, and I have come to set you free."

"Set us free?"

"Set us free!"

"Yes, set us free, please."

All the voices resumed speaking at once.

"Please, I cannot understand when you speak at once. Can one of you speak for all?" Mordred requested.

"Yes, I will. I am Mestocrites. How is it you can hear us?"

Mordred didn't know the answer. "I do not know, but I was drawn here. I am undead."

"Undead? What are you?" Mestocrites asked.

"I am a vampyre."

Silence.

"Hello?" Mordred asked, unsure how to continue.

"We have no need of a vampyre," Mestocrites replied. "We will not become a party to evil. Leave us."

"But he has said he will set us free, Mestocrites," another voice called out.

"Yes, he can let us go. Please."

Mestocrites spoke again with authority. "We are souls who have wandered these mines for ages, but we are not in league with evil and I will not have us made evil by consorting with a vampyre."

"I'm a half-vampyre actually. I'm also part human."

More silence.

"The other Hollows here want to free you. They have asked me to help," Mordred offered.

"Others? There are others like us? Above ground?"

"Yes, many others," Mordred replied, still having a hard time believing he was communicating with dead soldiers from centuries ago.

"And what would you ask of us in return?" Mestocrites asked suspiciously.

"Only that you pledge your loyalty to Xanthius, the king of the Hollows."

"You want nothing for yourself, vampyre? That is unusual.

I must think on this."

Mordred feared that if the beings had been trapped this long, Mestocrites' thinking might take awhile. "I don't have much time."

"You? You are immortal. Time is of no consequence to you."

"Not exactly. I am on my way to save a friend."

Mordred heard laughter. "A friend? Vampyres have no friends," Mestocrites stated. Several other voices echoed the sentiment.

Mordred was quiet for a moment while he considered the comment. Did he consider Dugald a friend? If so, what did that mean? Wasn't he just doing what was right? There was nothing deeper at work here, he convinced himself.

"I will repeat myself this once: I must leave soon. I can bring the Hollows back once the sun sets. They should be able to release you now that I've found the entrance."

"It isn't as easy as you think. The Romans who left us here to rot also cursed this ground. It cannot be disturbed by mortal or immortal hands until we are judged worthy to be released."

Confused, Mordred rubbed his eyes. "I'm not sure I follow."

"Our souls have been bound to this earth because of the curse. Even if the other Hollows dig through the mines, we cannot be set free. You must find the ones who have the power to bring us to rest."

"Christ! Is nothing simple any more?" Mordred muttered. He rose up and kicked at the ground with his sandaled foot, sending a cloud of dust into the air. As he watched it filter away, disappearing into the rays of sunlight that touched the earth, his eyes noticed movement in the distance.

Quickly, Mordred crouched and narrowed his eyes, peering intently through the tall grasses. His horse had moved away and was hidden from view by a stand of gnarled trees.

As soon as he identified the figure fast approaching, he groaned and rose. Saracles had not listened and stayed behind. Then he realized the Fane's timing might be opportune. He waited the few moments it took for Saracles to arrive. Strangely, the voices below had quieted as well, as if in expectation.

It was Mordred who started the new round of conversation. "Why am I not surprised to see you?"

"Because you were hoping I would follow despite your gruff commands to do otherwise?" Saracles offered with a tentative smile.

"No, more like I expected you wouldn't listen and I am immediately reminded of the words 'bird brain'."

Saracles ignored the barb. "So, why have you stopped?"

"As if you didn't know," Mordred growled before

stalking past Saracles. Bending, he touched the ground. "This is the entrance to the lost mines, and why do I think you've known this all along? Why am I suddenly thinking you are far more aware of the situation than you would have me believe?"

"I, I . . . Well, I . . ."

"Stop it. You know the other Hollows are here. You must also know they require the services of your precious Warders to release them, but you have resisted revealing this information because you think you are keeping the souls in check. You believe the Hollows don't belong in a good place. Right? C'mon Saracles, what gives you the right to be judge and jury to beings you don't even know."

It was Saracles' turn to be riled. He stalked toward Mordred, but Mordred turned with an expression of fierce anger. "No, don't even try to justify your behavior to me. If you had come across me in any other situation you would have damned me, too. You think the world, this world, the next and the ones we cannot see are all simply black and white? There's no such thing! I am living proof of that. I will not allow you or any other entity to condemn souls that do not deserve to be condemned in the first place!"

Spitting his anger to the ground, Mordred shook a fist. "The Hollows were children, Saracles. Children sacrificed because they were not found worthy by their own parents.

How is any of this their fault? How could any entity think they are evil? Because they have rotted and decayed but still retain a look of humanness? And these soldiers in the mines were murdered, buried beneath the earth centuries ago. Who are you to decide if they are evil or not?

"I am, by far, a worse monster than any of them and if there is anyone to be condemned then it should be me. And yet here I stand, the Chosen One."

Saracles remained silent.

"I will get your damned feather back tonight and when I do you will fly to your Warders and demand they come here. And if they don't, so help me, Fane, I will find a way to make them listen to me. Now, go back to the Hollows so they know we have not deserted them, and I charge you to reconsider how you view them. It is unjustified and it disgusts me."

VIII

Chapter Eight

It was the time when night and day were joined. That hour when the world still lay bathed in the glow of the setting sun, and the moon announced its presence as a silvery orb of cool light. Mordred found himself pulled back in time to a memory of Celtic twilight in his Scottish homeland. Vaguely, he saw fleeting images of huge dolmans and stone circles, of ancient groves of rowan trees, of an endless sky splattered with stars.

Here, in this place, was that familiar feeling of the mysterious ebb and flow of supernatural currents as the sun surrendered to the coming night. To add to the atmosphere, the legions of Hollows came marching across the grasslands in several columns. Their heads down, focused on moving as one giant force, they came to a stop in front of Mordred. He noticed how they looked almost human in the dying golden light.

Leading the Hollows was Xanthius, the only one whose head was raised, red eyes haunted with hope, staring at the spot where Mordred remained. His bearing whispered of a lost king, one who, if he'd been given the chance, would indeed have been legendary. Mordred was struck once again by the sadness of the place. So much tragedy, so much death. It was oppressive.

The others in the mines had quieted in the passing hours, waiting expectantly for release, not daring to believe finally, after many lifetimes, their desire to be freed might be fulfilled this night.

Mordred focused his thoughts on the task ahead. He watched a lone figure moving quickly some distance away from the Hollows. It was Saracles.

Sensing wariness from Xanthius, Mordred realized the king was mistrustful of the Fane. He knew Saracles felt his kind belonged with the darkness and with all things vile and profane, but when he brought his eyes to Mordred's, there was only trust.

"Xanthius? I trust Saracles has informed you of a little problem?"

The Hollow king smiled. "I like your way with words, Mordred. A small problem indeed. Do you think the Fane will be able to convince a Warder to come to us?"

"I think the Warders are already aware of a problem. I

think they've been aware for some time but they have been reluctant to intervene. They prefer things to follow a preset order. We are now disturbing that order."

The king kept grinning. Despite his gruesome appearance, Mordred could clearly see the man the king might have been, and found himself smiling back.

"I knew you were a good man, even if you are also a vampyre."

"There would be many who would disagree." Mordred laughed.

"And there will be many who will never understand you, but I am one of your believers and know that in the future, if it is within the power of the Hollows, we will aid you in your own quest." Xanthius bowed his head.

Mordred sobered. "First things first. You return Saracles' feather. He will go to the Warders. In the meantime, your men can begin digging at the entrance to the mines."

"And what of your werewolf? Do you not wish to bring him back?"

"Aye, I do, but I also know that if we release these men, your numbers will swell and perhaps a simple show of force will get Dugald released. I'd prefer not to have to wage a battle," Mordred said softly.

"I think they will not harm Dugald. In fact, if I know the Carlini family well enough, I think they will do the same thing we did with you: Strike a bargain to get the wolf to aid them."

Nodding, Mordred finished. "Let's hope you are right. Now, please give Saracles his feather back."

Reaching into his rotted leather chest plate, Xanthius withdrew a beautiful feather colored in shades of blue, from deepest midnight to brilliant sapphire. Just looking at it one could tell it held a great magic. He handed it to the Fane.

"I am truly sorry for causing you undue pain. I only want the chance for all of us to be judged properly."

Saracles nodded and took possession of the feather. "It is I who owe you an apology. I should not have been so quick to think Hollows were less deserving of the light. Like birds, there are many different creatures in this world, and while you may look like something darker, you should not be held accountable because of it. You have shown me how very wrong I was."

Saracles rolled up the sleeve of his black shirt, revealing the strange blue tattoos that ran across his skin. He brushed the feather across his lower arm. A shimmering silver light sparked and then grew around the feather, and soon it enveloped Saracles in its brilliance.

The light grew to a point where almost all of the Hollows, including Xanthius, and even Mordred, shaded their eyes. The image of Saracles captured within the confines of a silver border held for a moment longer before a blinding flash occurred. Then Saracles simply disappeared.

Everyone looked around the area where the Fane had been last seen, but there was nothing to indicate he had ever been there. Mordred was the first to glance at the darkening sky. There, flying toward the setting sun, was a beautiful blue bird, large wings outstretched, gliding on the air currents. As the sun vanished below the horizon, so too, did the bird.

"How long do you think it will take him to fetch us a Warder?" Xanthius asked, breaking the silence that had fallen over the entire crowd.

"Hopefully, not too long," was all Mordred could offer in the way of encouragement. For now, they would spend the hours of darkness digging through mountains of rock and dirt.

Mordred walked over to where a bunch of Hollows stood and without a word took a crude shovel and began to dig. He watched as those with tools similar to the one he held started doing the same. Hundreds of Hollows knelt and began to remove the dirt with their gnarled, bony hands. As one enormous beast, the group focused on their task.

"Mordred Soulis, I can hear our brethren. Are they coming for us? Will we be released?"

It was Mestocrites.

"I can only hope Saracles brings one of the Warders."

"You have the power to summon one of the Guardians? Who are you?"

Mordred couldn't help laughing; the Hollows paused to stare at him in bewilderment. Xanthius moved closer to Mordred, "You hear them? You hear our kindred?"

"Yes. Xanthius, meet Mestocrites. Hopefully, in a short while you will finally meet face to face."

Xanthius clapped his skeletal hands together. "Can you tell them we are waiting for their release? That we have waited for centuries, too?"

Mordred nodded and spoke the words to Mestocrites, who in turn had a message to relay back. Mordred smiled. "Mestocrites would like you to know his pleasure at his release. He asks for what boon you would claim for this task."

"Boon? I do not know this word."

"He's asking you what reward you would like. Now would be a good time to ask him to join you. With his army, and who knows how many have been trapped in the mines, you could well rule Sicily," Mordred suggested.

"Of course, of course. Please ask him if he would consider joining forces with us," Xanthius replied.

Mordred, who had never been one to stand on ceremony, found himself feeling as though he were brokering a treaty between two kings. Each was conducting this as if their lives depended upon it, and then Mordred realized their future did indeed.

He spoke to the soldier below ground and conveyed Xanthius' wishes. He was rewarded with a hearty cheer and acknowledgement that the others in the mines would think nothing less than joining forces with the legions who sought to release them.

A resounding cheer above ground soon matched the trembling below. The earth and all the area nearby, the shrubs and trees, vibrated with a strange energy. Suddenly the ground, large portions of rock, sand, and mud fell away to reveal a large pit.

In the enormous hole, exposed as the dirt settled, was a stone archway and a set of wooden doors. The doors were barred with iron spikes. Roman words and strange symbols were carved in both stone and wood.

It took Mordred only a minute to understand their meaning but in that time Xanthius had already spoken them aloud. "May those who die here remain forever denied their rightful place beyond until their day of judgment."

Mordred fell to his knees as a wave of desperation hit him like a physical blow. The past came to life beneath his closed eyes. He felt anguish, pain, betrayal. Every emotion tearing at his guts. Sadness, death, the absence of hope.

The sounds of crying from grown men, sobbing and

screaming, roared in his ears. Pleading and praying. And then he saw them, the Athenian soldiers, shoved at spear point in groups, in chains, into the dark tunnel entrance. Hundreds of men, perhaps thousands were forced to endure a slow, suffocating death. He saw the light of hope snuffed out of their eyes as the heavy wooden door closed and the Romans sealed them in.

A magic user had carved the stone and wood while those inside begged not to be left to such a horrible fate. Then the image of the earth being shoveled up and around the entrance came to Mordred and he felt himself gasping for breath as he relived the experience of the Athenians.

Finally, the cries of the men were muffled as the ground covered them. All signs that they had ever existed were gone. Men and boys, husbands, brothers, lovers, all gone in one violent act.

Mordred felt a hand grasp his shoulder as he remained with his head hanging. It was Xanthius.

"I feel it, too, vampyre. But we have found hope again in the most unlikely of places, haven't we? Come, now it is time to open the door and to allow these souls the chance for redemption."

Mordred brushed a hand across his closed eyes, feeling the moisture trickling down over the back of his hand. He drew in a deep breath, snapped his head back and rose slowly, aware all eyes were on him.

One Hollow approached him carefully, slowly, as if in awe of Mordred. He held his hand out. In his grip was something that resembled an ax. He was offering it.

"Take it, Mordred. Take it and set these soldiers free," Xanthius commanded quietly.

"Halt!" a booming voice rang out.

Mordred glanced around. The Hollows appeared confused as well.

"Go no further with your interference, vampyre!"

Peering into the darkness and seeing nothing, Mordred said, "Reveal yourself!"

"I take no orders from the undead. You should not be here. You had no right to interfere with the balance of souls."

Realization washed over Mordred. He stood with his feet braced apart, arms crossed his arms over his chest. "And I take no orders from something that does not show itself plainly."

"You are nothing to me. I could smite you where you stand if that is my wish. I am a Warder, one of the Guardians of the Gates, and you have no power to command me."

At this new threat, Mordred pulled his Blood Sword from its place at his back. He held the blade high, allowing it to shimmer in the silver light.

Another voice, equally as deep and commanding, spoke

from the shadows. "Oh, stuff it, Michvallae. This one is in my realm and you'll have to come through me first to get to him. Now, get out of the clouds and let's get this resolved. We can't be gone long from our posts."

Unbelievably, the shadows of night moved and undulated, coming together. A blackness, so deep it swallowed up the light of the moon, revealed itself. Two glowing orbs blinked. "I am Bachnel, Warder of the gates Below. I am here to determine if these spirits deserve to be freed."

A bright light erupted behind Mordred, and he turned from the shadow thing. He squinted at the place of glowing luminosity.

"I am Michvallae, Warder of the gates Above. I, too, have been summoned to judge these spirits. Stand down, vampyre, you are no longer needed. Consider yourself lucky that your champion arrived when he did."

Already, Mordred knew he didn't like the Warder named Michvallae. There was an arrogance, a haughtiness about him. It was as if Mordred were merely an inconvenience.

"That is exactly what you are, vampyre," the Warder sneered as he plucked Mordred's thoughts.

"Oh, he's much more than an inconvenience. Look at the sword he holds. That, my light-bearing friend, is the Blood Sword. There is only one being that can wield that. This is the Chosen One."

"Bah. The Chosen One would not be a vampyre. It would be human at the very least," Michvallae spat.

The Warders were speaking as though Mordred weren't present. It irritated him. "Look, I didn't want this job any more than you want me to have it, but unless you have a way of changing things, I'm what you've got as a savior. That being the case, and knowing you will indeed need me in the future, let's get this problem solved so I can continue on my own quest."

"Oh, my, the vampyre has done his research."

"Stop being such a pill, Michvallae. You're just mad because the champion didn't come from your side of things."

"And I'll never understand that."

"Dark must fight dark. You know the rules."

The light that was Michvallae wavered and then shone more brightly. "Speaking of the rules, this is against them. We do not do interventions. These spirits belong right where they lie. If they are released they are your responsibility."

Mordred had had enough of being ignored. "That's where you're very wrong. Look, I don't give a damn about balance and harmony. And if either of you were really doing your jobs, I wouldn't have been created in the first place. So, here's the deal. You will judge these beings as belonging on the side of good so they can be released from the mines, and," Mordred held up a hand, "you will judge the Hollows above ground. Neither of these groups has been dealt with fairly. They have suffered for centuries because you failed to notice their plight."

"Enough, Mordred Soulis," came the voice of Bachnel. "We are here because one of the Fane summoned us. He claimed you were responsible for getting his feather back. Because you brought one of our soldiers back to us, we do owe you one favor. We cannot judge both parties, therefore you will have to choose. The soldiers in the mines, or the Hollows."

Mordred heard Xanthius gasp. He stood with his back to stand before Mordred, facing the two Warders.

"Listen to me well, Warders. You are not the end or the beginning. Let me tell you what we are and how we came to be, and if after hearing the story you do not think we may leave this haunted existence, we will allow abide by your decision."

"Xanthius, no," Mordred said, his hand upon the Hollow King's shoulder. "You are far more worthy than many men I have known. Do not allow them the choice. Demand your freedom."

Bachnel laughed. "I can see a good choice was made when you were picked, Mordred, but allow the king to tell his story. Maybe he can convince us a mistake has been made. Besides, as a creature of the darkness, can you say it is that bad?"

Mordred was ready to answer, anger filling his mouth like a vile poison he longed to spew at both beings, but a look from Xanthius stilled him.

The Hollow King had never been given the chance at life. He'd been robbed of his future. It was only fitting that he should be allowed to prove his worth. This might be the one time he could actually be a king and could, just this once, control his destiny.

Xanthius spoke to the Warders of the days in his memory when he lived as a babe, newly born in the world of men. He told them of the way his life ended in infancy because of the whims of men, and of how he had suffered all these centuries living in an empty shell. He talked at length about how each of the Hollows had only the wish to die fully so they could be reborn, but until they were deemed worthy of the light, that could not be.

It was a soulful speech from a being that was said to have no soul. Mordred himself was moved by the passion shining from the king.

As he watched Xanthius plead for his release, he realized the king was filled with a golden light. Where his skin was missing, it shone through and pierced the darkness.

Mordred turned to gaze at the other Hollows and noticed they all were bathed in the same glorious light. Abruptly, the door to the mines exploded, shards of metal and wood simply dissolved into ash before hitting the ground. A beam of brilliant light shot from the opening.

Soldiers spilled from the depths of the earth, clad in ancient armor. They were pulled from the pit by the Hollows standing on the edge. When the Hollows touched the Athenians, the gold light turned to blinding white.

"Well, well, it looks as though Xanthius has pleaded his case quite well," Michvallae said, the light pulsing and throbbing, hovering over the ground.

"With a little help from the dark side, thank you," Bachnel chimed in. "And, because of that we will release the soldiers, too. Michvallae, we'd better get back to our own problems and, rest assured, Mordred Soulis, we will meet again, when you are ready."

With that, both the shadow figure and the light disappeared, allowing the moonlight to reach the ground once more. The glow was gone from all the men and instead of looking like rotted corpses, the Hollows looked quite real, except that Mordred could see through them.

"Now what?" Mordred asked, not at all sure if he fully understood what had just happened.

"We go get your wolf back. Then we will begin a new chapter in our existence," Xanthius replied.

Mestocrites nodded. "Aye, it is time to begin again."

Chapter Nine

hen the Athenians and the Hollows merged, they became a mighty force. By all appearances the beings, having been reborn in soul, looked like living, breathing men. They stood side by side, some still wearing the ancient armor of the Greeks, while others remained cloaked in their decayed clothing.

It was a strange army. The soldiers had found their weapons and carried spears and short swords. The Hollows carried no weapons, but their looks alone could easily freeze the blood of mortals bearing witness to the amazing display of strength.

The day had dawned with the absence of sun. Swollen gray clouds hugged the horizon, and a mist slithered through the lowlands. Further out to sea a heavy fog sat upon the waves, shrouding the island in mystery.

The massive army marched over land straight to the

border that brought them into contact with the Main-landers. There could be no hiding, or quiet surprise, with a movement of men this large. They knew they had mas-sive numbers in their favor. Even if more Mainlanders had crossed the channel in the past few weeks, the enemy would not be able to raise the kind of force required to fight the ghost army.

For Mordred, there was only one main concern . . . Dugald. Once he was safely back, they could resume their journey and leave this unexplainable place behind.

He warned Mestocrites and Xanthius not to go head-long into battle. That would surely damn their souls. He urged them to try and intimidate the Mainlanders into leaving of their own free will. If there was no blood on the hands of the troops they would be free to leave this plane and move forward as they should have long ago.

Each leader agreed, knowing full well the sacrifice they had already made in terms of time.

Cresting the last rise, Mordred saw Dugald in the center of a graveyard. The half-wolf, half-man was chained to a large stone. Where the silver touched his skin, burn marks had appeared. Large blisters and welts from the poisonous metal broke open and spilled both a yellow ooze of infection and Dugald's life blood. The quantity alarmed Mordred.

The site of the blood stirred his vampyre-self from its

slumber. Since coming to the island the beast had lain dormant, quietly biding its time until it might overpower the human side of Mordred once more.

His stomach growled in response to the dark thought of feeding. His vision clouded and wavered before coming back sharply into focus, but it was colored crimson. He knew he was changing.

He had no fear for the undead with him. Though they had been freed of the prison of judgment that had sentenced them to wander as haunted shells of their former selves, or stayed buried beneath the earth, they were still dead and, Mordred could not harm them. He assumed the Mainlanders would also suffer no fear from a vampyre.

He was quite wrong. In fact, it was because Mordred was a vampyre that the enemy left in such a hurry they did not even try to take Dugald with them.

"They still hold the fear of their mortality," Mestocrites said when he saw Mordred's puzzled look.

"But I cannot harm them now. They are dead."

"Yes, that is true, but even in death some fears are never released. They still war with their own demons. I don't think they will be back any time soon." Xanthius laughed watching the horde of invaders turn tail and run. They headed for the shores of the island, to the channel where the incoming fog swallowed them.

As the large contingent stood in awe of the fact that the island once again belonged to them, and happy that no war had started, a brilliant beam of light shot through the darkening clouds. It touched the earth just in front of the leaders and quickly grew, enveloping all the spirits in its golden light.

Just as fast as it had come, the light disappeared and when Mordred looked back, he was completely alone. All the hundreds of lost souls were gone. Stolen away in the blink of an eye as if they had never been. He knew all of the dead, Athenians and Hollows, had moved to the next plane. They would begin again as Mestocrites had said.

A groan from Dugald alerted Mordred he was conscious. Mordred pulled his sword from the scabbard at his side and raising it high above his head, he brought it down on the chains, breaking the links. He threw the blade down and made quick work of the remainder of the metal holding Dugald prisoner.

The man fell forward limply into Mordred's arms, but his eyes opened.

"What took you so long?" he whispered, the bare hint of a smile breaking across his face.

Mordred returned the smile and lifted Dugald, helping him walk by bearing nearly his full weight. They moved to a nearby cave with ornately chiseled walls and ceiling and

Mordred helped Dugald to the ground.

"Rest, friend. I'll find some coverings and we'll spend the night here. When you are better we will continue."

Dugald's eyes fluttered closed and then opened once more. "Did we do it? Did we save the island?"

"Yes, we did it."

Sighing, Dugald drifted off leaving Mordred to wrestle with the vampyre aching to be released. It would be a long night by denying the transformation, but Mordred was determined not to change.

✝ ✝ ✝

Dugald awoke in the morning. Clouds still darkened the sky, but he was eager to be off. His wounds had already healed. Such was the magic of a shifter. Mordred's horse, Sleipner, had made his way to them sometime in the night, bringing news that not a single entity other than mortal stirred on the island.

As Mestocrites had said, it was time for Mordred to begin again. Fearing they had lost precious time in their hunt to find the second vampyre king, Mordred focused on what might await them in Rome, where he had decided to head. Straight to the Vatican. If Vlad had been brought forth by men, there were only a few he felt would understand the laws of resurrection.

If they did not find what they were looking for in the Holy City, Mordred would move on to the Carpathians as Kabil had suggested. Vlad was at work somewhere and if he would not show himself, Mordred would be forced to go in search of him.

He had no idea where they might go after reaching Transylvania. Kabil had told him Lir could not be found. The second Vampyre King would come to Mordred when he was ready.

Finding passage to Italy proved no problem. The problem was having humans near Mordred. He fought every second of the journey with his vampyre side. He kept his distance, shrouding his face, and found himself clinging to the rail of the ship every time his body started to undergo the transformation.

Each time the familiar pain erupted, Mordred clenched his jaw and swallowed the darkness that bubbled in his throat. Lost in his own private hell, he watched his fingers become claws, then change back to fingers as his human side won the battle.

It was a long, exhausting journey to Rome. And, for Dugald, there was nothing he could do except watch over Mordred when he was in the grip of his black madness.

When they neared the Holy City, Dugald urged

Mordred to change his clothing. After leaving the ship, they made a stop and purchased breeches, shirts, and capes. Mordred chose black and Dugald chose brown.

When they approached the gates of the city, Mordred whispered something into Sleipner's ear and the horse moved off in the opposite direction. Where they were going they would have no need of the large beast.

Rome was a sight to behold. It was once again the Holy City thanks to the return of the Holy See, they learned from a merchant who was only too happy to offer his opinions on having the papacy moved to France.

Splendid monuments and tall buildings filled Mordred's vision. Though very different from the Egyptian architecture, Rome was no less amazing. Fountains and churches were on nearly every corner. Streets lined with stone opened to areas of greenery and beautiful statues of ancient gods and goddess.

Mordred was in awe.

The well known Coliseum rose to great heights, dominating the skyline. An enormous marble arch appeared to touch the heavens in another area, and still more temples and columns competed with the city's more modern buildings. Even in their state of ruin the remains of the once vast and mighty Roman Empire held a magical allure.

Settled among the magnificence rose fancy palazzos

that housed the wealthy. Neatly built merchant shops lined the twisting streets. And people filled every space. Again, Mordred tamped down the beast that ravaged him, looking for an escape.

Amid all the splendor there was also an undercurrent of tension that coiled itself in Mordred's stomach. This was the seat of the Roman Catholic Church. The same church that had sanctioned the Crusades. The same church that condemned beliefs other than their own. The deaths of hundreds of thousands were planned without a care for their suffering. It was here the fervor of religion was the strongest. It was here, in Mordred's way of thinking, evil held court.

For what but evil would see the destruction of humankind to such a brutal degree? What but evil would seek the total annihilation of cultures other than its own solely because they are different? Endless wars were being fought over an ideal that could not be proven. It had been this way for centuries Mordred knew, but he didn't like it.

In a city that should have been bathed in a light from some otherworldly source, Mordred felt only cold. He was uneasy and wished he were invisible until it was the time to reveal himself.

To make matters worse, he had the feeling he was being watched.

Dugald and Mordred made their way through the

streets and alleys trying to appear as nothing more than two simple men, not worthy of notice. The plan had been to head straight through Rome. They were not sure exactly where they would find the Vatican City, so they stopped to ask for directions.

A merchant smiled and pointed to a tall rounded dome in the distance.

Vatican City was the palace of the popes. Though St. Peter's had fallen into disrepair when the papacy moved to France, it was now, once again, returning to its former glory.

Mordred knew it was within St. Peter's or the Vatican he might find answers as to who had unleashed Vlad on the world. He would rather have avoided it. Though thousands of followers came each year to the holy place for blessings, he highly doubted a vampyre would be welcome.

At first the pair did not notice how long it was taking to reach their destination. Always in the distance, the dome of the basilica wavered like a desert mirage.

Finally, Mordred stopped.

"Dugald, do you sense something strange at work?"

"It appears no matter how far we walk, we cannot get to the place we seek to enter."

"Exactly. But I know of one way we might gain entrance. There are catacombs beneath St. Peter's housing the bones of the dead. If the church itself is warded above, I doubt it will be so below. Come."

Mordred moved off in the opposite direction. He had heard rumors of a supposed crypt beneath the church where the popes were buried. He hoped, with his ability to hear the dead, they would lead him there. Not that he expected to hear the popes, but there would be more than just holy men buried beneath Rome. After all, the crypts had stood for centuries.

The voices came en masse, as expected, when they rounded a corner leading to a dark alley. Mordred stopped.

"I hear the dead whispering. They do not speak to me, however, but to each other. I see visions of things I cannot understand. It is as if I can look at these buildings and see how they were along time ago. There is anger, bitterness, sadness, and danger here. And there are the smells. All the scents both present and from the past. I cannot make sense of any of it."

"You mention danger. Do you mean something otherworldly, like Vlad? This is a holy city. Surely, with the power of the people believing, like Jerusalem, evil has no home here."

Mordred stayed silent, not responding immediately to Dugald's reasoning, trying to decipher all the different feelings and thoughts rushing past him. Ironically, though Rome was now the seat of the Holy See, and all things connected to the Catholic religion, he could not shake the presence of darkness. Just beneath the surface of the visible lurked something else. Something far beyond the realm of mortals.

"Mordred? Did you hear me?" Dugald asked again when he had failed to respond.

"I don't think Rome, or the Holy City are warded like Jerusalem. There three different belief systems came together as one and because there was such variety, it somehow closed all the holes that might let evil in. There is only one way of thinking and it might not be enough to keep the darkness at bay. If Vlad was summoned by those here, this city would be a nest of evil."

"What do we do now?"

Mordred looked ahead and sighed. "Come."

A narrow gate, barely visible between two stone walls, beckoned. Its lock presented no challenge to Mordred, and in a moment he was inside. Beyond the gate a stone stairway led in a spiral down, beneath the earth, into shadows. Mordred walked cautiously into the gaping mouth of black. He let his eyes adjust to the darkness.

The voices of the dead grew louder. Dugald, though unable to hear the spirits, felt them. "Where are we?" he asked, as a shiver coursed through him.

"This is the necropolis that will lead us to St. Peter's."

"Can you hear them?"

"Yes, but I cannot pull one voice from the others. It is all noise at the moment. Wait. There is one that rises above the others. It is strange, though. It doesn't sound like the others."

"And?"

"His name is . . . Simon, I think, and he is telling me I have not found the truth of my origins. Until I do so I cannot hope to save mankind."

Dugald put his hand on Mordred's shoulder, less for support than to avoid being lost in the cavernous underground cemetery. "Here we go again with the riddles. Just what the hell does that mean?"

"I don't know. He keeps repeating his message and does not answer me. It's like he is not with the rest who are buried here," Mordred replied and continued moving forward.

"Maybe he is not speaking to you?"

"He said my name so I think it must be me."

"The why doesn't he respond, Mordred?"

Mordred made an abrupt left. Dugald followed close behind. "I don't know. He, it, is guiding me. This voice is different from any I have heard before. It feels so alive . . ."

"Wait, I am to meet someone. I am to find another Simon. A false man. A priest. This other Simon has knowledge I need."

"How do you make sense of these constant riddles?

You are speaking with a Simon, but you are to meet a false Simon. Well, that explains everything, doesn't it?"

"Shhh," Mordred whispered. "The voice is still speaking and I can't hear it over your blathering. Simon is telling me to go to Castel Sant' Angelo by way of a secret passageway near here. I am to look for the door with the peacock to find the truth."

"What the hell does that mean?" Dugald couldn't resist. "Sorry, but right now, I'm waiting to simply ignite into flames for being an abomination."

In the darkness, Mordred let out a soft laugh. "You would have to believe you were an abomination in order to allow a holy place power over you, and as far as I can tell from knowing you only the short time I have, you don't think you have anything to apologize for."

He heard Dugald echo his laughter and then grow quiet. "Okay, you're right. I don't think there is anything wrong with me, but what about you? You've often said you aren't worthy of this quest."

"And I still believe I am a poor choice, but I also do not believe that this religion has the power to decide my fate. I have sinned as much as the next man, but doing so does not condemn me any more than the next man, either. I am learning to have faith in what I cannot see, but my ignorance does not in itself condemn me."

Mordred weaved his way through the darkness. His field of vision was clouded and several times he shook his head as if to clear his mind. There were times when he touched dirt walls and yet he could see right through them to what lay behind. Hundreds of bodies were buried beneath St. Peter's. Mordred doubted even the church knew what lay hidden in the ground. If so, surely greed would have prompted digging and plundering. Here, though, the ground remained largely undisturbed save for the narrow passageway,

At one point Mordred detected a faint glow coming from somewhere beneath the earth; it changed to red and back to white. Again, he heard the man Simon's voice: "*Vampyre, you have much ahead of you that will temper and strengthen your soul. You have not lost that part of you which all mankind has been blessed with, but you must believe that both the good and evil within you are necessary for you to succeed. Do not deny one side at the expense of the other. Choose wisely. Even now you have free will. Choose wisely.*"

"Why do I hear you above all others?" Mordred asked.

"*I am the one closest to that which you think eludes you. Trust in yourself. The truth will be known to you at the time you will allow it. But until that time, trust only yourself. Others will come to you in the guise of friends, yet they will betray you. Beware of the man named Simon. Find the truth.*"

Confused, Mordred replied, "But you are Simon."

The voice drifted away and blended with the others in cacophony of sound.

Abruptly the path ascended. Mordred saw a set of stairs leading to a wooden door.

✠ ✠ ✠

Father Simon sat behind his desk scribbling notes on the inventory of ancient relics that had just been brought to him. The cataloging of all the items the Vatican acquired was almost beyond comprehension. The priest knew that long after he was gone the task of inventorying the treasures would continue.

All at once, he heard the voice in his head hiss a warning. *"Something is coming. Something familiar and dangerous to you and me. I cannot make it out, being trapped in this human form, but you need to prepare yourself. It is blasphemous, the thing that is approaching."*

Father Simon dropped his quill and rose, nearly knocking his wooden chair to the marble floor in his haste. He strode into the hall. One of the Swiss Guard, clad in his colorful yellow and blue uniform, saw him. "Father? Is all well?"

The priest did not answer, but continued past as if in a trance. He walked down the stairs and through the familiar corridors of Castel Sant' Angelo with purpose, although he, himself, did not know what it was.

The voice in his head had stayed with him since the time in the vaults when he accidentally conjured it for the secretive Order of Red Caps, into which he had been initiated soon after. He was to have traveled east to the Carpathians to learn of the man called Vlad the Impaler, but the Keys had delayed his departure for reasons he was not privy to.

While once he would have given anything to become a member of the elite society, now he was not so sure about it. They wanted the gift of immortality but even in their own religion there was only one way for the soul to become immortal and that was through death and the acceptance of Christ. What did it mean that men, high in the Church, sought other ways to obtain the gift? Ways that would keep them on this earthly plane instead of in the realm of heaven.

Father Simon was confused. There were moments when he was lucid and found himself wishing he had never wanted the gift for himself. Moments when he found himself nearly in tears from the fear of the thing that possessed him, for possessed he was.

The thing that shared his mind controlled him almost entirely. He found himself forced to witness unspeakable horrors in the form of torture within the walls of the Castel on an almost daily basis. Once he'd thought it justified.

Torture was sanction to protect the Church and the Order from its enemies. But having seen the inhuman acts inflicted over and over, Father Simon questioned the sense of it all. So much death weighed heavy his soul.

He was going mad, and he lived in complete fear. There was the constant dread that the Keys would know there was something wrong with him. The worry that the thing, the voice that controlled him more and more, would one day take over. He worried that he had somehow damned his soul for eternity.

He was a wretched man. He'd lost his appetite. His skin was sallow and his eyes sunk deeply into his thin face. His hair fell out in clumps. There were times when he swore he foamed at the mouth. It was the work of the devil, this thing inside.

Even now he watched himself like he was gazing through a window, while he tread the familiar paths to the ancient vaults, and it felt like he were watching someone else.

The voice of Vlad, as it called itself, had whispered incessantly in Father Simon's mind since that day not long ago when it had come to the vaults. Sometimes it spoke so loudly the priest caught himself clapping his hands to his ears, while others stared at him strangely.

He moved deeper into the less traveled areas of the Castel. He knew it was not of his own volition. Where once the thing could only infiltrate his mind, now it controlled his body as well.

He came to where a staircase ended. At the base of the stairs were two doors. One led to a crypt few knew about. Even the markings on the door gave no evidence as to whose remains were contained within, unless one knew the code. Father Simon knew the code. He'd only recently been privileged to receive it after killing the man who claimed to be a Soulis.

It was here the bones and bodies of every Soulis that had been gathered were dumped. Hidden from the world for all time. It had been thought that the family line had died out centuries ago, until the blasphemous man Father Simon had been forced to murder.

Now the church discovered its worst fears were coming true. One line. One tiny branch of the family tree had gone undetected in the wilds of heathen Scotland.

So, the Church sent its minions to eliminate all remaining members of the Soulis family. They would not tolerate the existence of a single one, a single man who could bring about their destruction, as claimed in one of the secret passages that had been conveniently removed from their good book.

But it was not the Soulis crypt that the voice in Father Simon's head was concerned about. Nay, it directed him to the other door. The hidden passageway that connected the

Castel with St. Peter's. Few knew of its existence. It was built as an escape route in the event the Vatican or the Pope fell under danger. It had already been used several times.

Father Simon unbolted the door. He opened it, grimacing as the hinges squealed in protest.

The father was greeted by a wall of darkness. Thick and black it gave away nothing of what might be coming toward him from the other side. He peered into the void trying to see a flicker of light, or shadow . . . and waited.

But, for what, he was unsure.

✟ ✟ ✟

Mordred was grateful for his keen eyesight. He could easily see the walls of the passageway, slick with moisture. Occasionally he stepped over a lone rat and then listened as Dugald cursed. Clearly, the werewolf did not like the company of rodents.

He wasn't sure where they were headed. He only knew this was the right direction, the only direction they could take after entering the tunnel. The voice named Simon had instructed him to continue on to the Castel St. Angelo through this passageway.

As they moved beneath the earth, Mordred could not shake a heavy feeling of foreboding. Once again, the presence of death and hopelessness was heavy in the air. He found it odd that in a place of worship, where people could be absolved of their sins for the right price, that there would be such a dismal atmosphere. Then he heard the voices.

This time they came to him from outside his mind, and Dugald heard them, too. Screams of pain and horror. Sobs of despair from both men and women. Anguished cries. Pleading and begging. Some, Mordred thought, asked for release but their voices were so full of desolation he could not fully understand them.

"Where the heck are we?" Dugald asked, slowing Mordred down by pulling him back. "Do you think it is safe?"

Mordred tugged himself free of Dugald's grip and continued. "We don't have much choice. We can either go forward or back, and I don't think back is the way I'm supposed to go."

"But I thought you said we were to go to a castle?"

"That's what I was told."

"Well, what kind of castle makes these noises?"

"You mean in what room would you hear these sounds?" Mordred shuddered as he pieced together where they might actually be headed. Clearly, the noises, coupled with the emotions in them, indicated they were very close to a dungeon.

Mordred was not unfamiliar with dungeons. Being a mercenary soldier in his past human life, he had spent many

Castel Sant Angelo

unpleasant days in various hell holes beneath the walls of fortresses, or in pits dug in the sand.

But these weren't simply the sounds of people imprisoned. Nay, these came from people undergoing excruciating agony. People being forced to endure the heinous experience of torture.

Mordred slowed. "Having second thoughts?" Dugald asked.

"I think we're headed to a bad place."

"I was afraid you'd say that. Now what?"

"I don't know. Why would I be sent here?"

"You mean, why couldn't we just have gone through Rome without incident?" Mordred offered, reading Dugald's mind. "You know this isn't your fight. Maybe you should go back."

Dugald snorted. "For once and for all, I am not leaving your side. Well, not yet anyway. Not until I have some indication you don't need me, and right now, you need me."

Mordred agreed as they came around a bend in the corridor and he saw a ghost. Or what he assumed was a spectral image of death.

An older man clad in black robes stood at the arched opening at the end of the passage. Beyond the stranger, Mordred saw a set of stone stairs heading upward.

A cool breeze drifted by, bringing with it the smells of

human waste mixed with fear and the scent of burned flesh. And the intoxicating scent of blood. Immediately Mordred's own blood surged through his veins as his pulse increased.

The figure had clearly not seen them, continuing to squint into the darkness.

Then, suddenly, he spoke and it was in a voice Mordred would never forget.

"Mordred Soulis, I was wondering when you would surface."

The voice belonged to Vlad, but the person speaking was not Mordred's creator. He watched the stranger's eyes glow a red fire and his face distort when he spoke. He realized the voice did not match the speaker who was clad in the robes of a priest.

"How is it you have taken possession of him?" Mordred demanded, coming to a stop mere inches from the holy man.

Laughter filled the small room, echoing off the walls of the tunnel. It was a deep, wicked sound that would easily strike terror in the hearts of mere mortals. Mordred remained wary and confused.

"Maybe you should ask the father how it is that he has summoned me? You see, I was fine waiting for you to surface in the world again, when Simon conjured me and commanded me to appear."

Mordred surveyed the priest. He seemed entirely too

unassuming to be dabbling in the dark arts, but Mordred was well aware a certain group of holy men had brought Vlad to life in the first place. Had he found the order?

"You are such a clever one, Mordred Soulis. Again, I offer you a chance to join with me. You and I could rule the world. We've no need of the human race."

Mordred ignored the taunts. "How is it you took control of this priest's body?"

"Ask him."

"Will you allow him to speak to me?"

The red fire blossomed in the speaker's eyes and disappeared, leaving the wide-eyed gaze of a very fearful man. "It cannot be. You cannot exist. All of you have been destroyed. The Church could not have made another mistake," he stuttered nervously.

"What the hell . . .," Mordred questioned warily. "What do you mean? By the Church? Why?"

The priest rambled incoherently.

Mordred redirected his question. "How is it Vlad commands you?"

"Vlad? Who is Vlad?" Father Simon tried to affect an air of innocence, but Mordred saw the truth.

"You already know him. You have tampered with something beyond your understanding and now he has possessed you."

"No. He is not with me all the time. In fact, he claims he has been . . ." The priest let out a loud groan and crumpled to the floor. His head bent back in an unnatural angle and he gazed up at Mordred. "It is of no importance for you to know where I am. I am everywhere and nowhere. I am around you and inside you, Mordred Soulis. You cannot run from me. If you choose not to join me, then you leave me no choice but to destroy you."

"You? It is I who can cause damage to you in this form. Are you so all powerful that you possess a human? Or are you weakening, failing?"

Laughter filled the alcove. "Destroy me? In this form? I don't think so. You don't have the nerve to slay an innocent. Though I don't believe Father Simon was ever innocent, since all mankind is born with the Original Sin, eh, Mordred? Be careful, pup. I made you and I can unmake you."

"We should go." Dugald said quietly. "It would not be good to be discovered here."

The priest fell silent but rose and when he did, he screamed loudly. "Guards! Guards! Help! There are intruders within the Castel! A Soulis is here! The Pope is in danger!"

"Holy Christ," Mordred growled, drawing his sword. He tried to pursue the priest, but the old man proved too nimble and shot up the stairs.

Something caught Mordred's eye and stopped him cold.

"What is it?" Dugald asked, sensing the change.

"This door, it's marked with the name of my ancestors. And the priest mentioned that my clan is dead? Why?"

Dugald was just as confused, "Clearly, the priest is insane. How could you know what the door says? All I see on the door are a bunch of marks and symbols."

To Mordred's eyes the symbols and marks literally danced and moved on the wood, repositioning themselves until they spelled "Soulis". He couldn't explain it to Dugald. Not now when he heard the guards coming.

The sound of booted feet rang out across the stone hall. Soon the noise became thunder as the guards made their way down the stairs. "We'll have to fight our way out."

"You don't think we could go back the other way?" Dugald asked, drawing two gold short swords.

Just then they heard men approaching from the tunnel.

"Dugald, you fight those coming through the tunnel and I'll attack those on the stairwell. We'll need to stay back to back and force our way up the stairs. If we are quick about it, maybe we can get to an upper floor that will lead us out of the building. And try not to kill them, just injure them enough to stop attacking."

If Dugald thought Mordred's last statement odd, he held his tongue and readied himself for the confrontation. His back against Mordred's, he waited the few moments before the rush of men spilled from the tunnel.

Mordred began a steady climb, trying to get up as many stairs as possible before he was stopped by a wall of armed men.

The first problem he encountered was the Swiss Guard's long pikes, staves of wood at least as tall as a man, tipped with wickedly sharpened steel. He held his long sword in one hand and wrapped his cloak around his other arm. With luck he could get several pikes tangled in his cape and then strike blows that would cause the guards to reach for their swords. The trick was to continue to press forward.

They were outnumbered, but the guards were not prepared for such expert swordsmen. Within moments the clatter of pikes was heard as Mordred yanked on his cloak wound about the heads of several of the weapons. He found he had taken at least four of the pikes, and swiftly began the process all over again.

Those who had lost their staves reached for short swords, but Mordred's blade was longer and none were willing to come within striking distance of his weapon.

When he had reached the first landing, Mordred heard Vlad screeching through the possessed priest.

"Get them! Kill them! They are unholy and seek to kill the Pope. One is a Soulis. He must not live!"

Before Mordred could call out a warning, the priest

grabbed a sword from one of the guards and attacked his own man. Blood spurted from a fatal chest wound, covering the stairs in a slick mess. Other men tripped over the body of their fallen comrade as they lost ground to Mordred's onslaught.

The air grew thick with the sounds of steel on steel, grunts and groans, but also the scent of spilled blood. Mordred knew the change was coming. The blood, coupled with his battle anger, created a lust for feasting that became unbearable.

This time however, instead of dropping to the floor, vulnerable, Mordred bit his upper lip and kept fighting as his body cramped and contorted in pain.

"What is wrong with him?" called one of the guards.

"He is unholy! Kill him!" the priest yelled. "He is a vampyre! He must be destroyed!"

Mordred roared, opening his mouth to expose his long canines. "Leave now and you will remain alive. Fight me and you will all die."

The guards stood paralyzed with a mix of fear and incredulity. Several dropped their weapons and pushed through their own men to escape into the Castel.

Others made the sign of the cross while still holding their weapons.

The priest continued. "He lies! He is a creature from

the bowels of Hell. He must be killed!"

It was then Mordred noticed that the guards' weapons shimmered more brightly than they would have if they were steel. At first, he thought perhaps they were simply kept polished for presentation, but now he knew . . . the weapons were made of silver.

He cursed. Not for himself, but for his companion. "Dugald, watch those blades," he growled while fighting off the few half-hearted attacks coming at him.

"I know. I've already taken one hit and I'm losing strength."

Mordred glanced over his shoulder and saw a large spot where blood stained Dugald's cloak.

"I will give you one more warning before I move, but I am going to get out of here alive. You will either let me pass or die foolishly in your efforts to prevent me from escaping. You cannot stop me. I am a vampyre. Look at me. Look into my eyes. I cannot die. Move!"

The guards remained at the ready, but none sought to come at him. The priest, in his anger appeared to be at a loss for words.

Suddenly, he crumpled to the ground, unconscious.

Mordred bent, lifted the man and threw him over his shoulder, still wielding his blade.

"You cannot take the father," one of the guards cried.

"He is possessed of a demon. I can release it from him,"

Mordred replied.

"But *you* are a demon!" another guard called following Mordred and Dugald through the lower levels of the Castel, as Mordred searched for a way out.

"Someday you will learn that appearances can be very deceiving," Dugald yelled still standing with back-to-back with Mordred.

Mordred saw a door. "Does this lead outside?"

Silence.

"Tell me! Does this lead outside?"

"Yes, but only to the river."

"Is there a boat?"

"Yes."

"Open the door," Mordred commanded.

"We cannot let you leave with Father Simon."

"I'm leaving with the dear father. You should pray for his soul. Now, get out of my way or I will kill you all."

The guards parted and allowed Mordred and Dugald to pass. As soon as the party reached the boat, they heard the alarm go up from the Castel.

"We'll have to get out of Rome in a hurry. They'll have the entire city crawling with guards."

"And let's not forget a fine bounty on our heads for abducting their beloved priest," Dugald added as he slumped into the boat. "I'll row as far as I can and then . . ."

He stopped talking as the boat moved by itself. Mordred looked over the side. "A current maybe?" He tied Father Simon with rope he found in the boat and left him in a heap.

"Dugald, watch out!" he called as they approached a bridge. Already Swiss Guards, along with the city guard, were amassed and stringing arrows into bows. Soon the air was filled with the hissing of the tiny silver barbs.

Dugald crouched into a ball against the bow of the boat, hoping to be spared another injury.

X

Chapter Ten

ordred used himself as a shield to protect Dugald from further harm while their small boat sailed swiftly down the Tiber River and out of Rome. By doing so he received multiple arrow wounds. None of them were fatal; silver had no effect on him whatsoever.

It wasn't until the boat came to a stop at a tiny tributary Mordred finally saw what had caused them to get out of the city so swiftly, and it had nothing to do with the currents, which they had been going against since they left Rome.

The surface boiled and bubbled until several beings appeared. At first Mordred thought he was looking at women, stunningly beautiful women. Stunningly beautiful naked women. Then he saw the great fish tails, and before he could utter what he was thinking aloud, Dugald came to the rescue.

"Bloody hell, they're mermaids. Well, hello, ladies," the

The Mermaids

man-wolf called in greeting.

Mordred watched as they waved, and then erupted in a fit of giggles. Several horses emerged from beneath the dark waters of the river, but they, too, had long, large, scaled tails that curved and looped behind them. It was an odd scene and Mordred's mind had a hard time absorbing the image.

"The Dark One doesn't think he really sees us," tittered a blond beauty.

"Why is that, Mordred Soulis? Why would you think we don't exist?" asked an amused redhead. "Once you believed vampyres and werewolves didn't exist and now look. Why not mermaids and mermares?"

"I, ah . . ." Mordred had never felt so at a loss for speech, and that included meeting Vlad for the first time.

More laughter and slapping of tails. Droplets of river water hit his face, but still he couldn't seem to get his tongue to work in harmony with his brain.

It was Dugald's turn to laugh. "I wish the father could see this. He'd probably pass right back out. Wouldn't need to knock him on the head with a sword hilt."

Mordred glanced at the unconscious form of Father Simon. He wasn't sure what he was doing with the priest. He only knew he couldn't leave him in the Castel. He had to find away to stop Vlad's possession. And perhaps the father could reveal how it was Vlad could enter humans.

For now, however, he had been knocked unconscious. When he had come to, he'd made such a fuss, he had nearly toppled the boat.

"Well, ladies, since my companion is clearly dumb-struck by your beauty, I'll introduce myself. I'm Dugald. You already know Mordred. We owe you quite a bit for getting us out of Rome. How can we ever repay you?" Dugald asked, grinning.

Even though he looked like a ragged mass of tangled hair, with an unshaven face, and clothed in a bloodstained cloak, he acted as though he were a prince among men. Mordred couldn't help smiling.

"You are hurt, Dugald. Let us tend to your wound," the blonde replied.

"Yes, let us. We have a poultice that will remove the silver poison," said a ravishing brunette with breasts that could have made a man weep. They had a slightly lesser effect on Dugald, but not much.

"Ah, well, I could be convinced to rest here awhile."

"No," Mordred stated flatly. "We must continue on. We've lost much time and there is even more urgency now that Vlad's able to possess people. We need to stop him. We need to get help for Father Simon. We must move on."

A black-haired beauty with dark blue eyes swam up to the side of the boat. "You still don't believe, do you? Running away from us will not make us a figment of your imagination, Mordred. We are as real as you."

"How come I've never seen you before? I've sailed lots of rivers and many oceans and I have never seen you until now."

"Other men have seen us, but humans laugh us off as dreams from sailors who've been at sea too long. That is just as well for us. But, Mordred, you have seen our kind before."

"When?" He demanded.

"When you were little. Remember? Go back to when you were small and you played in the waves. You saw us all the time. But then, as with most humans, a veil came across your understanding of what could really be, and you began to see only the things you felt could truly be real. Along with us went lots of other creatures. You stopped seeing us, but that didn't mean we went away. Fairies, pixies, goblins and ghouls, Fanes and vampyres, all exist. Open your eyes, Mordred. See us all."

Mordred shook his head, but couldn't help thinking back to a vague whisper of memory, being alone on a hill and watching what he thought was a white horse galloping through the trees. It was a magnificent beast with a long tail and full mane. And it was swift. Mordred gave chase on his little pony, but the horse kept ahead of him. And then, suddenly, a rare burst of sunlight broke through the everpresent clouds of his homeland, and he thought he saw a gleaming golden horn.

He'd never told anyone about that incident, knowing his friends and family would laugh. Even though they told the tales of the Finn Folk around the fires at night, there was no way they would believe Mordred saw a unicorn.

Lost in thought, Mordred was startled by the touch of the mermaid's hand. "You did see a unicorn, Mordred. You saw lots of things the rest could never see. You saw dragons, and trolls and sprites and red caps. You didn't dream them."

Suddenly within his mind, flashes of all those times returned, coupled with a pain so intense Mordred brought his hands to his head.

"Hey," Dugald shouted. "What did you do to him?"

"He is simply opening the door to his past. To memories he had forgotten. Keeping this door open will allow him to more easily accept all the other creatures he has yet to meet. Denial will be used against him. It is good he believes."

Dugald groaned as he leaned back in the boat. Mordred looked up at him to see fresh blood soaking through his tunic. He glanced back at the black-haired mermaid, now only visible from her shoulders up. "Can you help him?"

"Yes. Will you let us?"

"Yes."

In moments, Mordred helped Dugald out of the boat to the soft grasses at the edge of the river. He took a handful of what looked like seaweed and crushed shells from one of the merwomen and did as instructed. After putting the thick substance on Dugald's wound, he wrapped several lengths of a different kind of water plant around his waist.

"This will hold the paste in place. By morning it will be as if he was never injured." The black-haired smiled.

Dugald murmured his thanks. Mordred also uttered his appreciation.

"When you come down from the mountains and reach the sea, our sisters will be waiting to take you across the waters so you can continue your quest. You need only find a small unmanned boat and call on them with this." She handed Mordred a small nautilus shell.

"Wait," Dugald said in a daze. "You never told us your names."

The merwomen erupted into another fit of giggles. "We can never reveal our names to land creatures, or else you would have control over us."

With much splashing and snorting of the merhorses, the entire group of wondrous creatures slid beneath the surface of the water, just as the sun, too, disappeared below the horizon.

Mordred had spent the night watchful and aware. Now that he knew he had far more to be concerned with than Vlad, undead armies, and mankind, there would be no time for rest. It was as if his eyes had finally opened. Did a refusal to believe in mythical beasts make them less harmful? How was it that humans never saw these creatures?

Only as children were mortals allowed to part the veil between what could be seen and what could be imagined. Mordred had not simply parted the veil, but torn it away. He would see things that would continue to war with what his human mind accepted. A chill raced up his spine. Who knew what lurked in the shadows of a rainy day now that he had opened his eyes completely? What new thing might they encounter to prevent them from reaching their destination?

Once again his world had been spun upside down. This time, Mordred feared he might never come back to reality, for what was the reality he existed in presently? His thoughts were interrupted by the frantic voice of the priest.

"What have you done? Who are you? Where am I?"

Mordred ignored the man's questions and asked his own in a gruff voice. "How is it you know of Vlad? How has he come to you?"

He watched the man fidget with the bindings at his wrists. Fear rolled off him in waves. Fear, and deceit, but not necessarily evil, Mordred thought.

"You will not be allowed to leave until I permit it. You can stop struggling. You are tied up for your own good. The entity called 'Vlad,' how do you know him?"

Father Simon whined, "Are you going to kill me? Who are you?"

"Do you not remember the scene at the Castel?" Mordred asked while watching the man's face to detect the hint of a lie.

"I remember being in that room with the Keys, and hearing a voice in my head. Then, I heard the voice telling me to go to the dungeon and that man, that horrid, horrid blasphemer."

Mordred was about to direct the man back to answering his questions but he hesitated.

"That evil, vile, man in the dungeon. The Soulis. It couldn't be. It is impossible. We destroyed that line." The man was rambling, unaware Mordred had to clench his teeth to keep from showing his anger at the use of his surname in such unsavory terms.

Thankfully, Dugald lay sleeping deeply from the medicines the merwomen had given him, otherwise Mordred feared he would blurt something that for the moment he wanted to remain unknown.

"Go on," he encouraged. "I would hear more."

As if Mordred hadn't spoken, the priest continued his ravings. "The Church determined it had destroyed the lineage of the Soulis clan, and yet there he was claiming to be connected to that family of the Devil. I heard the voice tell me to kill him. The voice told me the man did not belong. I thought it was the voice of God." The priest broke down and brought his hands to his eyes.

"I thought it was God telling me to do away with the man. But then the voice came again and it told me to do unspeakable things. Bad things and I couldn't, but when I refused, the voice hurt me."

Father Simon looked up at Mordred, his tears of remorse leaving streaks across his dirty face. "Please, I, I want it out of me. It is not God that possesses me, but something else."

"Something very, very evil. You have somehow summoned the entity Vlad to you, and he has found a way into your mind and body. I'm not sure how we can get him out."

"I think I might know. We must find Vlad the Impaler," Father Simon stuttered breathlessly. "Yes, we must. Maybe if we confront the person he has taken possession of, and kill that person, we can get him out of me, too?"

Hopeful eyes implored Mordred. Clearly, Father Simon had no recollection of the chaos in the Castel, and did not remember he was in the company of a vampyre and a werewolf. Fleetingly, Mordred wondered what the holy man would think of that, but he had no time to ponder it further. Something the priest said had caught his attention.

"To the Carpathians?"

"Yes. To the east far into the mountains. The lands of the Turks and gypsies. In lands full of heathens there lives a man, a prince who is striking terror in the whole of Europe. He has committed great atrocities against both his own people and his enemy, the Church. He has disavowed his faith and fallen to the darkness."

Mordred stood up and walked over to the priest, knelt beside him and offered some dried meat he had found in the boat.

"Bless you my child," Father Simon said as he hungrily ate what was offered.

Biting his tongue, Mordred kept his thoughts directed on the problem at hand. "Tell me more about this Vlad."

"His name is Vlad the Impaler, as you mentioned. We must pass through the Forest of the Damned to get to him. It is said he allows no trespassers. I am afraid of what he would do to a priest."

The irony that a human was called the same name as the entity was not lost on Mordred, but he focused on the rest of the apellation. "The Impaler?" Mordred wondered at the grisly name.

"Yes, the Impaler. It is rumored he impales those who displease him. Women, children, and men, especially holy men, he impales on sharpened stakes and leaves them to die in misery. They say you can hear the voices of those tortured souls miles before you get to the forest. Most won't set foot in the woods, and none have yet overtaken his castle. Even the dreaded Turks fear him. Though it is rumored they are the cause of his madness. He was once taken prisoner by them."

Dugald groaned, and Mordred turned his attention to his companion.

"Finally you wake. I thought you would sleep for weeks. Dugald, meet Father Simon."

"But, I thought," Dugald started, and then stopped when he saw the look Mordred gave him.

"Father Simon, meet Dugald."

The priest nodded, greeting Dugald. "I am truly sorry you two have to suffer from my ills, but I hope you can free me of this thing that has possessed me."

Wisely, Dugald kept his mouth shut.

✛ ✛ ✛

The journey was now even slower going than before. Father Simon, being wholly human, could not withstand days without rest, or the extremes in temperature that Mordred and Dugald could.

More regularly than Mordred liked, the travelers made

their way into small villages seeking food, clothing, and hospitality. There was a strong sense it was much easier to track the party. They moved slower and left a trail. Their human companion was a liability, but Mordred was not inclined to simply leave the man to Vlad's machinations.

Carefully, they made their way across the mountains and down the other side to the sea without incident. Mordred, always on the alert for anything normal or abnormal, felt he was now completely paranoid at the slightest noise or movement.

More than once he nearly beheaded Dugald when the wolf came ambling toward him, away from the sight of the priest.

"Christ, Mordred, what has you so jumpy?" Dugald finally asked one evening as he was yet again confronted with a dangerously on-edge vampyre. "Ever since we met the mermaids you've been acting like every little thing is out to get you."

Sneering at Dugald's naiveté, Mordred snapped, "Isn't it?"

"Well, if I think back to all the beasties we've encountered I'd say it's a mixed bag. Vlad is a bad one, and then the Kraken and, well, okay the Ammut, but they actually didn't harm us. I don't know, Mordred, I think we've less to fear from the supposed mythical creatures than we do the humans. Though I'm not very anxious to see a dragon, thank you."

"Easy for you to make light of a terrible situation, or do you just not get it? Even now we could be watched or stalked and then, the moment we let our guard down, we'll all be maimed, or killed. And maybe some of these things do know how to kill a vampyre properly."

Dugald put on his clothing and boots. He peered at the moon, haunting the sky behind a mass of thin, vaporous clouds. He cocked his head, still staring at the orb, as he replied, "Aw, gee, Mordred, now you know what it feels like to be human again. I mean, look, I can be harmed by the silver of mankind among other things. I take nothing for granted. No minute, no day goes by where I'm not wondering if this might be the end for me. Such is the way of all creatures."

"Not vampyres," Mordred bit out. "We're supposed to be immortal."

"Yeah, well, maybe if you'd stop thinking you're going to live forever, you'd get a clue." Dugald kicked at a rock, finally turning his gaze from the night sky. "You know, instead of thinking this whole thing is a curse and all, maybe you should see the blessing it brings."

Mordred narrowed one eye while the other shot open in surprise. "I should feel blessed that I must drink human blood or go mad for want of it? I should be grateful that I will live for centuries watching the years pass by while everyone around me, my entire family, my clan disappears. I am like a ghost among those who feel they are always on the edge of death. I am not afraid to die, I would welcome death but for this weight."

Dugald sat on a log and rubbed at his face. "I'm just saying that while in your mind this isn't the most perfect situation, maybe it isn't the worst, either. You would be dead right now. How do you know what waits for you there would be better or worse than this?"

"It's easy for you," Mordred bit out caustically, "you were born a werewolf. You weren't changed against your will. You weren't made into a monster."

"Really? Once, a long time ago, my people roamed the earth without fear. No one loathed us. We were simply other creatures that belonged, but now? Now, we must live isolated and away from humankind, because it is humans and their inability to believe in what they cannot see that has led to the persecution and almost total destruction of werewolves."

"If you dislike humans so much, why help me save them?"

"Good question. I suppose I see it as helping you, not humans directly. I owe you my life."

"You repaid that debt."

"No, not really. You continue to allow me to accompany you and that is far more meaningful than you will ever know.

You make yourself an outcast gladly and you revel in your isolation. I *am* an outcast and would go mad without the companionship of others, if not werewolves, at least you."

Mordred didn't answer. He simply let out an exhalation of breath.

"So, now what?" Dugald asked. "We storm the castle of this Impaler fellow and then what?"

"I have no idea. I only know somehow this earthly Vlad is the vessel for the entity Vlad. I'm hoping we'll learn more before we encounter either of them."

✛ ✛ ✛

The pair, along with Father Simon, sailed the sea without incident. They found a small boat as instructed and when they unfurled its sails, both Dugald and Mordred knew it wasn't the power of the wind that got them across so swiftly.

It still amazed Mordred he was to simply accept the existence of yet another creature of his dreams as a reality, but this time he did smile when he saw the half-women, half-fish beings. They waved their greeting and set to the work of moving the boat across the open water.

Once they reached the shore they led Father Simon to a spot on a hill and went back to thank the women. There was much splashing and giggling, some of it Dugald's as once again he had a silly grin plastered on his face every time he looked at one of the mermaids.

If Mordred didn't know any better, he'd have sworn Dugald was smitten with the entire race of mermaids.

Once across the sea from Italy, the trio moved inland. They crossed several mountain ranges and made their way slowly through dense forests. They forded cold streams and followed the course of rivers. Always, Mordred let some unknown source within him guide them.

Fearing even humans, Mordred only allowed them to enter populated places under cover of night. He knew that was the time Vlad's minions would be searching for him but he also knew the priest would need to eat and rest. Always, he maintained a silence within himself. He quieted his thoughts and slowed his breathing, heartbeat and pulse until he blended completely into the surroundings. He could leave nothing to chance. Vlad would be able to detect even a thread of thought from Mordred. He was determined to keep his entire being as still as possible.

He fed, when he felt the urge. Always on someone he determined was either ill or of bad nature. Sometimes after feeding he purged the contents of his stomach, as if the bad blood was too poisonous to absorb.

And always he remained alert to the presence of evil. He knew they were getting close when they entered a vast, jagged mountain range heavily forested with ancient trees.

Mordred left Father Simon alone at their campsite while he went to meet Dugald, back from his nightly foray. The pair were just returning when they heard Father Simon scream. Dashing up the slope, Mordred stared at the scene revealed to him.

Father Simon was trussed up in rope and being slung over the back of a horse, none too gently, by an unsavory looking stranger. Around him were others wearing heavy furs. They looked like animals themselves.

Mordred moved rapidly toward the group. "Halt! Leave that man alone!" he shouted.

The men stared at him silently for a moment and then laughed. They unsheathed their wicked looking blades and pointed them at Mordred.

"And what do you think you are going to do about it? The Impaler has offered a hefty bounty for any men of cloth caught in his woods. We are bringing him the priest. What concern is it of yours?"

"He is part of our party. We are heading to Vlad; perhaps you can show us the way?"

This last was met with more derisive laughter. "What need do we have to allow you to join us? We serve Vlad only. You are of no consequence. Be gone with you. The Turks are about and you would do well to avoid this area at night.

There are things in these woods that no man should want to meet up with."

Having no choice, Mordred pulled his sword from his side. "You don't understand. I cannot allow you to take the father to Vlad without us. So, we will either join you, after you've untied the priest, or we will kill you."

The leader, a giant bear of a man, smirked, unafraid. "You think we have fear of you? Who are you to threaten us. We should kill you just for wasting our time."

Dugald stood next to Mordred, brandishing his golden short swords, one in each hand. "Well, let's have at it then, shall we? Or are you guys all talk?"

The big man slapped the horse Father Simon was tied to, sending it dashing away. "Do not fear, the pony knows his way home. The priest will be greeted by Vlad shortly, but first, we must make you die."

The men, all twelve of them, dismounted and strode forward. Their weapons caught the dying sunlight. They did not wait for a signal, but rushed Mordred and Dugald in a frenzy.

"Dugald, you should shift into your wolf form and go after that damned horse before it reaches Vlad."

"No," Dugald retorted, "look at the size of these men. You'll need my help here."

Mordred glanced at Dugald. "After I change, go after

the priest. You can't let Vlad the Impaler find him until we know what to do."

This time Dugald agreed. He moved to the front, covering Mordred, while Mordred called forth the vampyre. It was different this time. His human side did not fight against the beast, and therefore there was no pain. Easily Mordred became the creature of nightmare.

He growled through his long, sharp teeth, telling Dugald to leave.

When Dugald stepped aside, leaving Mordred in clear view of the attackers, each paused. One man made the sign of the cross while others remained frozen, their faces contorted in horror.

"What the hell is that?" one of the men asked in a voice filled with fear.

"It is a vampyre. Kill it!" urged another.

"How? We do not have the proper weapons."

Mordred slammed into the group, catching them at their weakest. They fought as a group but were not organized. Each fighter slashed and hacked without aiming. Most of the blows went past Mordred.

One stroke caught another attacker, splitting his skull.

Body parts flew everywhere. Mordred threw down his blade revealing his sharp claws and canines. In moments, he tore the throat from one man, spraying flesh and blood over the others. Some turned to run, but it was too late.

Mordred dispatched each in turn, slicing into their necks, savoring the taste of the salty elixir. He gorged himself on the dead, licking his lips and his fingers until he had sucked every last drop of blood.

Not a single man was left alive. There would be none to report his coming.

Mordred picked up his sword and quickly cut the heads off all of the victims, ensuring they could not come back to life. Then he moved off into the woods at a run, praying he could reach Father Simon in time.

Chapter Eleven

he bodies were everywhere. They rose from the ground on tall pieces of wood. Hundreds, if not thousands of them. All human. All impaled through the groin, and up through the skull, the point of the sharpened stakes piercing bone, muscle, and flesh.

Mordred felt ill.

The stench was suffocating, filling the forest of humanity, clogging Mordred's nostrils and making him want to retch. He swallowed several times as his vision blurred and cleared. It was as if his human mind and even his vampyre mind were struggling to accept the sight.

He'd been on crusade and he'd seen the carnage that men could do against those considered the enemy. He'd walked through streets running with the blood of the newly slain, but this was different.

Men, women, and children were all staked. Some had

Forest of the Damned

been dead for a time and their eyes had been plucked out by the great horde of ravens that descended on the forest with much squawking.

Oddly, though there were thousands of dead, tortured souls, what haunted Mordred the most was the absence of their voices. Usually when he came to any place of burial or death, he could hear them talking, or he felt an energy, but here there was only the overwhelming blanket of sadness.

What kind of man could do this? What would drive a man to do this?

The answer came back as quickly as the question was asked. Vlad. Not the Impaler, but the entity. The human Vlad was simply a pawn in a deadly, macabre game and Mordred an unwilling player.

Then he heard the moaning. Some of the victims were still alive. Some were bearing the excruciating pain of being impaled and then having their flesh torn from their limbs by the carrion eaters.

It was unbearable. Though Mordred worried about Father Simon, he knew he could not leave the dying. He must do what he had done more than a century ago. The thing he hated most. The thing he felt had damned him the first time.

But this was different. He wasn't putting soldiers, hardened men who'd seen the horrors of war, out of their misery.

Nay, this time he would be sending what he assumed were innocent men, women, and children to their maker.

It was genocide of the worst kind and Mordred was the only witness.

This truly was the Forest of the Damned.

Mordred pulled his great sword from its place at his waist and walked between the stakes determining those who were still in the throes of agony. When he found a person still alive, he hefted the stake from the ground gently trying to not cause more pain and stabbed each and every suffering soul through the heart until once again, as centuries ago, he waded in the blood of the dead.

Once again, as before, he questioned the belief that a god, any god, would allow such a travesty. How could God stand by, silently bearing witness to the destruction of thousands of innocents? Even those found guilty of crimes should receive a quicker death. This was unforgivable. This was torture for someone's perverse pleasure.

Cursing and sweating, Mordred continued to work. Hours slipped by, then days. The sun rose and set behind him. And always, he heard another moan.

Sometime after the fifth day and night, exhausted and full of pent-up anger and sorrow, Mordred finished the grue-some task. Only once had someone opened their eyes to look at him as he completed the work. A small child, a boy, who looked remarkably familiar to Mordred, gazed at him and offered a small smile. A whispered word of thanks, and the child was gone.

He sat on a log. His nose had by now grown used to the disgusting odor that filled the valley and his eyes had grown blind to the images of suffering. He felt nothing. He sat in silence, unmoving, his mind devoid of any thought.

And when he looked once more at the frightful scene stretching leagues beyond him, he saw, at the edges of his vision, small balls of golden light. They were no bigger than a man's fist, and at first Mordred thought his mind was playing tricks on him.

The lights grew more plentiful and larger and hovered over all the fallen. They multiplied into pairs once the orbs had enveloped a body. Mordred heard the sweetest sound. It was as if hundreds of children were singing a beautiful but melancholy song and it stirred something deep within Mordred. It was the keening of angels.

And then he wept. His body shook with the force of his emotion. He felt helpless and hopeless. What purpose was there in saving the human race if they would simply destroy themselves in the end?

Dugald stood transfixed just beyond the clearing where Mordred sat. He watched as the orbs of light completely surrounded his friend. Mordred was unaware of the incredible flares of golden beams that touched and shot through him.

It was something far beyond the understanding of a werewolf, but Dugald knew he would never forget the image of Mordred with his head in his hands weeping, completely enveloped in the wondrous ethereal glow.

He glanced around at the hundreds of bodies still held in place by the sharpened stakes and realized the full measure of the cruelty of mankind; he, too, felt the confusion and pain that had only been Mordred's to bear for centuries.

Why, if humans possessed this kind of brutality toward each other, save them?

Dugald reflected they were the only species that went to war over belief systems instead of food and shelter. They did not respect one another or the place they had been given in the world. They slaughtered each other and other species as fast as dry grasses were swallowed by a fire. What purpose to create a breed of creature that held no regard for any other thing, living or dead?

As much as he was confused by the creation of humans, he no longer questioned why Mordred had been chosen for the quest. The half-man, half-vampyre who sat, before him was a complete contradiction of who he thought himself to be. He mourned for the loss of life, for the souls of those who had to suffer.

Mordred Soulis might indeed be a vampyre, a creature steeped in darkness and secrets. A blood-hungry beast driven to madness if deprived of the life-giving essence, but he was also a man, and for the first time, Dugald understood what Mordred faced.

Someone had to bear witness to the passing of mankind. Someone had to chronicle and weigh and measure each passing hour against human thought and feeling. Someone needed to remain, if only to let those who came after know of the plight of men. Some things were better never repeated and if the human race was indeed a mistake, a flawed breed, and something took the place of humans, as was the way of nature, it would be for that new creation to know what came before.

Mordred was that Chosen One. The lonely soul who would time and again watch mankind turn on itself. He would be forced to see horrors repeated over and over, and if only to keep him from madness, Dugald thought, perhaps there was a reason for his becoming a vampyre.

He vowed to do whatever was in his power to assist his friend. No longer did Mordred simply represent the companionship Dugald so desired. He felt humbled to be allowed to travel with Mordred.

And while Mordred wept for the souls of the departed,

Dugald leaned against a tree and softly wept for Mordred's lost soul.

✠ ✠ ✠

They did not speak of the dead. They did not speak of Father Simon and his likely death. The days were subdued. There was no sun to break through the clouds.

The pair had left the Forest of the Damned, but still they were surrounded by dense populations of enormously tall trees and nearly impenetrable undergrowth. Yet, the tops of the trees appeared devoid of leaves and vines seemed to be choking the life from the woods.

Oddly, they saw no evidence of animals or forest creatures, both of their realm or any other. Dugald reported having to range far into another valley to find even small prey.

A fierce wind whistled through the branches, making all but the most necessary conversation difficult.

An everpresent mist crept across the low areas, curling and snaking into every crack and crevice. There was a dampness that would not go away. It was a dankness that seeped into pores and settled deep within bones; no amount of physical movement could warm the body.

Mordred decided against the lighting of fires. He also made it known he would not rest until he had found Vlad

Tepes the Impaler's fortress. Surely, a man who committed such atrocities would not be hard to find.

The few inhabitants they did encounter resembled startled deer at finding strangers in their midst. Suspicious looks were cast at the pair and many people refused to even speak to them. Mordred felt a weighty blanket of fear smothering the area.

The peasants, those that could be approached, simply pointed ahead and whispered in hushed voices that the Mad Prince lived in the castle at Tirgoviste beyond the next rise.

Even the gypsies refused to come near, holding up their symbols of protection. Mordred wasn't sure they did so because they knew he was undead, or if they simply felt anyone foolish enough be heading in the direction of the Impaler could only be evil.

A thick feeling of dread fell over both Dugald and Mordred though neither voiced their fears. They traveled together in silence, concentrating only on the task ahead. When they saw the spires that marked the roofline of the towers of the castle at Tirgoviste, Mordred spoke at last.

"I think it wise you shift into wolf form and remain that way until we can assess the situation."

At the look of disagreement Dugald gave him, Mordred held up his hand.

"I need you to do this. Vlad, the entity knows we are

coming, but he may not know just when and we need every advantage we can get. Vlad the Impaler will only know what the other Vlad tells him, so there is a chance he may not even know we are this close."

Instead of arguing, Dugald nodded. He dropped his pack.

"I'll bring clothing and your swords should you need to be human, but I think it would be in your best interest if you simply remain a wolf."

Dugald grasped Mordred's forearm and Mordred returned the gesture.

"You don't have to do this," Mordred said gazing into the golden eyes of the man he was fast considering his friend.

"Yes, I do." It had become a familiar statement to Dugald. Someday maybe he'd tell Mordred about the exact moment that he had decided his part in this adventure became more than one of simple companionship. He'd tell his vampyre friend of the day he became honored to be included. That day in the Forest of the Damned.

But for now, he merely smiled. "I'll see you on the inside."

Mordred nodded and watched Dugald remove his clothing and silently shift into the sleek predator that was his race. The wolf glanced back once more at Mordred before racing off into the dense curtain of trees.

Alone, Mordred mentally prepared himself for the confrontation ahead. He knew he would have to continue to hide his thoughts and block Vlad from entering his mind to gain an advantage.

Kabil had told him he had only grown a little in all the time he was asleep. He would continue to grow into his vampyre-self, but for now Mordred doubted he would prove strong enough to destroy Vlad. Realistically, the best he could hope for was to inflict enough damage to slow him down for awhile, buy time, and then hope Lir would show up so he could find the other Vampyre kings.

In Mordred's mind came the voice of the one he missed the most. Jakob.

"Go forth bravely, Chosen One. It is your destiny, and your design, to be here. You have the might and faith of the Templars within you."

Mordred wanted to ask what would happen to him if he failed, but the voice drifted away as if it had never been. It was enough, however, to remind him that he must at least give all he had; if he went to this challenge with doubt in his mind, he would indeed be defeated.

Inhaling several deep breaths, Mordred gazed to the sky, waiting, as if to see some heavenly sign that God was on his side, but nothing appeared. No magic, no glorious light, no divine intervention.

The wind ceased its incessant howling and silence descended on the forest. The world stilled, as if holding its breath. Waiting to see who would be victor in the battle.

Among the ancient sentinels, shrouded in damp mist, one lone vampyre stood. He dropped his head to his chest and brought his hands to the necklace given to him by Anubis. He had no words for prayer. None of his prayers had been answered in the past and he wasted no time thinking God would hear him now.

Rather, Mordred reached mentally to Kabil and Lir, asking for guidance from afar. He had no idea where he would find the next king, but he hoped, as with Kabil, that if the vampyre was powerful, he would hear Mordred's call.

Breathing deeply to still his racing heart, Mordred tried to calm his mind. Clear it from all thoughts save fighting Vlad and whatever else hid behind the walls of the castle.

Mordred divested himself of his sword belt and the scabbard on his back. He removed his gauntlets, boots and tunic. Then he summoned the armor that Jakob, the Master Templar, said belonged to him by his calling. It had been brought to him in an ornately crafted silver trunk and when he had first seen it, though beautiful, he had assumed it would be like any other armor.

Jakob withheld critical information from Mordred, preferring the Chosen One discover the armor's true magic himself. The suit was crafted of a supernatural force, and was with him no matter where he found himself. The entire suit of black armor melded with his skin. He only had to don the protective covering once, and it remained dormant beneath the flesh of his body until the time it was needed. The armor aided in battling both the undead and Vlad.

He learned through trial and error the armor could not simply be called forth to fight any foe. Only those of the dark realm caused it to appear. Now, as he stretched out his arms in preparation to receive the gift, Mordred felt the air around him change.

The wind rose up again, more forcefully, scattering dried leaves and dead brush, reminding Mordred of the death rattles from the tortured souls he had dispatched in the Forest of the Damned.

The clouds grew thicker overhead, and hung lower. Flashes of light ignited the dark sky, followed by the rumble of thunder, sounding like a waking beast. A hungry beast.

Lifting his palms upward, Mordred waited. All around him chaos erupted as the storm hit full force. Rain fell in a torrential downpour, soaking him, but still he stood. And as the earth shook and trembled and the elements slammed into one another above him, he continued to call forth the armor.

Mordred watched through half-closed eyes as droplets of water hit his face, stinging him as the skin of his hands began to undulate. The motion continued up his arm until the entire surface of his body was rippling and changing. The armor appeared. Black as night it molded to him, became his second skin. Even his hands and fingers were protected by articulated pieces of the strange metal.

Clad in the magical pieces from the neck down, Mordred pulled on his boots and strapped his Blood Sword across his back. He yanked his long, wet, dark hair, behind him, tucking the mass beneath his *gorget*. Then he reached for the helmet that appeared on the ground beside him.

It was a massive piece of exquisite beauty, expertly crafted and molded to reflect the image of a grotesque demon. Its narrow eye holes allowed Mordred to see, but completely protected his face. The only area not covered by armor was his mouth. This, he knew, was deliberately left open so when he assumed the change and released the vampyre within, as he would need to do to battle Vlad, his long incisors would be able to inflict their terrible damage.

It was time to go. Mordred walked slowly toward the castle looming in the distance. The storm continued to exert its forces around him, but he paid it no heed. It would take more than the elements to dissuade him from his course.

All at once a brilliant streak of light stretched overhead; jagged and forked it ripped across the fabric of the sky, shredding the clouds and all else in its path. It hit the highest tower of the castle, rocking the ground as stone exploded.

Another bolt headed toward the castle, but before it hit

an eerie, glowing red shard of light split the bolt, sending it harmlessly to the ground.

More strange red light knifed through the clouds heading straight for Mordred. He inhaled once and drew the Blood Sword from its scabbard, raising it high in the air. It caught the pulsating streak of energy, and the force of the direct hit was almost more than Mordred could bear. Somehow, he managed to stand his ground.

He'd brought the shield that matched armor and helm, and in the moment before the next attack Mordred pulled the round hammered metal from his back and donned it.

When the scarlet light came again, it was in the form of massive rolling orbs of fire. Mordred deflected them with both the shield and the Blood Sword, feeling his strength sapped each time the evil energy came at him.

Yet, somehow above him the lightning from the natural storm seemed to counter the bolts coming from the castle. Mordred watched as time after time they hit the castle, dislodging stone and exploding windows and rooftops. He wasn't sure if he was just lucky and the storm was exceptionally violent this night, or if there was some other force behind it. He was grateful nonetheless.

Pushing forward, Mordred came to the gatehouse, but instead of finding soldiers, he saw on the sloping ground surrounding the massive fortress more visions of the evil men do. Countless bodies were staked and left to die in slow agony.

Mordred refused to lose focus. He strode between the dead bodies and concentrated on the large iron doors of the castle. They opened in invitation.

As Mordred entered the courtyard, he saw Father Simon. The priest had been spitted like all the others, but had been left upside down. His flesh appeared to have been burned and his mouth was twisted in a final cry of pain. A crucifix had been nailed through his head. Mocking Mordred.

He couldn't breathe for a moment, couldn't think. He had brought Father Simon with him in hopes of reversing the possession. He was now responsible for his death, the death of someone who might have held keys to Mordred's own past and who might reveal clues to explain why he was chosen to be the savior of mankind.

Laughter erupted from all around him. It was Vlad.

"Welcome to my lair. Father Simon served me well, but in the end he could not free me from this earthly form and had to pay for his crimes."

Mordred ignored the taunt. He must focus.

"I'm so delighted you have decided to come to my home. Here I hold all the power. Fool. You were not worthy to stand beside me. You've never appreciated the gifts I've bestowed on you. Look at you wearing the armor of the holy.

Do you think faith in your god will help you now? Your god forsakes you, Mordred Soulis!"

The ground trembled, sending loose stones tumbling from the high towers.

"Come and get me if you think you can," Vlad taunted.

Mordred saw the door to the interior of the castle open. As he walked forward he heard the sound of nails clattering on stone and knew without looking Dugald had arrived.

"Watch yourself, Dugald. Find Vlad."

The beast pushed past Mordred like a loyal hound and tilted his head up to sniff the air. The animal's wet coat stood on end and a growl pierced the eerie silence. The wolf took off across the great hall.

Mordred followed. He passed portraits hung on the stone wall, and burned the image of the man in them into his mind. If Vlad was in human form, this was who he must look for.

The pair raced through the castle, but something odd was happening. Each time they appeared to be making progress and found a stairwell, or a hallway, or reached a landing, a new hall would appear or stairs would abruptly reverse direction. It was as if the fortress was a living, breathing, entity, constantly changing the floor plan.

Doors opened to reveal stone walls, stairs led to nowhere

and halls shifted direction right beneath their feet. At this rate they would never find the object of their search. Mordred tried to collect his thoughts, all the while trying to create a wall around his mind so Vlad couldn't prowl in it.

All of the sudden, he felt the building shake. At first he thought Vlad was causing the tremors. But Dugald came to a halt and reversed. He raced right past Mordred, down the stairs they had just climbed. He raced behind the wolf.

A strange moaning sound filled the air, bouncing off the wood and stone in a gruesome chorus of death. At the bottom of the stairs came several hundred revenants. Each of them bore the look of those Mordred had passed outside. They had large holes in their skulls and parts of their flesh were missing.

Some had no eyes, while others were devoid of tongues or fingers. They were the victims of Vlad's diabolical machinations. And Mordred had no idea how he was going to take them all on.

Stumbling over one another, they made their way to the stairs and climbed slowly upward, groaning in deep guttural tones. Dugald had come back up ahead of the masses, and stood growling and snapping as the revenants came at them.

"Looks like it's now or never, Dugald. Let's see how many we can take."

Mordred glanced over his shoulder where once he had

seen another hall leading off to the right; now there was nothing but a stone wall. Between the castle and the undead horde approaching, there was no escape.

Instead of waiting for the flesh-eating army to come to him, Mordred charged using the stairs to his advantage. He kicked out, hitting several in the chest. They took the direct hit and fell backwards, buckling the line of revenants behind them.

Mordred hacked and slashed with the Blood Sword, glowing red and vibrating with his energy and adrenaline. He had no fear of the sword being dislodged from his grip. Like the armor, it melded with his hand.

Heads were cleanly severed from bodies, green and yellow viscous fluid spewing forth, coating the stairs in a slippery mess of ooze. Arms, hands, fingers, legs and torsos were cut and chopped. Skulls were cleaved in two, but still the revenants came. Mordred looked down into the room at the base of the stairs to see it was filled with still more. A sea of them surged forward and as fast as he could decimate them, they multiplied.

He knew this could go on endlessly. He had to get past them and find a way deeper into the castle. He glanced again over his shoulder. Maybe it really wasn't a wall. Maybe his mind was seeing what the castle wanted him to see. There had been a hall there when he had first come to the top of

Dugald Transformed

the stairs.

"Dugald, hold them off. I'm going to find a way out of here." There was no answer; Dugald was clearly intent on inflicting as much damage as possible.

Turning, Mordred ran and prepared for the impact of slamming against the stone wall. He went through and found himself in a different hall. He was still able to hear the battle as the sounds bounced off the stones, but knew that had merely been a distraction. He had to find Vlad.

As he was fighting the revenants, Mordred had been struck with a thought. If Vlad had been bound to a human form, perhaps his powers had been curbed somewhat. Mordred prayed he was right.

He came to a spiral staircase. As it closed over into yet another wall, Mordred jumped at it and took the stairs two and three at a time. He kicked down a wooden door and found himself on top of the remains of the tower that had been blasted away by the lightning.

The storm had not let up. Sheets of rain fell, coating the stones with a slick sheen. Where a crenellated battlement should have been was a gaping hole. The wind raged. Mordred was keenly aware of what a fall would do to him should he lose his footing. He was about to go back down the stairs, thinking he had been led to a dead end, when he saw a shape move from behind a pile of stones.

"So, you have proven to be not so stupid after all. Foolish, yes. What do you think you can gain by trying to destroy your creator? You and I are one. If you vanquish me, what becomes of you? How can you think to have good in the world without evil, Mordred? How would you know good if not for evil?"

Mordred tried to block Vlad's voice rasping inside his skull. He knew the thing was trying to cause confusion, hesitation, searching Mordred for a sign of weakness. He did not respond, but took up a defensive position, waiting for the first strike.

"This human I've become was already well on his way to meeting the Devil, Mordred. How can you save the world from darkness if darkness is what it wants? Why save them from themselves? You see what they do to one another. And that's without my help. There is still time for you to join me. You will join me, son."

Mordred hissed, "Never."

"Vampyre, you belong to me!" Vlad stretched out his hands and Mordred felt as though someone reached into his chest, encircled his heart and squeezed it. His lungs deflated. Like a doll, he felt himself falling under Vlad's power.

He knew there was only one way to resist. Mordred forced the change. It had been gnawing at him since he had put the armor on, sensing it would be called forth. Now it burst through Mordred like a rampaging beast, slashing and clawing him.

He gasped for breath and felt the sharp teeth rip through his lips. The taste of blood trickled over his tongue. He charged just as Vlad, revealing his own set of nasty looking canines, made his move. They hit and the air around them erupted into a violent crash of thunder.

Mordred felt Vlad's hands wrap around his neck, hauling him toward the opening in the battlement. He pulled himself back and turned them both so Vlad was the one on the edge. Vlad released his grip and brought his elbow up, slamming into Mordred's mouth and even with the armor he felt his nose break.

More blood spilled, driving Mordred crazy with the lust that came with the hunger. Bringing his head back, he suffered another blow, this one to his midsection, and he stumbled backward.

Vlad came at him again, black robes billowing out behind him. Lightning struck inches from the evil entity and Mordred thought he saw a brief flicker of fear the eyes of the human shell. He brought the hilt of his sword up to bash it against the side of Vlad's head, and fell. Mordred jumped to his feet and brought the sword over his head, but Vlad rolled to avoid the strike.

While Mordred recoiled from his miss, Vlad shoved

him, hard from behind, sending him sliding across the stones. He felt himself go over the edge, but he caught the fragmented stones.

Vlad appeared, arms crossed, smiling. His black eyes were devoid of warmth. He stepped on Mordred's hand. He hung only by the fingers of his other hand.

"Join me," Vlad called.

"Never."

He felt the boot crush the bones in his other hand. Enduring the pain that ripped through him, Mordred willed all his strength to him and let go of the stones. He ascended for just a moment and snaked out his arms to grab Vlad's legs. The momentum of the fall pulled Mordred backward, and with him came Vlad.

He saw the surprise in Vlad's eyes. Oddly, the entity trapped within the man, did nothing. He was not indeed, as strong when in possession of a human. With all his remaining will, Mordred turned himself in mid air. In his mind's eye he saw himself rolling so Vlad was beneath him.

They hit the sharpened stakes one right after the other. Vlad skewered first, Mordred immediately after. As his body shut down to prolong consciousness and limit the damage from the new wound, he felt his vampyre-self recede. With his eyelids flickering and threatening to close, Mordred forced himself to look down at the face of the man beneath him. It looked human. There was even an expression of pain frozen on the face, but Mordred knew he had not destroyed Vlad. A shadow spilled out of the dead man's gaping maw.

A shade, or spirit-thing, moved and formed into a large bird before disappearing into the storm.

Mordred's mind went blank. He thought he heard Dugald yelping. His last thought was that he had failed once again. His world and his being went still. A flash of lightning ripped through the sky, hitting him squarely in the chest. Mordred was unconscious.

XII

Chapter Twelve

hat Mordred hated most about injuring himself so badly so that he slept for days, weeks, months, or possibly years, were the dreams that haunted him. His mind was aware, to some degree, of the things around him, but his body was helpless while it repaired itself.

Kabil assured him the healing would occur at a faster rate as he grew older in his vampyre years, but for now he had no idea how long he would swim in the blackness of his unconscious state.

As he climbed the steps to join the living once more, snippets of the time before the injury flashed through his mind. Like shards of a much larger work of art, Mordred was unable to make sense of them individually. He knew he must wait until he was fully awake.

Until that time the dreams would tease him and make him mad with the desire to know what had happened to him. Who was the dark-haired stranger battling him in his mind?

"Move away, damn women, he's been asleep too long for the Chosen One!" A rough shout broke through Mordred's rest. The male voice boomed around him.

Another voice, a female's rang out. "He belongs to us until he awakens of his own accord. You can bellow and bluster and call down the thunder for all we care, Lir, but he belongs to us now."

"And I say, WinterKil, you will obey me this once and release him to me. All your coddling and cooing has done nothing but make him not want to wake. He is a child suckling at its mother's teat, and has no reason to join the living."

"When have I ever coddled a warrior? If not for me, you would have lost him to that evil thing he hunts. I was the one who heard his call. I was the one who convinced you to call down the lightning. We are allowed to keep him until he is fully ready to join the others in the hall."

Mordred found it interesting that two voices were arguing over him. The woman wanted him to stay where he was, while the man wanted him to wake, as if that was so easy to do. He groaned at his own frustration.

"See," barked the male voice, "he wakes. It is time he furthers his training. Vlad injured him greatly this time and the whelp is in serious need of my help."

"We'll bring him to you when he is ready to join the others, and not before then." There was a marked stubbornness in the woman's voice.

"You'll get one more day from me and not a moment more. If he is not fully awake, I'll force him out myself."

The sound of heavy footfalls receded.

Mordred opened his eyes and closed them as the bright light stabbed into his skull.

"Easy there, Chosen One, you need to do everything slowly. You have been lying still for a long time and your body needs to catch up with the rest of you. If you come out of this too fast, you could harm yourself permanently."

Keeping his eyes closed, Mordred asked, "You are WinterKil?"

"Yes. And you are Mordred Soulis."

"Where am I?"

"In Valhalla," she replied softly. "The hall of heroes. The kingdom of Lir."

Shock registered. He was in the abode of the second Vampyre King? "How?"

"That is an interesting story. Suffice to say you called for Lir, but the big oaf was deaf to your cries. We, the Valkyries, his Battle Maidens, however, heard you loud and clear. We convinced him to cause the storm to help you fight Vlad, and then when you fell in battle we collected you and brought

Winter Kil

you here."

Mordred's eyes shot open. "There was a wolf, Dugald, my friend," he stuttered.

There was a notable silence. A different sort of pain flooded his mind and squeezed his chest. "Do you know what happened to Dugald?"

Mordred felt a hand pressing down on him, reminding him not to move. Warmth radiated from the spot where the Valkyrie touched him and Mordred relaxed. He gazed up into what he thought was the face of an angel.

While she wore a silver helm decorated with wings on each side, her hair spilled freely around her heart-shaped face, pale blond, like sunlight, set off her incredible eyes. They were a mix of steel gray and deep blue and reminded Mordred of the hottest part of a flame. He found himself thinking that with her fair hair and eyes she glowed with an otherworldly radiance.

WinterKil wore an expression of sadness and something else indefinable. He watched her clench her jaw before responding. "There was no time to save Dugald. We could only bring one of you here, and we knew it had to be you. We are very sorry."

Something lodged in Mordred's throat, making it hard to swallow as the impact of what she said washed over him. Dugald was . . . gone?

It was true that Mordred had never exactly been happy about the werewolf tagging along. He'd had to get him out of trouble more times than he could possibly count and the shifter was a liability, making Mordred have to worry about more than just himself.

But Mordred felt a hole in his heart, a feeling he did not expect. He had assumed some of the more basic emotions of his human-side would fall beneath the raging of his vampyre-side. He did not expect to feel the great waves of grief rising in him.

"Go," he ordered in a voice thick with pent-up frustration and rage. "I want to be alone."

WinterKil nodded. "We understand. He was a good warrior. He will be remembered well." She motioned to the other women in the room and they all quietly left the chamber. Mordred noted all the women wore battle gear, complete with chainmail and armor plating. Each had a large axe strapped to her side.

The women were a myriad of colors: brunette, auburn, blond and ebony-haired, each could rival a goddess, yet there was something in the way they walked, in the way they held themselves, that spoke of strength and power.

Oddly, every woman wore a long cape that concealed what Mordred took to be something strapped to their backs. He assumed it was more weaponry, although knowing they only sought the dead after a battle he wondered just who they might have to fight that they needed to be so armed.

Alone, isolated, and full of remorse, Mordred's thoughts turned bleak. He railed at the fates. Who had determined Dugald should die? Show him the one who decided it was his time. He had been so full of life, so much like a pet hound and less the dangerous wolf he could become.

Memories whispered through his mind. The time he had met the werewolf. He had tried to get him to go home, but Dugald refused. He had helped Mordred find the Book of the Undead, and had fought alongside him in the first battle with Vlad.

After that first battle, Mordred had once again told Dugald he was free to go, but Dugald insisted he hadn't repaid the debt he owed for Mordred saving his life. The real story eventually revealed that Dugald had been driven from his pack, making him an outcast like Mordred. As Mordred had learned, it was a far worse fate for Dugald.

He would no longer see the great golden wolf racing through the trees, the sunlight dappling his coat and making him appear more magical than he already was. He would no longer hear the howls of isolation Dugald loosed when he was miles away and thought Mordred could not hear.

Mordred would no longer be challenged to be better than he thought he could be from just one look and lopsided grin from the werewolf. It grieved him to think he had never told Dugald he had finally come to accept him as a friend.

Too late. Too late Mordred realized the bond that had developed between the vampyre and the werewolf. Too late came the knowledge he never let Dugald know what his companionship had meant.

There was an intense guilt, a weight like a thousand stones on his shoulders, knowing he had sent Dugald to his death. It was Mordred who had left the hundreds of revenants to search the house for Vlad. He had thought the wolf would have followed, but that was the last time he'd seen Dugald, surrounded by the undead army.

Mordred shook his head as if to rid himself of the image. It did no good. A thousand talons of sorrow plucked at his heart as Dugald's face swam before Mordred's eyes.

The person who'd come the closest to being his friend was gone.

Mordred wasn't given long to grieve. In fact, it didn't seem he'd been given any time at all. Soon, he heard the sounds of the Valkyries. WinterKil appeared in the doorway, her face emotionless.

"It's time we bring you back to normal."

Shocked, Mordred's arched. "Heal me? I've just learned my friend is dead and you want me to simply move on?"

WinterKil didn't stop until she was standing right beside Mordred's pallet. She lowered herself, sitting on her haunches and bringing her face to his eye level. This time there was a definite look of determination. "That's exactly what you need to do. Lir has given us one more day and in that time we need to prepare you to do battle against him. He doesn't think you are the real Chosen One."

When Mordred would have interrupted, the Valkyrie brought her hand up to silence him. "It doesn't matter what another king thinks. Each will require that you prove to them, independently, that you are worthy, and to do so with Lir you must defeat him in battle. I doubt you can do that in your current state. You, vampyre, have no choice. I suggest you tuck your hurt away for a day when you actually have the luxury of feeling sorry for yourself. Until then, you have to remain focused on this quest."

"Austr, Vestr, bring the chalice," WinterKil ordered. Two other women dressed in finely wrought silver chainmail and helms came forward carrying a hammered goblet. They passed it to WinterKil who handed it to Mordred. "You must drink this. It will speed your healing so you can begin your training."

Mordred brought the cup to his lips and looked at the liquid swirling in the chalice. It was deep red in color and boiled as if it had been heated, but the cup itself was not warm. It remained cool to the touch.

When he hesitated, WinterKil added, "It is dragon's blood. I'd not waste a drop if I were you; it's hard to come by. Don't worry, it won't kill you, though I imagine after going a few rounds with Lir you might wish it had."

"Sisters, Mordred Soulis has come back to us, but let us not tell Lir just yet. He has given us one more day and he will need all the help we can give him if he is to measure up to the king's standards."

Rising to a sitting position with the assistance of several pairs of hands, Mordred did as WinterKil instructed. He swallowed every bit of the bitter liquid, grimacing when he reached the end.

"The cure is worse than the injury in this case, isn't it? Dragon's blood is not something a mere mortal can handle. It would be poison to your human-self, but your vampyre side is strong enough."

Mordred felt a fierce heat consume him. He heard the sounds of his body fluids churning, blood pumping, muscle, sinew, nerve and bone all fusing and repairing. His chest throbbed, his legs ached, and his head pounded. He felt as though he had just fallen on the sharpened stake again and he let out a groan as he writhed in new pain.

Hands held him down and through the red haze that had descended across his vision, he saw WinterKil's face.

"Your body is reliving the injury. I am sorry you must feel the pain again, but it is the only way to heal. Each cell in your body is releasing the memory so the injury will no longer exist within you in any way. You will be as you were before you fell, but first you must let all parts of your body experience the battle again. It will pass soon enough."

Her voice was a soothing balm to his heated soul and as he gasped for breath and felt sweat bead and roll down his face, he stared into her eyes and had the strangest sensation he was drowning in cool, no, icy waters. Her touch brought sweet relief to his anguished body.

Mordred had no sense of how much time passed while he continued to wander, lost within her gaze. It could have been minutes, or a year and a day. Nothing mattered but that he remain focused on the blueness of WinterKil's eyes.

As his mind cleared he became aware of the touch of several pairs of hands on his upper body. He then realized he was naked.

The lead Valkyrie answered his question before he asked. "Your armor, the special kind you summon, has receded inside you. The rest of your clothing was bloodied and ruined beyond repair. Odin is making you a new tunic and breeches. For now, you'll simply have to wear a robe."

"Odin?"

Smiling, WinterKil explained, "Valhalla is the house of

the Norse gods. Here they reside, and here they wait for you to be deemed worthy. A few, however, have already given you their favor. Odin is most impressed that you have lasted this far and has decided to gift you with the mail and tunic of a true warrior. Even though you are not a Viking."

Mordred was confused. He felt as though his mind was crammed to bursting with all the impossible things he'd experienced. Now, he was ensconced in Valhalla, a place only found in Norse legends and he was expected to believe the Viking gods were with him as well.

He felt like closing his eyes and succumbing to the urge to simply sleep forever. Knowing that was not a possibility, he decided to learn more about what was expected of him.

"What next?"

"You will come with us to the Fighting Hall. We will try to teach you how to fight properly," the Valkyrie called Vestr replied.

Mordred couldn't help himself. "Ladies, I do appreciate your willingness to give me some assistance where it concerns Lir, but I haven't made it this far without knowing how to wield a sword."

Laughter erupted in the chamber, rising in volume at Mordred's quizzical look.

"You may fight very well with a sword, but with Lir you will fight the true warrior way. You will fight with an axe,"

WinterKil explained, her mouth turned up in a haughty smile.

"An axe? I don't fight with an axe. Meaning no disrespect, but the people I've known that do fight with that weapon aren't exactly graceful and, well, they aren't . . ."

WinterKil rose and strode over to a wall where a white robe hung a peg. The garment was shot through with silver thread in the design of a dragon, starting from the neck and winding its way down to the hem.

She threw it at Mordred, who caught it in his fist. "Go on, you think an axe is a weapon for a barbarian, don't you? You think it is a tool from the Dark Ages and only those with no real fighting skill would use a bludgeoning weapon."

Smiling back, Mordred nodded. "It's just that I have never seen one wielded by anyone other than an oversized brute who used his size to smash through his enemy, but, in the end, he was felled easier than those who used the sword."

It was Austr's turn to laugh. Mordred watched the redhead cast a wink at her fellow sisters. Crossing her arms over her molded breastplate, she smiled. "Oh, so you think there is no grace, no skill required to use an axe, do you? Well, then, prove it vampyre. Did we choose correctly when we pulled you from the field of battle?"

The Valkyries all moved away from him, wearing a mischievous look on their faces. WinterKil remained in the chamber. "I will wait for you in the hall. Please put the robe on and then you will *teach* us how to fight, right?"

She strode from the room, her legs bare to the hip, exhibited the fine detail of a warrior's honed body.

Mordred knew the women were certainly shapely in the way only female fighters could be. He'd seen the muscles in their upper bodies clearly defined, the silver arm-bands serving to accentuate them further. But as fit as they were, he highly doubted they could do damage to him, a seasoned warrior. A man who had fought countless battles. A mercenary who had gained the attention of kings all over Europe for his prowess in battle. And as a vampyre, his strength had only increased.

Vlad was the only thing that could unseat Mordred. He had little doubt that he could beat not only the Valkyries, but Lir as well. Especially if the man wanted to fight with a clumsy axe.

It took Mordred only a moment to put on the robe which really only came to his knees. He wasn't sure he wanted to fight anyone in the outfit, but given no other clothing, and not wishing to fight naked, he readied himself and left the chamber.

WinterKil stood in the hallway. She had her cape pulled to one side, and it was then Mordred realized what it had covered. A pair of beautiful white wings were folded snugly against her back.

At his look of surprise, WinterKil smiled. "How else do you think we retrieve warriors on the fields of battle and bring them here? We are far above the plane of mortals, and without wings we'd be lost."

She noticed he had not taken his eyes from her and quickly pulled the cape back into place.

"You've been hurt?" Mordred questioned after noticing a spot on one of her wings was featherless. An ugly red gash marred the pink skin beneath. "How is it you were wounded? You come to the field *after* a battle, correct?"

WinterKil shrugged. "Yes, but sometimes we are not the only ones waiting to collect the fallen. Sometimes Death and his soldiers want the same warrior. Then we must do battle, and those from the underworld do not fight fair."

She walked down the long corridor, shining white and silver by the light of many torchieres, but as Mordred passed them he discovered they cast no heat, only light.

"By the underworld you mean the Devil?"

"No. The Devil and Death are two different entities. Death does not judge souls, but merely collects them until they are judged by the others. We take certain souls with us to Valhalla. The Viking souls. Those who die heroically in battle."

"But why me? I have no soul," Mordred said.

"That's where you are wrong, vampyre. There may

indeed come a day when you forsake your human side, but for now, when I cheated Death of you, I was able to do so because my kiss cast aside the winter from your human soul. It would not have had such power if you were not in some way still human." She paused for a moment as if considering her next words. "It is why you feel grief at the loss of your friend."

Mordred did not respond, but merely walked alongside the Valkyrie, taking in the strange palace that appeared to be made of crystal. He would have thought it ice, but there was no coldness.

WinterKil stopped before two silver doors. She opened them and then waited for Mordred to go through first. "Time for you to prove to us you can beat Lir."

"Am I not to be given anything more than this?" Mordred asked. The women were suited up in their armor and mail and all he had was the thin fabric of the robe.

"You don't think we could actually get a strike in against you, do you? After all, the axe is such an unwieldy weapon and we are simple barbarians," the Valkyrie named Vestr goaded Mordred.

"Are you not from Scotland?" asked another. "Have you not fought in a skirt before?"

Laughter filled the large, circular room.

"It is called a kilt and it was a far better choice than this garment," Mordred retorted.

"Well, then, if you don't like the weaving of the Norns, the Sisters of Fate, we'll let them know and you can fight naked and pray they don't cut short your own life-giver."

It was WinterKil who boldly threw the barb that caused everyone to erupt into a fit of husky laughter.

Mordred knew when he was verbally outwitted, and outnumbered. It was time to get down to the business of fighting, something at which he greatly excelled.

"Let's see if all your boasting is a true representation of your skill," Mordred taunted. He smiled when several pairs of eyes narrowed.

The women circled him, but gave him wide berth. He mistakenly thought it was from a fear of him and what he might be able to do even with an axe.

WinterKil handed him a weapon, one with a heavy steel head that could easily have felled a large tree with one stroke.

"I can't fight with this," Mordred sputtered.

"Too heavy?" she asked him.

"No. I'll kill you if I hit you."

"No, you won't. You won't even come close."

She pulled her own axe from its place at her hip. The other women did the same. The odd silver light that filled the chamber bounced off each metal head, refracting it. As it hit the walls it was split again and redirected into a kaleidoscope of color.

As Mordred admired the light source and the pattern it produced on the ceiling, he narrowly missed have his skull crushed by WinterKil's first swing.

"Boody hell!" he shouted angrily.

"Rule number one when fighting with Lir; never, ever lose your focus," she instructed, readying for another swing.

Soon all the ladies cast their own weapons forward and back while circling Mordred. He had no choice but to raise his axe, if only to ward off the oncoming attacks.

Someone kicked a wooden shield at him. It skidded across the floor, and Mordred looked for an opportunity to grab it. The women did not let up.

A momentary break in the rhythm of the Valkyries' strikes gave Mordred the chance he needed. He slipped his left hand around the grip and raised the shield just in time to stop a crushing blow. It glanced off, but Mordred's arm vibrated with the force behind the strike.

He was amazed. First, at their prowess, then at their strength. He realized he had severely underestimated his opponents.

WinterKil must have seen the look on his face as he fended off another attack that would have dropped an ordinary man to his knees. "Rule number two when fighting

Lir; never underestimate him. He may look the bear, but he is swift as a deer."

Mordred had yet to launch his own attack.

"C'mon, fight! Or are we too much for you?" WinterKil yelled as she swung her battleaxe high over her head. The others followed and tightened the circle.

"Look, I don't want to hurt you," Mordred began again.

"Don't worry," WinterKil shouted over the thundering sound of her axe slamming into Mordred's wooden shield. He was grateful the shield was designed with a small metal circle in the middle. It would protect his hand from damage should an axe blade make it through the wood. WinterKil continued, "As I've already said, you can't hurt us. Now, fight like your life depends on it, because actually, it does. Lir is going to do battle with you. He has every intention of proving you are not deserving of his help."

It seemed the fight went on for hours. Sweat was streaming from Mordred, soaking the white fabric of the robe. Many times he had to wipe his eyes, leaving him to bear the brunt of another attack.

WinterKil swung her axe hard to Mordred's right shoulder, but he spun and deflected it with his shield. The other women moved in more closely, caging him.

With the circle getting tighter, Mordred had no choice but to fight back. He took the handle of his axe and used it like a stave, knocking one of the women to the floor.

She grimaced, but stood back up as if the blow had done her no harm.

"Don't worry about her. Fight!" WinterKil shouted. "You have to learn to use that axe. It is not a sword. It is weighted differently and you'll have to work with it differently. Possess the axe, Mordred."

She was right on one count. The axe felt clumsy in Mordred's hand. However, he was learning fast that barbaric or no, those who really knew how to use the weapon could be quite proficient.

"Rule number three; never allow yourself to be cornered. We could have ended this a long time ago. Instead you are slowly tiring. You need to get in and get out. Don't let Lir toy with you as we have done."

Another blow glanced off his shield and hit the side of his head. Though the shield had taken most of the impact, Mordred swore he saw silver stars. He shook his head to rid them from his field of vision and turned on the one who had scored a lucky shot.

It was WinterKil. "C'mon, Soulis, use that axe for more than chopping wood."

"Why can't I use my sword again?"

"Because swords aren't what we fight with here."

"WinterKil!" A loud voice broke into the melee. "How

dare you cheat behind my back!"

Mordred brought his weapon up in a defensive posture as he watched the other women, a few moments ago hacking and slashing like the most agile of warriors, suddenly become frightened children. They all stood behind their leader.

WinterKil brought her chin up slightly higher than was necessary, striking a haughty pose. Mordred realized she was all muscle and fire, a perfect match for him. Then his thoughts came crashing back to reality as he heard a real crashing sound.

The wooden door slammed against the wall with the force of a blow, and Mordred stared at the figure of a man larger than any he had ever seen. In fact, the king was not only larger and broader, but stood at least several hands taller than Mordred, and Mordred was taller than most men.

The burly giant was bare-chested but for a long cape of what looked like wolf fur tucked into an enormously wide silver belt around his narrow waist. His legs were clad in silver mail and his feet were swallowed up in furred boots. Bare arms revealed bulging biceps, wrapped with several silver bands that looked, when Lir flexed his arms, as if they would easily break apart.

He wore a silver helm that only covered the upper half of his face. The lower revealed a thin blond beard separated into three braids. Additional braids came down either side of his

Lord of Darkness Lir

head, while his hair, long and full, hung well past his shoulders.

He was definitely the picture of pure muscle. And Mordred, though not a young boy in his own strength, suddenly felt like nothing but a squire, facing off against a well-seasoned knight for the first time.

Blue eyes shot fire at him from beneath the helm. "How dare you cajole my ladies into helping you?"

Mordred tried to find his voice. "I did no such thing."

"Well, surely my WinterKil and her sisters would not pull a trick worthy only of Loki? Nay, they are far too innocent."

"Oh, quit your bellowing, Lir. Yes, we did trick you. We knew you were planning on making Mordred prove himself, and it was only fair he have some training in axe fighting. You know as well as anyone that this is not his weapon of choice. It gives you an unfair advantage, you a man who needs no advantage. Unless . . ."

Lir strode forward and came to within inches of WinterKil. Though he towered over her, she did not back down.

"Unless what?" the king shouted.

"Unless, you really are worried that the Chosen One might best you?"

"What?!"

Mordred looked at WinterKil, wondering just what the devil she was up to. He didn't need her help if getting Lir riled up was her idea of helping.

"Come with me, whelp. We'll see how much you've learned." Lir reached out and dragged Mordred forward. He found he had no choice but to follow the king from the room.

XIII

Chapter Thirteen

he giant king said nothing as he strode hastily from the Fighting Hall. Mordred tried to keep up with him but it seemed for every stride Lir took, Mordred had to take two. Again, he had the vague notion that he was only a boy compared to the king's imposing size and might.

They arrived at the end of a long corridor and entered a massive hall. Silver light shone from every conceivable place. Huge pillars of silver rose from the floor to the ceiling, though the ceiling disappeared in a thick mist.

Row upon row of tables faced a large arena. Above what was the first floor, there were several seats that looked down on the room. The seats themselves were thrones, ornately carved and encrusted with jewels.

Mordred was yanked into the arena, and had to narrow his eyes from the brightness of his surroundings. As he did, he realized the hall was not empty. It was filled with rough-looking men clad in fur and skins. Each was of a size similar to their king. Mordred could not help thinking the Norse surely must be a race of giants.

He had no time to contemplate his next course of action. The slight hissing sound of a blade cutting through air came to his ears just in time and without any warning, Lir cast his first strike.

Focusing on the object coming dangerously close to him, Mordred saw that while it was indeed an axe, it had two heads. Each one was sharpened to a very fine edge.

The split second it took Mordred to focus cost him dearly, and he felt the side of the axe connect with his shoulder, sending him crashing into one of the silver columns. He wasn't sure what hurt worse; the actual blow from Lir's axe, or hitting the immovable tower.

"Don't think, vampyre, fight!" Lir shouted as a rousing round of cheers filled the hall.

Mordred pulled himself upright and adjusted his balance. He bent his knees slightly and readied himself for Lir's next move.

"Soulis? What are you waiting for? Strike!" Again, Lir thrust a powerful blow at him, and again, even though Mordred was able to raise his shield to bear the brunt of it, the sheer strength behind it brought him to his knees.

Lir continued to hammer at Mordred until he could

do nothing but fall on his back and pray the king would relent. It was utterly humiliating for a seasoned warrior to find himself felled by a weapon he had never before considered dangerous.

"WinterKil! Get your vampyre out of my sight. He is not the Chosen One. Not today. Perhaps tomorrow a real champion will face me."

Lir turned and stalked off into the hall amid much laughter and joviality. Mordred was left to pick himself up off the floor.

WinterKil came for him and helped him out of the hall.

"Thank you," he whispered, barely able to find the strength to stand, much less speak.

"Save your strength. I did nothing but what Lir commanded." Her jaw was clenched.

"Well at least you helped me out of the hall."

"If you don't rise up to his challenge tomorrow, there will be nothing left of you for me to help. Mordred, you must beat him. You must bring him to his knees using his own weapon. You can't do that if your mind is elsewhere." She brought Mordred to his chamber and allowed him to enter while she remained in the corridor.

Mordred turned to face the woman. "I did my best today. The man is an absolute giant. And my thoughts were right there in that arena."

She made a scoffing sound.

"You don't believe me?" he asked.

"No. I think you are still mourning the loss of Dugald, and I think if you cannot put that aside, you will not pass this test."

Angry, Mordred stalked back to her. "Don't tell me what I'm feeling. You couldn't know what it's like to be me, knowing I brought that man to his death."

WinterKil did not flinch at his harsh tone. She remained toe to toe with him, challenging him with her fierce blue eyes.

"Mordred, you no more sacrificed Dugald to the legions of undead than you were responsible for the destruction in the Crusades. To blame yourself is both a waste of your time and foolish. Dugald knew the risks he took remaining with you. He didn't want to leave your side, and don't you think he was able to make up his own mind? He stayed behind in that castle, not because you ordered him to, but because he knew only one of you was going to survive. He did what had to be done."

Mordred spun on his heel away from the Valkyrie. He smashed his fist into the doorframe and bent his head. "You speak as if there was no choice."

WinterKil put her hand on Mordred's shoulder and once again the soothing feeling flowed through him, tamping down his anger, easing his sorrow.

"He chose to be with you. He honored the quest by remaining with you. He knew the risks, but he also knew what the ultimate goal was. He could not have stopped himself from following you.

"Mordred, he was a noble creature. A beast with a heart of gold who gave of himself, knowingly, willingly, so that you would live one more day. Even in the knowledge of his death, he had hope. Do not let that hope be destroyed by your own pain. Fight this, fight Lir, do it for your position as the Chosen One. Honor Dugald. Let him know he did not die in vain."

"My destiny controls me. I am helpless to the whims of my fate," Mordred growled softly.

"As are we all."

"But if I could only have allowed Dugald the chance to get away. If I had stayed and fought . . ."

"It wasn't meant to be. What can I do to convince you?"

"No," Mordred replied acidly, "it wasn't meant to be. I want to bring him back."

It was WinterKil's turn to look confused. She removed her hand and walked further into Mordred's chamber. He watched the play of emotions cross her face.

"You can't get him back."

"Like hell I can't. You were there to bring me here and

it was you who said that there are times when you must do battle with Death for the warriors intended for Valhalla. Well, it's time to go to Death's door and retrieve that which wasn't meant to be. Dugald deserves another chance."

WinterKil became silent and worried her lower lip in agitation. "I can't. Lir would have my head for claiming a soul he has not already deemed worthy."

"You said Dugald was noble. You said he gave his life for me, for the quest. Is that not the mark of the truest of warriors?"

"But, the journey is not an easy one and there are demands to be met, and that's if Death will even agree. And, Mordred, Dugald may not be the same person he was when he left the earthly plane."

Mordred cocked his head. "What do you mean by that?"

"The longer a person remains in the underworld, the more they become unreachable, unsalvageable. We don't even know if he is still there. He could have already been judged and moved on. No, it's too risky. Besides, how do we explain your absence to Lir?"

"You tell him if I can bring Dugald back, then I will have more than proven myself in his test of strength."

"He won't be willing to sacrifice you if you are the true Chosen One."

"That is not his choice to make. If I am the true Chosen

One, then I should be able to not only make this journey, but succeed."

"Mordred, it's not that easy. There are laws and rules. Otherwise Valhalla and all the other destinations the noble go would be crowded beyond belief. How would it look if we dispatched an army to the realm of Death and demand he release souls? We have to respect each other, and it's a tenuous peace we keep, at best."

Mordred approached WinterKil. He brought his hand to her chin and raised her head so she looked into his eyes. "If I know one thing, one single thing, it is that it was not Dugald's time to die. He belongs with me. I am going to find a way to bring him back and I will go with you, or without you."

She smiled, but there was sadness in her eyes. "You cannot go without me. You would never find the way. I am the only one who can take you."

"Was it Death who wounded you?" Mordred asked softly.

"Yes," she replied in a whisper.

"It was his intent to keep you?"

"Yes."

"Do you not want the chance to exact revenge?"

WinterKil turned her head away, but Mordred brought her back to focus on him. "Please, I am begging you. Please, help me. I will do whatever Lir and every other Vampyre

King commands of me."

Mordred brought his lips close to hers. He would have kissed her, but she pulled away. "Know that I feel the attraction as well, but you cannot kiss me. My kiss is only for the dead."

"A part of me is dying for want of your lips, and surely I will be dead soon from the desire." He stroked her cheek and watched as her eyes fluttered closed.

WinterKil leaned into Mordred and he wrapped his arms around her, careful of her injured wing, and did what he had most wanted from the moment he had first seen her. His lips met hers softly, the barest whisper of contact. It was not a kiss born of lust, but of something deeper. Something more solid and time-worthy.

She allowed him the kiss but for a moment, then she pulled away.

"You know not what you ask of me. I pray it is not so much that you will live to regret this decision, but I will help you. Meet me in the Fighting Hall when you hear the bells of Valhalla ring three times."

And then WinterKil was gone.

✠ ✠ ✠

Mordred paced in his chamber until he heard the bells ring.

He felt like beast in a cage, restless and edgy. He wasn't exactly sure his decision to go to the underworld was a smart one, but he'd met Anubis in the Egyptian underworld and had come back unscathed. He touched the familiar necklace and said a silent prayer that if Anubis should hear him, he might be guided and protected.

The chimes rang out through the halls and shook him from his thoughts. He left his chamber.

Trying to remember how to get to the Fighting Hall proved difficult. Each corridor looked like the next and he feared he was getting himself hopelessly lost. He also feared running into Lir and having to do a rematch before he was ready.

Just as he was about to retrace his path yet again, Vestr came to his rescue. "Here, follow me. She waits for you and time is short. I cannot believe she has agreed to this. You are a fool to try to cheat Death. He is not one to allow the slight." The Valkyrie sighed. "But she has spoken to us of her thoughts of you and it is rare that WinterKil takes to anyone, so we will honor our sister's wishes knowing the price that might be paid."

"What will you tell Lir?" Mordred asked as he walked beside the woman.

"The truth. But only after you have a head start. He could very well decide to come after you both, and then there would be real hell to pay. Know this; when you come back, you will still have to face him and he will be none too pleased."

Mordred wanted to tell her he cared little about Lir, but decided to hold his tongue. It was clear Vestr was not happy with the choice he had forced WinterKil to make. He did not want to push any goodwill remaining.

She stopped outside a door that would have looked like any other to Mordred and pushed it open. Entering, he recognized where they were.

At least ten Valkyries stood to one side. WinterKil sat on a low bench with tall wooden wings framing her. In her lap she held something. At Mordred's arrival, she raised her hands to show him.

"This is Odin's gift. It is finished early. He does not know where you are headed, but he told me that after watching you fight Lir he felt you could use all the help you can get. The mail is fine, but stronger than any you have on your plane, and unlike your armor, you can use it to protect you both from mortal and immortal foes."

Mordred took the pieces from her. They consisted of a pair of mail leggings, a pair of cloth leggings, a soft white tunic, and a shirt of delicate looking mail. Though the rings looked as though they would weigh no more than a feather, they proved to be far more substantial that he had at first thought.

He looked around for a place to change.

WinterKil smiled. "You are far too modest for a vampyre. You forget we have seen all kinds of dead men. Naked ones, too."

"Well, I . . ."

The women laughed at his hesitation to strip down in front of them, and as one spread their wings and formed a circle, enveloping Mordred with their downy feathers. They faced outward, giving him the opportunity to change his clothing.

Only WinterKil remained on the bench, though she politely turned her head.

"Done," Mordred said after slipping the mail shirt over his head.

One of the women produced a silver hair ornament attached to a band of leather. Several others enfolded their wings and turned to stand behind him. He felt them working with his hair, gently taming the mass of black waves by braiding them into one thick length.

Another woman brought forth a mail coiffe, the top part metal. It had a strange shape to the face guard, covering Mordred's eyes, nose, and forehead, but keeping the mouth visible. On either side of the helm were wings.

Looking down at the white tunic Mordred noted it was not made of cloth as he had assumed, but rather tiny feathers woven together with silver threads. He looked up to meet WinterKil's gaze.

"You would challenge Balder, the Sun God, with your new armament. You wear the protection of the Valkyries, for whatever it proves worth. It is always a good thing to greet Death in a manner befitting a king. He would waste no time on one who could not pay his price."

"Do you know what the price will be for Dugald?" Mordred asked, watching as her gaze fell away from his to meet several others. Each avoided looking directly at him. They were hiding something. "You know."

"No. Only that Death does not give up souls easily, and even if we succeed, as I've said before, there is no guarantee he will be the same man you once knew. Now, we must hurry. There is only one time each night when we can make the descent to your world, and we must continue to the next plane. It is a long journey."

She stood then, as regal as any battle queen, dressed in her armor and mail, her axe strapped to her side. A long white cape was pinned at her shoulders. Her helm shimmered as did her whole being, and for an instant Mordred felt he was in the presence of angels.

Gleaning a measure of his thoughts, she said, "Nay, Mordred, we are not angels. Only Battle Maidens."

"WinterKil," Vestr said, "we wish you the speed of all

Valkyries. May each of our gods protect you and keep you safe. Mordred, guard our sister well."

The women walked forward and encircled both Mordred and WinterKill with their great white wings before moving back to their original positions.

"Good luck," they said in unison as Mordred and WinterKil began their descent to the underworld.

"We must not stop. No matter what you see, we cannot remain on the mortal plane or we will be trapped. Are you ready?" WinterKil glanced at Mordred. They stood at the very edge of a tall cliff. He had no idea where he was and only knew that when he looked down he could not see what lay below. They were above the clouds. She had told him they were in a realm in which only immortals could exist.

"Wait," he said. "You have wings, but how will I travel?"

She smiled. "Has no one taught you how to fly?"

Kabil's image swam before Mordred's eyes, goading him. "Well, yes, but . . ." Mordred was afraid to reveal that most of his flying episodes ended badly. He still had to work on his concentration.

"No fear, Mordred. You have been given a most important gift. One that shall remain with you. You had the wings, you just never knew to summon them. We've done that for you."

She reached behind him and he felt her patting his back.

"Did you not find it the least bit strange that Odin made a shirt of the most delicate design, yet he left two large openings in the back?"

"I thought perhaps he had been in a hurry and didn't have time to finish it."

WinterKil wore an amused look and laughed softly. "He would be horrified to think you didn't believe he had finished his garment. Now, there is one more thing. Thor, our God of War, is the only god who knows about the journey we are to undertake. Because Thor is always up for a good fight, he has lent you his war-hammer. You see, you cannot use your weapons against Death.

"Your blade crafted by mortals would shatter at first contact against Death, or his soldiers. Your undead blade would have no effect because he is Death, not dead or undead. So, you need a weapon of the gods. This should help should it come to fighting."

WinterKill searched behind the nearby rocks and lifted a sack. She handed it to Mordred, who opened it.

The hammer did not look magical in any way. The head was made of stone, while the wooden shaft was carved with many strange symbols Mordred knew to be Runes. He stared at them, and they rearranged themselves. Soon he was able to read the inscription.

"May the wielder of this blade never fall in battle. May the thunder of war bring safe journeys to the bearer. Only in Ragnarock will this soul be judged."

"Ragnarock?" Mordred questioned.

"The Doom of the Gods," WinterKill responded. "A time when good will battle evil a final time and the gods will be called to take part. Come, Mordred, it is time to go. Spread your wings and fly."

Before he had time to protest, WinterKil stepped off the precipice and plummeted toward the thick layer of clouds below. Mordred felt a sudden weight on his back and a sharp throbbing pain and then, unbelievably, he was unfurling a set of large black wings.

He took only moments to stretch them, letting his entire body get used to this new part of him. Then he, too, jumped into the unknown.

As WinterKil and Mordred sped through the air, they were shrouded in a thick gray-white fog. It was so heavy at times Mordred lost sight of the Valkyrie and could only hope he was meant to continue the downward circular spiral she had started.

Flying was an absolutely foreign feeling to Mordred. While he had done it in the past, it had been simply an act of levitation rather than a soaring motion. But this time, he felt the wind moving through his feathers. It caressed him as he allowed himself to be buffeted on the air currents. Hot and cold air mixed and swirled around him. It felt very much like swimming, except there was no water.

He was thankful the bank of clouds was so heavy he could not tell how far they were from ground. It was one less thing to distract him and he knew even in this state he could easily lose focus, especially if he knew how high they were.

The howling of the wind was all around him. At one point they must have flown straight into a storm, for Mordred saw flashes of light and heard a low rumbling. Water pelted his face, but as soon as he felt it, it was gone.

There were moments when, for a split second, he looked in one direction and saw visions of things he wasn't sure he understood. Once, he watched as bizarre silver beasts roared to life and took to the skies near him, but they vanished when he looked back. Another moment he saw strange buildings that touched a blackened sky, while a fire burned at the edges of the horizon.

He swore he caught a glimpse of the edge of the world, where a piece of earth just simply disappeared into an abyss of nothingness. Gaping jaws of jagged rock bled the life from a barren land above. The whole of the world was torn, and bloody.

He wanted to stop, entranced with things he had never

before witnessed. Things that could only come from dark nightmares, images of prophecies he could never believe in. But, as if sensing his desire, Mordred felt WinterKil's hand reach out to him and pull him onward.

Shaking his head, the fog returned to comfort him with its opacity. It hid the dangers and the darkness.

"Prepare to stop," WinterKil yelled out over the shrieking wind.

Watching as her great white wings beat several times up and down, Mordred mimicked her movements and slowed, coming to a halt as his booted feel struck something. He folded his wings behind him and waited.

"We are here."

Mordred stood on black rocks at the edge of a raging sea. From what he had ever heard about Death, he expected a boat and a skeleton figure to be waiting. He saw neither.

WinterKil offered him a smile, as if apprehending his thoughts.

"Turn around," she instructed.

Realizing they were in front of a door, Mordred gave her a quizzical look.

"Go ahead. It is always polite to knock. Death doesn't really expect many visitors, but he also doesn't like surprises."

Mordred balled his gloved hand into a fist and pounded three times, listening as the sound echoed through the stones.

The door creaked slowly open, but no one appeared.

"Remember, he is king here. Whatever your feelings or opinions about what has happened, you must offer him respect. If he senses you mocking him in any way, he will refuse. Death has no reason to agree to this and if he denies you, you must honor his decision. We will leave. It is dangerous to stay here any longer than necessary."

WinterKil walked through the doors and waited for Mordred to follow. "Oh, and one more thing . . . Don't eat or drink anything while you are here, no matter what he offers you."

"You just told me not to offend him," Mordred pointed out.

"Yes, that's true, but you can politely decline. He has been known to be a very sore loser when a soul is, basically, robbed from him. He hates Valkyries, and I wouldn't put it past him to try to get you to remain here."

"I'm undead. I don't think I could stay even if I wanted to."

"Don't be so sure of that. If there is someone who could change your condition, I would think it would be Death himself. And try not to bargain. Making a deal with him will never be to your advantage."

"But, I have to bargain with him to get Dugald back."

"True." WinterKil paused and turned to look into Mordred's eyes. "Just know that in the end he always gets what he wants. You may get Dugald back, but for how long, you won't know."

Mordred mulled over her words. He was surprised to see that Death's domain was not full of sorrowful souls wandering lost or chained to cold slabs of stone bemoaning their fate. Instead, he strode through the halls of a very well-cared-for palace. Where he expected to see black and gray, Mordred was stunned at the brightness, the light shimmering everywhere. Reds, gold, blue, even violet, peeked out from tapestries, cushions, and furniture.

In fact, if Mordred did not know where exactly he was, he could have sworn he was walking through the halls of a manor on Earth.

At the end of a long corridor of polished marble a figure appeared, striding toward them. He was handsome, with well-defined features, blond hair, and a beaming smile.

He was clad in a purple tunic and hose. A long purple cape with an underside of red flowed behind him. The most striking thing about him besides the silver armor he wore, molded to look like bones, was his gray eyes. They glowed from an undetected source.

"Mordred Soulis, as I live and breathe." The man held out his hand and started laughing. "Well, all right, you caught me. I'm not living really, or breathing for that matter, but I am truly surprised to see you."

When Mordred hesitated clasping the man's hand, he

Death

added, "Go on, I don't bite. You've obviously got me confused with the Devil. I'm Death. It is good to see you again."

More laughter.

Mordred looked at WinterKil, who nodded. Only then did Mordred reach out and touch the man's hand. That was when he felt the entity beneath the façade.

A searing coldness invaded Mordred's veins, causing his heart to seize. He choked as breath froze in his throat, and quickly released himself from Death's grip.

"Oh, I am so sorry. I hadn't thought I'd have such an effect on an Undead. You are the first vampyre to walk in my world."

Finding his voice, Mordred asked, "You mentioned we've met before?"

The man never stopped smiling. Death met Mordred's gaze and winked. "It was to be our little secret, but it appears the cat's out of the bag." Death glanced at WinterKil with a look of disdain. "Yes, we've met before. Where do you think you went when you died in the desert?"

It dawned on Mordred that he had died. Really, truly, he had passed on. "Then why the hell did you let me go? Why did you let Vlad take me?"

He would have throttled Death, but restrained himself due to the strange reaction he had when he'd first touched him.

"Come, let's go to my chambers. There are some things

you clearly don't remember. You can leave your bodyguard behind."

"I'd prefer she come with me."

"Of course you would." Death frowned and met Mordred's gaze again. It felt as if he was being sized up, measured, but whether it was as an opponent or for a coffin, he couldn't be sure.

Death turned and led them up a set of winding stairs to an enormous, colorful chamber. He offered them seats at a large round table. There were names etched into each place setting which first Mordred couldn't read. They were ornate carvings that included a skeleton wrapping around letters that looked vaguely like something he should know. Then magically the images moved so he made sense of them.

Though there were many names he was not familiar with, Mordred was able to recognize a few. Anubis was there, as was the Norse god, Loki. Both the Warders' names were present, and a name he would have been just as happy not to recognize, Lucifer.

"Yes, yes, we all sit round this table, the table of equals, and we have a fine good time discussing who goes where and why. There are debates, and arguments, and sometimes things get downright ugly, but eventually all the dead get sorted out. Well, except for the ones the Valkyries steal."

WinterKil lifted her chin and faced Death, a slight narrowing of her eyes the only evidence she was not comfortable. "We take only those who deserve to spend their time in Valhalla. And we only take the Vikings."

"Not, exactly . . ." Death directed a pointed stare at Mordred, eyebrows raised.

"He wasn't dead when we found him, but undead and in a state that required healing. You couldn't have taken him."

"A small technicality. One I'm sure the others would have overlooked." Death replied smoothly. "Would anyone care for something to drink? I am parched."

"No, thank you," Mordred responded.

"I see, you've already been warned by the Winged One. My, my, WinterKil, you make a fine guardian." A smile crept across Death's face, different from the ones he had bestowed on them before. In this one Mordred detected a hint of malice.

"Oh, dear, how awful . . . Your wound has opened again. You really should have had someone see to that before coming all the way here." The subtle shift in tone was not lost on Mordred. Death was not happy with WinterKil.

Mordred looked at WinterKil sitting a bench, and saw the stain of blood soaking the white feathers of her right wing. "You need help."

"No, Mordred. I'll be fine."

Death watched the two for a moment, silent, calculating.

"So, let's get down to business."

"Not before you help her," Mordred interrupted.

"Oh, I'm sorry, that I cannot do. You see, there are the rules. If I touch her, she stays." He paused to allow for a dramatic effect. "Of course, if you insist."

Death rose. Mordred rose, too. They stood, evenly matched, studying one another.

It was Mordred who spoke first.

"Don't touch her."

"I really wish you would make up your mind. I never knew vampyres could be so fickle. Now, on to business, since I know you wouldn't want to stay too long . . . Why do you pay a visit? Who do I have that you want back? Oh, don't look so surprised, it's a pretty easy deduction. It's not like Death's Door is the first place everyone wants to go. Now, spill."

Mordred remained standing, despite the fact that Death returned to a throne chair made of polished silver molded into human bones. Everywhere Mordred looked he saw the skull and skeletons. Some were hidden in the ornate tapestries, others subtly blown into fragile glassware.

Death saw Mordred taking full measure of his surroundings. "It's a little joke I like to have at myself. After all, I'm the guy no one wants to see, right?"

"Can you blame people?" Mordred asked, curious that

Death seemed to be bemoaning his title as King of the Dead. "You are the last person anyone would want to see."

"Well, no one lives forever, Mordred. Even you will, at some point, tire of living in your torn state. You once begged to die. Do you still wish for death? Do you still call out for me in your sleep? You used to every night."

Mordred shrugged. "Yes, I did wish I had died. And, yes, sometimes I still do."

"I could change that for you. I mean, I could arrange to keep you here, if you really don't want to go on."

For a moment, one fleeting blink of an eye, Mordred considered it. He could end it all now. He could fade away to nothingness and the weight of the world would no longer be on his shoulders. He could be free of mankind's burden, one he had never asked for. Perhaps he would find the peace in death he so longed for in this twisted life he led. Would he rest in peace, as the saying claimed?

Or would he spend an eternity regretting the decision? His hesitation did not go unnoticed by Death, or WinterKil.

The Valkyrie stood, grimacing as the motion caused her injured wing to move. "Don't even think about it. You are destined for greater things. You cannot cheat the outcome. If you give up the fight, it still goes on. But without you, all will be lost. Do you want to spend forever knowing you failed?"

"I could fail anyway," Mordred replied, the bitterness in his tone unmistakable.

"True, but at least you'd fail knowing you did everything you could."

"The outcome would be the same. Why not simply end it now?"

She walked over to him and tilted her head, searching his eyes. He felt as if she were prowling his interior, searching for his heart and soul. "You are not this person I hear talking now. Do not be seduced by Death. It was not your time before. It is not your time now."

"I hate to break up this touching scene, but time is passing and decisions need to be made. WinterKil, if Mordred is tired of being everyone's hero, who can blame him? He has lost much to become the Chosen One. Hell, he's lost part of his human side."

The Valkyrie faced Death. "But, he hasn't lost it all and it is not his time. Mordred, look around you. Look at everything you see. Is this really what you want?"

Something in Mordred stirred. Something he hadn't felt in a long time. He didn't care about being heroic, and he wasn't sure this quest wasn't a product of madness, but he wasn't sure he wanted to remain dead, either.

As he turned to look at Death, he noticed the image of the man had changed. He saw the entity beneath the glamour.

Though he shimmered and glistened, even he couldn't hide who he really was. It brought Mordred out of the strange seductive spell that had been cast over him.

"No, I don't wish to stay. Nor do I wish Dugald to stay either. I have come for my friend."

"Ah, the werewolf. Well, see, it isn't that easy," Death said. "He wasn't exactly human either, which presented a challenge."

"Wait a minute," Mordred interrupted. It was as if a gust of fresh air had blown through Mordred's mind, clearing his cluttered thoughts. "How is it you have Dugald? Isn't he also immortal in his wolf form? The only thing that can kill him in that form is silver, right?"

Mordred glanced at WinterKil, who shook her head. "I don't know, Mordred. I know nothing of the Wareckyn beyond that they are shifters."

Looking back at Death he noticed a slight twitch in the man's clenched jaw. Mordred moved closer. "You know. Tell me."

"Or you'll what? Kill me?" Death laughed and waved a hand in the air. "Really, you are amusing coming here all blustery and demanding. Where is your respect for the dead, Mordred?"

Mordred reached inside his mail and tunic to pull forth the chain around his neck. The golden scarab glimmered in the light. "Ask Anubis. Summon him, and while you are at it, summon the Warders, too."

"Aw, bloody hell, you are smart, Mordred Soulis. Okay, there's no need to summon everyone over a little mistake."

Eyes opening wide, Mordred brought himself to within inches of Death and snarled menacingly. "A mistake? You took my friend and you call it a *little mistake*? Someone needs to correct this little mistake, and if you won't do it, I will."

"Well, therein lies the problem." Death was clearly not in full command. In fact, he look thoroughly nervous and uncomfortable as he moved away from Mordred. "Once I realized we'd made a mistake, and there is a 'we' in this, we sent his spirit back. But . . ."

Mordred growled again. "But?"

"Seems the damn wolf has a wandering soul and instead of going back to where he died, the horrid creature went elsewhere."

"Where exactly?"

"A place you don't yet know about. A place you haven't discovered just yet."

Mordred slammed a fist on the round table. "No riddles. Tell me now or I'll call on the other gods myself."

"I am telling you," Death replied in a voice that was nearly a shriek. "You, your people, kind, humans from your country haven't discovered the place yet."

"Wait," WinterKil strode forward. "Do you mean the New World?"

"The New World?" Mordred echoed, confused.

Death nodded. "Yes. Exactly."

Mordred looked at WinterKil, but the Valkyrie slid to the floor, unconscious.

XIV

Chapter Fourteen

heck-mate," Death said coldly, penetrating the haze surrounding Mordred's mind when he bent to help WinterKil. When she did not respond to his voice, Mordred shook her. There was no response.

Mordred swept her up in his arms. "Where can I put her?"

"It won't matter, Mordred. She's mine."

"No." It was all he could get through his clenched teeth.

"Yes. See, unfortunately she failed to mention to you that she was warned when last we met that she could never be seen by me again. Once wounded by my arrows, you are marked for Death, and if you come within my sights, you forfeit your life."

"No."

Death walked over to Mordred, not making a sound. He looked into Mordred's eyes. "You must understand there is an order of things, and always there is a risk.

WinterKil knew the risk and she knew what she would sacrifice by returning."

Mordred shook his head and backed away, cradling the Valkyrie. He hadn't realized how fragile his feelings were for this woman. "You will bring her soul back. You will give her to me."

"No, I don't think that will happen. I don't sit here and judge souls, Mordred, I am merely someone a soul meets on their journey from here to there, wherever those places might be for each soul. I cannot bring her back. It was not my decision to take her."

"But, you just said it was your arrow . . ."

"Yes, that's true, but I didn't pull the string. I didn't fire the shot. I, too, was merely a pawn in a much larger game. Some things, Mordred, are even beyond me."

Gazing down at the angelic face in his arms, Mordred could not help feeling he'd made a big mistake. WinterKil had tried to get him to rethink his plan, but he had not listened. But, if he hadn't not come here, he would never have learned Dugald still lived.

Ah, but the gods had such cruel ways.

"I wish to be alone."

Death nodded. "Of course. You'll find, Mordred, I'm not an ogre."

"I don't want to find out anything more about you. If

you can't bring her back, if you won't help, then I'll leave. I will never call out for you again."

"Careful . . ." Death cautioned. "You never know when a visit from me might be preferable to something else."

"Never. Leave me."

Quietly, and without further discussion, Death left the chamber. As the sound of his boots echoed off the stones and receded, Mordred heard him whistling a strange, melancholy tune.

He was alone for only a short time with the body of the fallen Valkyrie when the sound of footsteps grew louder. Mordred didn't turn around, and as they grew louder, he called out angrily, "Damn you, I said give me a minute."

"You'll get no such thing from me, you ignorant vampyre!" a voice boomed across the stone hall.

Mordred whirled, shielding WinterKil's body lying on a bed.

It was Lir who spoke, or rather, bellowed. His anger rippled off him in visible blue waves. *"Bloody stupid idiot!* What the hell possessed you to come here, and why on earth did you bring WinterKil? She was warned never to return."

"I didn't know. I came for Dugald."

"Dugald? Are you mad? He isn't here. He was, for a an instant, then he was returned to the earthly plane. I was going to tell you we'd be sailing to the New World when next we met, but you decided to skulk out of my hall and head down here. Ah, by the gods, you have no idea what you've done."

Mordred wanted to fight back. He wanted to rail at Lir and tell him he really didn't care what the giant thought, but he hadn't strength. The journey to Death's domain had, strangely, left him feeling as though he might drift into a sleep from which he would not recover.

Lir frowned and peered into Mordred's eyes. "Did you drink anything?"

Mordred shook his head.

"Then how bloody long have you been here?" Lir's eyes flickered to the hammer at Mordred's waist. "Oh, shit, Thor's hammer? The gods knew you came here? Have I lost all control of Valhalla?!"

The Vampyre King's voice thundered through the halls and Mordred thought, hazily, he could certainly wake the dead.

"Look at me, Mordred. Look-me-right-smack-in-the-eye."

Mordred did as he was told.

Lir rolled his eyes. "C'mon. You've got to get out of here."

"But," Mordred protested, "what about WinterKil?"

"What about her? She's dead, Soulis. There's nothing anyone can do for her. She knew another meeting with Death would be her last, so you can rest easy knowing she gave her life to your idiotic idea of rescuing your friend. Come."

Lir turned and, when Mordred hesitated, reached back and grabbed him by the sleeve of his mail and dragged him from the chamber.

The king did not stop until they were at the doors. Closed, they didn't stop Lir, who simply smashed a large fist against one panel, sending it crashing outward to hit the stones surrounding the frame.

He forced Mordred through the door and, without pause, Lir rose into the air.

"Wait, I can . . ."

"Like hell you can. Just let me take care of this. Trust me, after your stint in the underworld you don't have the strength to snap your fingers, much less fly."

It was humiliating to have the Vampyre King take hold of the belt around his waist and hoist him unceremoniously into the air. But Mordred wisely kept his mouth shut.

He was puzzled.

"You mentioned going to the New World? Are you still going?"

Lir made a noise that sounded more like a rabid beast as he shot forward through the heavy clouds and mist with an inhuman speed.

"Like you would allow me not to go? Besides, we need to retrieve something very special and bring it back here."

"Something special?"

"Something your Templar friends hid in the New World."

"The Templars have been there? How is it this new land isn't known by many?" Mordred asked.

"That is a mystery you can solve yourself. I really don't care. I only know that before the majority of the Templars were destroyed, they left your continent for another and took with them several objects of great importance. They believed the objects would fall into the wrong hands if they remained on your soil. So they sailed across the ocean to a new world and hid them there. We will have to find them, and while we're there you can go searching for your dog."

"He's a wolf."

"Whatever. Now be quiet and conserve your energy."

✠ ✠ ✠

Mordred found himself in his familiar chamber safely tucked into the furs on his pallet. He cracked one eye open, then the other. Vestr sat nearby and rose as soon as she saw him wake.

"It's about time you came around. We thought maybe Death had managed to lure you back for good." She smiled, but Mordred saw her expression was filled with sadness.

"I'm sorry," he offered, knowing she and the other Valkyries would blame him for taking WinterKil to Death's realm.

Vestr brought a goblet from a nearby table and handed it to Mordred. He knew without asking it was more of the dragon blood.

"It was not your fault that Death claimed WinterKil as his own. He has coveted her since the first time he saw her. It was only a matter of time before he finally got his way. Besides, there was nothing anyone could have said to stop her, even Lir, though he thought otherwise."

Mordred finished drinking the blood in the chalice and set it near his pallet. He gazed at the brunette Valkyrie, giving her a quizzical look. "Why do you say nothing would have stopped her? It was my idea to go in the first place."

"Yes, but, there was nothing she wouldn't have done for you," Vestr replied softly. Her golden eyes filled with unshed tears, glistened in the light of the chamber's strange torches.

Feeling as though he had just been stabbed in the heart, Mordred grimaced and closed his eyes. In another time or place, WinterKil would certainly have made a fine life-mate. But, it was not to be, he being a vampyre, and she being a Valkyrie.

Neverthless, it didn't lessen the pain.

Vestr remained silent.

"I'm sorry." Mordred spoke in a voice thick with unspoken thoughts.

"You surprised us all, Mordred. We did not expect sorrow from a vampyre. We are sorry, too, for judging you. WinterKil was the only one who saw you not as something dark and destructive, but as someone filled with hope. Perhaps WinterKil has left her mark on us all.

"Now, however, it is time to do battle with Lir. Again, you must prove yourself worthy. After this last foray, he is not too pleased with you. Know that he will seek to crush you and prove you do not deserve the help of the Norse gods of Valhalla."

Mordred rose, realizing he was still in his clothing from the journey.

"Come, Lir waits in the hall."

Once again Mordred found himself weaving through the halls and corridors of the magical Valhalla. He had no idea what to expect; he only knew he had to defeat Lir.

Entering the vast chamber, Mordred noticed the tables were once again filled with hundreds of men. Each wore a heavy fur cap, mail shirt and leather breeches, along with fur boots. Each was also heavily armed.

As Mordred entered the arena where the fight would take place, a Viking approached at a run. There was no time for Mordred to get out of the way. He waited for the impact and braced himself.

Strangely, the impact didn't come. The man passed

right through him.

"You look surprised," Lir boomed as he loomed over Mordred. "They are souls, spirits only. They do not have a physical form, though to you they appear as human."

A light mist filled Mordred's mind as his human side warred with his vampyre side at the impossibility of all he had witnessed. Ghouls, mermaids, and ghosts existed in the same world as mankind, yet mankind never saw them.

It made him wonder again if what else he thought false would prove true.

Lir broke into Mordred's thoughts by slamming his axe on his shield. The loud crash reverberated across the hall. He threw the shield at Mordred.

"You'll need this more than I will, whelp. Come, let's get your beating over with. The gods are not happy you brought about WinterKil's demise. They look forward to seeing you gone."

Picking up the shield, knowing Lir was right, Mordred slipped it over his right hand. He reached for the silver axe strapped to his side and backed up several paces.

Lir's massive body vibrated with unspent energy. He stood like a giant, bare-chested, long hair and beard flowing past his shoulders, axe head gleaming. Mordred had no doubt he was in for a beating. Just by looking at the Vampyre King, he knew he was the object of his wrath.

The fight began. While Mordred avoided several blows that would have crushed a normal man, he also grunted with the exertion of staying upright. Lir, however, looked as though he was barely expending energy. In fact, the oaf was grinning.

"You can always plead for your life. Of course, it won't make the gods look on you with any favor, but, it will stop the beating."

Mordred grunted, "No," and readied his axe for a damaging blow. He missed. How could someone so large be so agile?

"Think, Mordred. Think before you strike. When you are involved in battle, do your damage as quickly as possible. Don't let the enemy toy with you as I am. You will end up losing your strength while the enemy may not have used any at all."

"Shut up." Mordred grimaced, allowing his arm to extend backward. "I don't need advice from you. I've fought in all kinds of battles and won."

"Yes, you wouldn't have gotten this far if not for your skills. But this is the ultimate test."

Wanting to tell Lir off, but knowing it would take away more of his precious energy, he bit back the scathing retort. Instead, he tried to focus.

It was no use. Mordred was slammed into a column

from one blow and sent sprawling backward from another. He narrowly missed have his skull cleaved in two by rolling just inches away before the blade struck the stones. He watched in amazement as the tiles cracked from the force of the blow.

Christ! The man was going to be his undoing.

Out of the blue it hit him. He could not possibly defeat a vampyre king while in human form. He would have to call forth his vampyre side. He ducked and feinted to the right, body shuddering from the beating. Mordred thought he heard the bones in his arm crack.

It would be tricky to continue fighting while summoning his dark side. He couldn't miss a beat while Lir kept hammering at him.

Mordred was brought to his knees. Lir backed off and waited.

Gasping, Mordred closed his mind to the outside world, to the crowded hall filled with cheering men. He shut down all his senses and sought the next strike with his mind.

Every bit of him was concentrated on the next maneuver, and on allowing the beast within to surface. Mordred only prayed he would not find himself helpless as he underwent the change.

Mordred could not determine if the snapping sound ringing in his ears was his body breaking from the force of

Lir's blows, or from the shifting. He hoped it was the latter and knew it was when his canines split his lower lip.

Dagger-like nails extended past his fingers, his body contorting internally to accommodate the beast. Mordred kept his wits about him although it was difficult with the red curtain descending.

Sucking in a gulp of air, Mordred hoped to dull the throbbing pain while remaining standing. His heartbeat steady and sure, much slower than it had been, he felt his pulse steady, his muscles bunched beneath his mail as he readied himself for his strike.

He saw Lir smiling. "Yes, Mordred, that's it. Let me greet your vampyre side. Send me a worthy opponent."

Mordred could only utter a guttural moan as he swung his axe. The flat side of the head found a home, slamming into Lir. Stunned, the king was forced to take a few steps back.

A hush fell over the hall. Only the sounds of the opponents breathing and the resounding crashes as their weapons hit stone and metal could be heard.

Mordred advanced on the king, swinging from left to right, and right to left, over and over. His sharpened mind swiftly plotted the best way to reduce the king's threat. He knew if he could keep Lir from returning his blows, he might just beat him.

And it worked. He hammered at the king, his newfound

weapon, the axe, acting as if it were an extension of his body. On and on he slammed it into Lir, forcing the king to grab a shield to ward off his advance.

He would have kept going, but from the balcony over the hall came a loud command.

"Cease! You, Mordred Soulis, have proven to us that you are indeed the Chosen One. Only the Chosen One could withstand as much from Lir and turn the tables. It is done. You have gained the favor of the Norse gods."

It was hard to simply stop. The vampyre wanted nothing more than to spill blood. It did not want to be denied the taste. When he rose to strike the voice came again, like thunder. "Cease!"

"Part of this test is about control. Are you able to maintain control over your vampyre side?" Lir baited him he stood with arms crossed, staring down at Mordred.

Snarling, Mordred tried to once again gain the upper hand on his vampyre side. Everyone in the hall remained quiet, watching his struggle, but soon he felt his teeth recede into his gums, and his lust for destruction became nothing more than a pang of hunger, reminding him he had not consumed human blood in a long time.

"Well done, Mordred," Lir continued, watching him. "You have indeed shown us that you are worthy. Tomorrow you will carry on your quest."

"No," Mordred replied softly. "Tomorrow, I will find my friend."

"The wolf?" asked the voice from above.

"Yes."

"You would delay your progress to find a werewolf?"

"Perhaps searching for his friend and continuing his journey will lead him in the same direction." Lir said. "Did Death not say Dugald's spirit was released back into the New World? That is where Mordred's quest will resume. We will search for the sacred silver box belonging to the Templars there."

Confusion settled in Mordred's mind and suddenly all the blows and physical energy he had spent in the melee took its toll on his muscles and bones.

Lir laughed, a thunderous sound. "I would ask you to stay and drink from the Horn of Plenty, but I see you are in need of some rest. Vestr, escort him back to his chamber. I will come for you when it is time to descend from Valhalla."

✛ ✛ ✛

It was dark and cold in the room far below the Castel St. Angelo. Several red-robed and masked individuals waited in shadow. One lone figure stood on the black marble dais as a monotonal chant echoed off the ancient walls.

They had been in the chamber for hours, and still the spirit Father Simon had called forth at their last meeting had not surfaced. Neither had Father Simon.

The man on the dais finally stopped chanting. The room fell into an eerie silence, broken only by the wailing of yet another heretic being tortured somewhere above.

"It's no use. However Father Simon conjured the entity, he's gone and it's gone. The guards reported seeing him leave in the company of two strange men, one a vampyre. I can only assume this is the being who will thwart our efforts to find immortality, for it was written long ago in the Dead Sea Scrolls that there would be a Soulis that would bring darkness to the world."

The leader did not reveal that he had read the prophecy incorrectly. He alone knew that the Dark One was to lead the world to the light, but the cardinal did not wish anyone but himself to save the world.

"Has Father Simon's body been found?" asked a robed figure.

Irritated that the members would doubt him, he bit back his anger and replied smoothly, "No, there is no body, but what other conclusion can there be? Father Simon was a devout member of the Vatican as well as our order. Only death would keep him away."

"What do we do now?" the voices chorused.

"We begin searching for the Dark One. We will initiate an inquisition throughout the realm that will expose him, and any who side with him. The populace will think it is about religion, but only we will know the truth. We will find him. For us to attain immortality we must find him. He will know how to reach the entity we seek."

"An inquisition? But where? How?"

"We'll start in Spain."

XV

Chapter Fifteen

he wind slammed into Mordred like a wall of icy stone, nearly toppling him on the deck of the Viking dragon ship. The vessel was built for speed and had a shallow hull which allowed it to ride high on the enormous waves of the churning sea.

Lir stood at the helm, legs braced apart, confident and calm. He was not unnerved by the viciousness of the vast ocean. In fact, Lir looked as though he had been born to the water.

Mordred made his way to the Vampyre King. "Are you sure you have sailed this sea before?"

Lir smiled, and yelled above the raging wind, "I've been sailing these waters for centuries, and with the Vikings since well before 1000 A.D., in your time. The seas haven't changed, only the people I sail with."

Mordred eyed the crew. The men were all human but

clearly unafraid of the storm. Each went about his duty with the efficiency of a soldier trained in battle. They expended little energy and were unhindered by the ship's pitching.

They were headed to the New World, a place Mordred thought of as another mythical legend. He'd always been told the world was flat and at some point one would simply sail off the edge. Seeing no land in sight, and having been at sea for several days and nights, it was easy to believe that over the next swell they would reach the edge and fall into oblivion.

Mordred had to face old fears along with learning things that might not prove true. Lir had laughed when he expressed his initial concern over sailing west. He tried to convince the Vampyre King there was no such land and all they would end up doing was reach Asia, if they didn't sail off the edge of the world first.

Lir broke out into his annoyingly loud guffaw, drawing the attention of the sailors. Barking an order, Lir had explained the truth of the world as he knew it. He told Mordred the world was round, never-ending, and that one could not sail off the edge into oblivion as Mordred had been taught.

Nevertheless, it was hard to put old beliefs behind. Mordred gripped the main mast and tried to ride out the storm like the crew. Waves sloshed across the deck. Cold water slammed into him along with the howling wind.

Just when Mordred feared he might never set foot on

dry ground again, he heard a shout. Amazingly, through the low, dark clouds and menacing waves, one of the men had sighted land.

Lir called out a few directions and soon the vessel, with two more following closely, sailed into an inlet of calm waters. Cliffs of rock speckled with greenery rose from the sea to impossible heights before them, while to the right a sloping hill dotted with trees blocked the horizon.

There was a scar that ran upward in the cliffs, and Mordred realized he was looking at a trail.

"Welcome to the New World, Mordred Soulis. Here is a place you have never been, but it belongs on earth and not in any magical plane." Lir spoke as he jumped into a smaller boat to row them to shore.

Mordred followed and soon the small craft edged its way to land.

"Now what do we do?"

"We search for the Templar treasure."

"It is here? How could it be?"

"You think the Templars disappeared because that French king persecuted them? The guardians of the Chosen One had help when they needed it. They required a safe haven, and they found the New World."

Mordred thought back to the Master Templar. "What of Jakob? Could no one have saved him?"

"Even we cannot interfere with what is written. Jakob's time was near and he would have suffered greatly had he lived."

"Suffered greatly? You don't think being burned alive at the stake was suffering?" Mordred asked.

"I'm sure he did suffer. I am also sure his god was with him when it was time for him to pass on. But I also know he was dying. His goodness was being snuffed out in his battle with the entity, Vlad. It was getting harder and harder for him to defend the Templars, and himself, against the darkness. You do realize it was Vlad that put the idea of persecution into the French king's ears?"

Mordred shook his head.

"And there was someone who betrayed him in the end. A man who gave the French the information they needed to plan a surprise attack against the Templars."

"Who?"

"A man you became acquainted with . . . Markus."

"No." Mordred allowed the shock of the news to overwhelm him. He felt as though he was drowning. "Markus was the holiest of the Templars, second to Jakob. He loved Jakob. He could not have been the betrayer."

"I am amazed at your ignorance of your own race," Lir replied. "You know humans are susceptible to all manner of evil, greed being one of the easiest ways to reach a man."

Still Mordred refused to accept what he had heard. There was no way Markus would have turned against the man who had shown him a new life. He could not believe it was true.

Lir broke Mordred's silent reverie. "Come, we go ashore to the old ruins."

Mordred followed Lir through the tall green grasses. The sun just touched the horizon, bathing all the world in one last burst of golden light before the orb gave way to darkness.

They walked for what seemed like hours. Mordred gazed at the sky and saw countless stars piercing the fabric of the night, sending glistening beams of silver light to the forest floor.

After they had crossed an expanse of beach, the crew climbed the narrow path in the rocks, and once above they moved cautiously across an enormous meadow. They were in the depths of the forest.

Mordred heard the voices of men speaking quietly. They were talking about the numerous trees and how many boats they would be able to build here if they settled.

As they continued into the heart of the forest, Mordred became aware of the presence of others. He looked into the depths of the shadows but could not make out what made him feel as if he were being watched.

Lir dropped back to walk beside him. "You feel them, too."

"Yes," Mordred answered softly, listening to the sounds of the leaves whispering in the cool night air. Something else spoke beneath the forest noise. Something quiet, watchful, and wary.

"We will be attacked shortly."

Alarmed, Mordred reached for his Blood Sword.

"No, you won't need that one. Use your axe. What comes to take souls is of human kind."

"Are you sure?"

"Watch."

Mordred would have called out a warning, but before he could give voice to an alert, figures emerged at a run from behind the trunks of the trees. Overhead, hidden among the branches, still more revealed themselves. A chilling whistling sound filled the air and Mordred knew it was arrows.

"Get down!" he ordered, hoping the men could see well enough to stay out of the line of fire. He heard the sickening sound of flesh being torn asunder, and the shouts of men as they were cut down.

The metallic smell of blood filled the air, thick, heavy and sweet.

While staying hidden, Mordred tried to hold himself in check. He needed to summon his vampyre-self to the surface to enable his sight to become clearer. He could only make out silhouettes and blurred shapes. They moved fast. Almost too fast to be considered human. But Lir had told him they were.

Risking the chance his vampyre-self would rampage among the dead or dying, Mordred knew he needed to call forth the beast if he was to stop the attack. He closed his eyes and felt the thing slither in the deepest part of himself.

All around him men were dying, blood was spilling, and within the blink of an eye Mordred entered the fray. He felt arrows strike him, but they caused no pain. His body cut off all feeling from his nerves.

He felt only anger and hunger. Both proved deadly.

The things attacking them were all too human. But they were clad in an odd manner and used crude weapons. Mordred fended off the blows from several clubs. His hand shot out and grabbed an attacker by the throat and squeezed, lifting him off the ground. Crushing his windpipe, Mordred threw the him down and reached for another.

The hunger built until it burst through, making it impossible for Mordred to focus on anything but drinking blood. The next enemy he caught hold of he brought close to him. Struggling, the attacker put up a fight. Mordred smelled fear wafting from him and looked into the strange black eyes and saw terror. He sank his formidable canines into the victim's throat, tearing flesh and muscle, sucking and swallowing the warm blood.

Gorging himself, Mordred killed again and again. He was heady with the unfamiliar sensations pouring through him, visions he didn't understand. It was as though he was drunk. He saw tent-type dwellings and small birch bark water craft. He saw men with long dark hair and black eyes gathered around in a circle.

His mind showed him images he could not fathom, he saw things he was unsure were real, or a product of his imagination And still, he killed and feasted.

He was brought short by the whispered words of his next victim. The man was bare-chested, but wore deerskin breeches. Around his neck hung a leather thong filled with the teeth of a wolf. He had no fear. He pointed to the sky as Mordred held him and uttered words in a deep, guttural tone.

"You seek the man-wolf. His soul is lost to you. He is missing, wandering the world, searching for his spirit. It is not here."

It took Mordred only moments to assimilate and make sense of the language he spoke. He shoved the man away from him in shock.

Still, the man pointed to Mordred as if in a daze. His dark eyes shone brightly beneath the moon emerging from the clouds. "You and he are the same, but not so. He looks for you."

Before Mordred had a chance to ask a question, Lir approached, blood running in rivulets down his chin. He grabbed the enemy and without a pause, sank his fangs into his neck. After a few moments of twisting and turning, the body went still and Lir pushed it toward Mordred.

Angrily Mordred stepped over the body and faced the Vampyre King. "What the hell did you do that for? He knew about Dugald. Why did you kill him?"

Lir crossed his massive arms across his chest, and stood smiling, totally unaffected by Mordred's fury. Calmly, he said, "Drink his blood, Mordred, for the answers you seek."

"What the . . . ?"

"Do not betray ignorance. The blood contains the memories. Drink it to learn more about your wolf. You must hurry, as with the departing spirit go the memories."

Still in his vampyre form, Mordred fell to his knees and pulled the body toward him. There was no point in bemoaning the fact that Lir had killed the stranger. He was dead and there was much to be gained by absorbing the memories, locked in his blood.

Mordred drank and the pictures came. They revealed his friend wandering aimlessly, first as a wolf, then as a man. He was confused, running, and afraid. Where was Dugald?

He stopped feeding and rose.

Bodies littered the forest floor. Copious amounts of blood had been spilled, turning the dirt to a red mud.

"What were they?" Mordred asked, realizing he hadn't used his axe at all.

"A different race of humans from those of the countries you come from. These people live close to nature and worship other gods than the one you have known."

"But why did they attack? We meant them no harm."

"Didn't we?" Lir queried, wiping a stream of blood from his mouth. "The Vikings have been coming here for over four hundred years, and like any other place they travel to they only know how to conquer and subjugate. They tried it here, but it has all but failed for them. They once thought to create a whole new existence for themselves in the New World, but these native peoples who were here long before the Norse, felt differently."

They truly had found a New World and a new people.

He wondered then at the ignorance of those living in the countries of his homeland. There, the Church denounced anything other than their doctrine to be heresy. It kept people blind to the reality of the rest of the world and by keeping them blind, it rendered them harmless.

"So, the Vikings found this place long ago and didn't tell anyone?"

Lir laughed. "Why the hell would they? Other peoples,

other countries would only seek to take away what they discovered. The Norse are a lot of things, but they are not stupid."

"What of the native people? Have they always attacked?"

"Ever since the Norse struck and killed several members of the original band that came to greet them, yes. They have no love for intruders."

Movement to the right alerted Mordred that not everyone was dead. He watched two men drag the bodies of the fallen Norse. They stacked them neatly in a pile.

"What are they doing?"

"They will build a fire and bring a huge cauldron from the ship and fill it with water. Once it is hot enough they will boil the bodies."

Mordred arched his brows.

"They will take all the bones from the dead and bring them back with them on the ship. When they reach a location where there is a church, they will bury the bones. They believe they must find consecrated ground."

"But, I thought Vikings believed in the gods like Odin and Thor," Mordred replied, curious as to why the men felt the need to find a church. He had always been taught the Norse were barbarians because of their belief in many gods and goddesses.

Lir sighed, and it was the first time Mordred saw something other than strength. The Vampyre King kept himself as emotion-free as a rock, but Mordred thought perhaps he detected a bit of sadness in his voice.

"It was that way in the beginning. The time before your time. Our gods and goddess ruled our world. I ruled the Viking world. Then came your Christianity, and the conversion of the Norse. Only one god could be worshipped, and so all the others were thrown out. The ones for harvest and fertility, the ones for luck in battle, and the ones that brought the rain were no longer considered necessary. All the different entities the Vikings once considered important enough to pray to died when Christianity came. The old ways were considered pagan and unworthy. An entire culture was lost. It is why the gods and goddesses now reside in Valhalla. They are no longer needed, and they won't be until the end time."

"What of the Valkyries that take the heroes from the battle fields?"

"In your world they are angels. Once, they were battle maidens who soothed the newly deceased in their passage from life to death. You see, every aspect of the previous culture of the Norse has been replaced, used and changed, and cast out. Valkyries become angels. Important days of the past become Holy Days in your church. Some day, I will show you how similar the ancient cultures are to your new religion.

"Still, despite all Christianity has done, it cannot stop the growing threat to its own kind. Even after the removal of all the other gods and goddesses, evil still lurks in the heart of mankind. It has always been there, and it will always be there. It is humans who harbor the evil, not the gods they pray to."

Mordred fell silent, thinking about what the Vampyre King had told him. This was the third culture he had become acquainted with that had been decimated because of the new church. Centuries-old ways of being, and doing, had fallen beneath papal decrees or the booted feet of Crusaders. Egyptians, Norse, and even the desert peoples, all paid the ultimate price not bowing to the European religion. And, for what?

The threat against humans was not one created by another culture. It came from a band of holy men discontent with the laws of life and death. They wanted immortality and sought to bend the rules to their bidding. All of mankind must suffer.

"Lir, why do you help me?"

A laugh echoed throughout the forest. Lir glanced down at Mordred and offered his hand, helping him to stand. "I did not say I would help you, yet. I am merely curious to see just how you plan to defeat Vlad, whom we call Loki. And, I am most anxious to see my brethren."

"You don't think I will succeed?" Mordred asked, not really sure he wanted the answer.

"At this time, no. But we will see how long you can preserve yourself and how much you will learn before Loki comes back for another fight. Now, still your vampyre soul and help the men gather the bones. We cannot stay. These people are connected with nature so thoroughly they will know your secret. It is dangerous to linger."

"But, we just arrived. Surely they cannot threaten two vampyres?"

"A vampyre and a half-breed," Lir corrected. "And, you will do as I say. I do not speak lightly of things such as this. These people are spirit walkers. They will know the truth of you and we cannot be sure they will not have a means to destroy you. Now, go, I will meet you at the ship at dawn. Should I fail to arrive, sail without me. You will need the two survivors if you are to get back to your homeland. They are good sailors and know the way. But, do not stay overlong. Should the native people come again there will be more of them and they will kill your navigators."

"Where are you going?"

"As if I would explain myself to you, pup? Never mind. I will be back at daybreak, otherwise, I will find you at some point in your quest. Now, go."

Mordred kept his eyes on Lir. One moment he was

standing tall and proud, and the next he disappeared into a flock of black birds that flew swiftly away in the night.

Morning dawned and there was no sign of the Vampyre King. The ship was filled with the bones of the dead men. It had been gruesome work boiling the flesh from the bodies, and dissolving the organs into a thick, putrid stew, but as the first fingers of light touched the beach the last man was brought to the deck.

Mordred scanned the expanse of white sand down from where the ship had anchored. Then he looked to the rocky slope with its narrow path and, finally, into the distance, searching the line of trees marking the edge of the forest.

Nothing moved. There was no sign of Lir. The two Vikings were nervous and anxious to be away. They felt it dangerous to linger in the daylight and looked to Mordred for a sign they might begin the sail home.

When the sun was high, Mordred knew he could wait no longer. He had no idea what had happened to the Vampyre King or more aptly, what *could* happen to a vampyre king, but he could not linger knowing his chance to sail home rested with the two survivors.

It was clear neither Norseman had witnessed his transformation. Or, if they had, they made no mention of sailing with a creature of the undead variety.

"It is time," he said to the men. Mordred wasn't even sure if the three of them would be able to handle a ship that had originally housed thirty sailors, but the Vikings assured him they would manage.

When they got under way and the vessel sailed smoothly out of the harbor, Mordred glanced at the beach once more. All that remained of their arrival was the two dragon prows they had buried in the sand. The other ships had been burned.

Slowly, the ship moved away from the strange New World and Mordred wondered just how long it would be before the people of his country would learn that there was indeed land beyond the horizon.

He wondered how long the New World would remain new. Was it only a matter of time before his kind, the human kind, came to the shores to despoil and foul the pristine location? Would the church seek a foothold here, too, strangling the life from its native inhabitants? Only time would tell.

The wind picked up once the vessel was clear of the harbor. They raised the striped, square sail and used the strong breeze to begin the journey home. They had no idea how long it would take or if they would even make it back.

The endless cycle of day and night was made more monotonous on the open waters. It had been smooth sailing for the most part until one morning the sky was filled with an ominous red glow. The two Vikings, Thorvald and Svenin, crossed themselves and told Mordred the heavens did not bode well.

Shortly after sunrise, the sky grew black. Ominous clouds gathered on the horizon and slowly edged their way closer to the ship. Without the sun, the men used other means to take their position. They checked the waters and made measurements with odd-looking instruments. Mordred wisely kept silent.

The rain came a while after the clouds had blocked out all light. It was a cold, driving rain that covered the deck in a fine, ice-like sheen, making movement across the surface extremely dangerous.

The heavens opened up, letting loose a deluge. Thunder roared across the sky and the darkness was rent by jagged bolts of lightning. The Vikings seemed not at all concerned. They explained Thor was their God of Thunder and he was speaking to them.

The wind howled furiously and the men thought it wise to furl the sail before it was shredded. Struggling, Mordred and Svenin brought it down. The ship swayed first from prow to stern, then from side to side, rocking dangerously low. Sea water poured over the sides, drenching everything that wasn't already wet from the rain.

Mordred saw real fear in the men's eyes. They desperately tried to determine the direction they were headed, but the boat was being flung from crest to crest as if it were no more than a wooden toy.

Just as the vessel headed down a wave several times taller than the mast of the ship, Svenin was flung across the deck. He tried to grab on to the railing, but it was no use. As the craft bucked and tossed, he lost his grip. Before Mordred could get to him, he was gone, sucked into the now-black sea.

He watched Thorvald cross himself.

"Come here!" Mordred shouted to be heard above the storm. "I will tie you to the mast."

The man's eyes widened.

"It is the only way you can keep from being thrown overboard like your friend."

"But what if the ship sinks? Then I will be drowned."

"If the ship sinks, you'll wish you were dead anyway. Now, come on."

Reluctantly, Thorvald edged his way to the mast and watched silently as Mordred wrapped a length of rope around him, binding him to the mast. He then tied a knot and backed away.

"And what of you?" Thorvald shouted.

"I will go back to the steering oar and try to plot a course."

"Look out for rocks. We've lost our bearings and Svenin was the navigator. I've no idea where we are now."

Mordred nodded. He would be happy to weather the storm. There would be time enough to figure out just where they were.

Soaked to the bone from both the sea water and the rain, Mordred wrestled with the waves. He continued to hold on, desperately fighting the storm as it tried over and over to suck him into the sea's hungry jaws. He didn't know how long the bad weather lasted, only that he was exhausted when it was over.

Dawn broke over the deep blue bringing with it a strange calm. There was no wind. No current beneath the boat. It was as if the vessel was on dry land.

Mordred untied Thorvald.

"We are in serious trouble," the Viking said as he looked overboard and then at the sun in the sky.

Mordred wanted to ask what else could go wrong, but it appeared Thorvald would tell him.

"There are no birds. There is no wind and there is no current. We're stuck."

"Stuck? How the hell can that happen?" Mordred growled.

"I've heard about these conditions, but in all my years of

sailing I have never experienced them. They say it can last for days, or weeks, or even months."

"Months?"

"Yes, and we only have food to last us a few days and even less water. Some of the other provisions were washed overboard during the storm."

Mordred wanted to ask about rowing, but in a boat that could hold thirty, he knew it would be impossible.

"So, now what?"

"We wait. There is nothing else we can do."

Mordred felt the sweat trickle down his back between his hauberk and his skin. The air was warm and sticky and there was no hint of a breeze. With the sun beating down on them mercilessly, they would be roasted where they stood.

A couple of days later, Thorvald felt the effects of starvation and dehydration. A long buried memory came back to haunt Mordred. He remembered the Crusade, and the men, and the wide expanse of the endless desert through which they had been forced to march.

He saw the waves of heat undulating over the sand. He smelled the scent of death and the stink of unwashed, ill bodies. He watched as the soldiers succumbed. Until there was only one left. Radoc. That was the last Crusader's name.

Mordred heard his voice begging for his life to be ended.

He told Mordred to drink his blood. Mordred saw himself bringing his sword down to stab Radoc in the chest. After he was sure his heart had stopped, he punctured Radoc's throat with a dagger.

There was a great cloud of dust whirling behind him and the sound of the wind was like that of a malevolent laughter. Vlad.

"Mordred, I cannot take this anymore. I'm crazed for want of water and food. I cannot stand this."

The voice snapped Mordred out of his thoughts. He looked at the thin, blistered form of a once robust Viking and realized Thorvald was asking of him the same thing Radoc had.

"Just hang on a little longer, Thorvald," Mordred said.

Another fear consumed Mordred. It had dogged him for days. His dark side wanted nothing more than to taste the blood of the lone Viking. His human side was sick with disgust.

"I cannot live another day like this. Look, even the sharks circle. They know it's the end."

Thorvald knew the boat had not moved far for many days. The heat worsened and the sun seared the flesh anew each time dawn broke over the water.

He hated himself for his thoughts. Quietly, Mordred damned himself for what he was.

"Please, Mordred, please, kill me. Please, take my life. Perhaps you can live on and tell my family what became of me. Don't tell them I begged you to take my life," Thorvald rambled in a hoarse voice. "I know the Valkyries will not bring me to Valhalla. I know this is a disgrace, but I cannot bear the pain anymore."

Worse than his own thoughts were the pleadings of a man driven insane by the conditions. Mordred knew the best thing he could offer the Viking was a quick death. He reached for dagger strapped to Thorvald's waist.

Mordred did not say a word. He brought the dagger up and slit the Viking's throat.

As much as he did not want to drink, he found he could not deny himself. Feeling the beast roar to life, he bent his head.

Mordred was clad only in his black breeches and hauberk, having divested himself of mail many days ago. He slumped to the deck after taking his fill, forcing the vampyre-part of himself to recede back to the bowels of his existence.

He had no idea where he was. All he knew was that he was now the sole survivor on a boat filled with the bones of the dead, in the middle of the ocean. And then he heard voices.

At first, he thought he, himself, was feeling the effects of the elements. He rose and saw a ship was nearing his vessel. Slowly, carefully, it edged its way closer.

Adrift

"Ho, there. Is anyone on board?" a voice called out across the water.

Mordred raised his arms over his head and waved. He saw the approaching ship was full of oarsmen diligently rowing in the otherwise still sea.

"Climb aboard and we'll get you safely back to port. It's been dead water for the past month out here. All kinds of sailors have died. You're lucky we happened across you."

The ship, larger than Mordred's and designed differently, bumped up against the Norse vessel. A rope ladder hung over the side. Mordred climbed it and slid over the railing to the deck.

A tall, red-haired man with a beaming smile held out his hand. "Peace, friend, you are saved. I am Columbus, Christophe Columbus, but you may call me Christopher."

Mordred shook the offered hand and smiled weakly, feeling incredibly tired. So much had happened to him over the past many months. He'd lost track of what year they were in.

"What is the date?"

Christopher continued to smile. "It is August the twenty-second, fourteen-hundred and ninety-two. You must have been at sea a long time to become so disoriented. Where did you come from?" He stopped, then and waved another sailor over. "Forgive my manners, Antonio, please bring water and food to our guest."

Mordred was about to reveal he had no need of these things, but thought better of it. Christopher walked to the prow and raised a hand to his brow, shading the setting sun from his eyes.

"You are lucky indeed that we happened past. There is no telling how long you might have languished before the currents and the winds returned. It is a curse, I tell you. A curse against the Church for their Inquisition . . . But, I digress. I am interested to hear your tale. Where were you coming from?"

Mordred paused, as a man came up to them and laid a flask and a loaf of bread out on a small wooden table nailed to the deck of the ship. Christopher motioned Mordred to sit in one of the four chairs, also nailed to the deck.

"You should start small. Sips of water and a few chunks of bread. Until your stomach gets used to the food and water. So, now, tell me, what grand adventures can you share?"

The man's blue eyes lit with amusement, but Mordred did not feel he was being mocked. Columbus rested both elbows on the table and leaned in, waiting for Mordred to begin.

"I'm afraid I don't have much to tell."

"Nonsense, good man, you can start with your name and how you came to be sailing a Norse ship in these waters. Did you truly come from the north countries, or were you trading in the south?"

Mordred paid no mind to the men nearby who were coiling great lengths of rope. At a further distance sat the oarsmen, rowing steadily, propelling the ship across the blue-green water and leaving his Norse vessel far behind.

"My name is Mordred, and I was on a trading mission," he lied. What else could he say?

"Please to meet you, Mordred," Christopher replied politely. He went on, excitement palpable. "So, which is it? Wool from the north, or exotic spices from the south?"

"Actually, we sailed west."

Christopher leaned back, arms dropping to his sides. His eyes grew even wider. Several of the men at work on the rope fell silent, too.

"Go on . . ." Christopher prodded. "Did you find Asia? Or did you sail to the edge of the world?" He let out a hearty laugh.

"You do not believe in the edge of the world?" Mordred asked.

"Listen, I've been a sailor all my life. I've plied all manner of waters and I say the earth is round. I'm not the first one to make that claim, but I plan to prove if you sail west you won't hit Asia. I think you'll find more exotic lands and countries and peoples. Am I right?"

As Mordred's hesitation, Christopher said, "Yes, I know

these are dangerous times and what I speak of could be deemed heresy, but I only want to prove that I am right. I've been petitioning the king and queen of Spain. They haven't come around yet, but I'm sure they will soon enough. What can you tell me that might help me plead my case?"

As the sun slid below the horizon and the boat moved swiftly over the water, Mordred told Columbus of what he had seen. It seemed perfectly normal to share the information. The man was right. It would only be a matter of time before others discovered the New World.

The pair, Columbus and Mordred, stayed awake all night speaking of Mordred's travels. When dawn broke, they had entered the harbor of a small fishing village. The men set to work mooring the vessel as the captain collected his gear and slung the sack over his shoulder. He motioned for Mordred to follow him.

"I've friends in this town and they can see to your comfort until you are rested. Then, we'll see if we can find a ship heading back to your homeland. Come, let's go have a real drink on land."

The pair jumped over the vessel's low gunwhales and walked down a wooden gangplank. Mordred wore only black breeches and boots, his own sack of belongings hung from one shoulder. Christoper wore heavy cloth breeches and a woven white shirt, his wild red hair was untamed. He pointed to a pub just on the other side of the main street.

"We'll quench our thirst there."

Mordred sensed something was not right with the town. The people all appeared subdued and hushed. Each merchant, each peasant, avoided eye contact. He had seen this before in the mountains to the east. It was the result of some tragic event, which left people afraid.

He was about to mention it to Christopher when he felt a hand slam down hard on his shoulder. Mordred spun around ready to take a swing at the offender, but halted in mid-strike recognizing the robes of a priest.

Surrounding him stood a group of heavily armored guards. Mordred was calculating his escape, determining how many men there were, when someone hit him over the back of the head. Though his vampyre-self was quick to rise to the surface, Mordred was not willing to reveal the beast until he knew what was going on.

Gritting his teeth against the pain from resisting the change and from the blow to his head, he closed his eyes and sank to the ground, unconscious.

XVI

Chapter Sixteen

ou have been found guilty of spreading blasphemy against the church. You claim there are lands to the west. How do you know this? And it was reported to us you murdered your kinsman on your vessel. For this you must be punished. I ask you again . . . what magic do you practice? Does the Devil possess you?"

Mordred only wanted to sleep. He didn't have the energy to lift his lids. Too much had happened for him to have the strength to continue. He needed to rest.

He ignored the voice, thinking it part of a strange dream he had been having.

Suddenly, Mordred choked and sputtered as cold water poured over him. Opening his eyes, he snarled. A brown-robed priest held an empty bucket while another black clad holy man made the sign of the cross.

"You will tell us your name, heathen, or it will be pulled

from you. We have the ways and means to make you repent. You cannot escape from us, and if you are the Devil's child, we shall know of it."

Confused, Mordred tried to wipe his now soaked black hair from his eyes, but found his arms restrained by heavy manacles. He struggled.

This brought laughter from the man in black.

"As I have said, you cannot escape the Inquisition. You are one of our prisoners now and until you repent, you will belong to us, body and soul. Especially the soul as that is most what we are interested in saving."

"The Inquisition?" Mordred queried.

"Surely you have heard of it. In Spain we are hunting down the enemies of God, such as yourself, and destroying them, or saving their souls."

Mordred heard a bloodcurdling scream and the scent of burning flesh filled his nostrils.

"I think I'm going to be . . ." He couldn't finish. Looking around he saw that there were all sorts of people in the same chamber. Some were chained as he was to a flat surface, while others hung on the walls, mouths stuffed with rags.

Mordred watched as a woman on one of the tables, stripped naked, was being burned with a red hot piece of metal. He struggled again at his bonds but made no progress in releasing them.

"You best stop trying to avoid the inevitable. God has brought you to us, my son. You are in need of salvation and we will give it to you. Now, who are you and why do you wear the mark of the Devil?"

"I don't know what you are talking about," Mordred rasped angrily, noticing that his clothes were missing.

The man in black smiled, but it did not reach his eyes. Mordred immediately sensed the priest was well acquainted with torture and would not hesitate to use it.

This wasn't the Crusade however, so why were people being treated in such a cruel way?

The man moved closer and revealed a gold chain. From it dangled the charm Anubis had given him. "You wear the mark of the Devil on your back and this trinket confirms it. How dare you bring your filth here? You must pay for all your evil deeds. Rest assured, we will cleanse your soul."

Mordred couldn't think clearly. By rights he could simply transform himself into the vampyre and break the chains. Then he might escape, but to where? He was in Spain, that much was clear, but how far away was safety and how wide reaching was this Inquisition?

His head was filled with a strange fog. It clouded his vision and his mind. He closed his eyes only to find himself the recipient of another bucket of icy water.

"No, no. You won't escape me. Each time you close your

eyes, I'll be here to bring you back. And next time, we'll try heat instead of cold. Now, tell me what I want to know." The holy man's voice rose higher and his look sent a clear message that he was fast losing his patience.

"I was in the crusa . . ." Mordred realized that story wasn't going to work. "That was a gift."

"A gift? From who?"

"I don't remember."

"You don't remember? He doesn't remember! Markus! Bring the hot iron over here. Perhaps we'll burn the truth from him."

Mordred's head turned to the right, but he could not make out the figure the priest had called Markus. As he turned back, he felt pain as the searing metal was applied to his chest. Roaring with anguish, Mordred struggled to break free of his bonds.

"Again," said the priest and the iron was placed on Mordred's chest. Now, he could smell his own flesh burning.

"Bring in the hammer. If he will not tell us willingly who he is, then we will force it out of him. Such a tiresome job."

Mordred felt his hands being pressed down against the table. His fingers were stretched.

"I'll give you one last chance. Who are you?"

It was impossible to tell the man the truth. Mordred knew from what Father Simon had said that the Soulis clan had some connection to the church. Some bad connection. He would not reveal his name. He was so exhausted and so filled with pain however, he doubted he could come up with a plausible lie.

The priest never took his eyes from him, apparently watching for a sign of treachery. When Mordred did not immediately answer, the man nodded to someone just outside his view.

He heard the crack of bone before a sharp jolt shot up his arm and into his head. It took a moment to realize someone had just smashed his thumb.

"Break each finger until he talks, and if you finish with his fingers and he's still not cooperating, move to his knee caps. Put him on the rack until every bone is pulled from every socket of his miserable body. If he doesn't die, we'll render him so useless the Devil won't want him back."

Several more fingers were broken. Mordred's mind was filled with red and the beast refused to heel any longer. The tired feeling plaguing him since he had sailed to the New World returned. He had no strength to prevent the vampyre from breaking loose in self-preservation.

His mind swam in a sea of crimson and he knew there would be a blood bath. And, oddly, Mordred felt no remorse.

Sneak Preview

L.G. BURBANK
PRESENTS

LORDS OF DARKNESS

VOL: III

THE
HEARTLESS

Coming October 2006

Prologue

elease Mordred Soulis at once!"

Lir the vampyre king bellowed before stepping aside to allow Odin entrance to the ornate hall. The Norse king wore garb similar to Lir's and looked just as fierce.

Their faces were thunderous masks of fury. Lir, clad in a thick, sleeveless, silver mail shirt and leggings, stalked across the polished marble floor toward the object of his anger. He clenched his jaw. His bare, muscular arms bulged as he balled his fists. Feet planted firmly apart, he waited for a response.

The chamber was filled to bursting with all manner of beings. Lir knew every one. Each, man, woman or thing, was a ruler in his own right. Each reigned over his dead. From the feather-covered Aztec king, to the leather clad Irish king, they were all assembled in this Court of the Dead to determine the fate of Mordred Soulis.

Mordred had officially died while enduring torture in Spain during the Inquisition. The fact he was only half immortal was cause for concern among several of the kings. Some felt the Chosen One should simply remain dead, while others thought his mission far from over.

Lir liked none of it. It rankled, the notion the fate of the one he was to protect rested in the hands of the other kings and queens. He fixed Death with a murderous glare.

Unaffected, Death rose from his throne of bones. He held his chin slightly higher than eye level, leaving him to peer down his helm-covered nose at the vampyre and his Norse god.

"No."

Steel gray eyes sparked with gold fire and widened in disbelief. "What? How dare you refuse me?"

"And how dare you burst in here thinking to tell me how to run my domain? I would never presume to instruct you on how vampyres should exist in this world. I would never dream of coming to Valhalla to treat you with such disrespect," Death countered.

Lir opened his mouth. Then, discovering he lacked words, closed it again though he continued to a send threatening glare Death's way. Odin mirrored him.

Hel, Germanic ruler of the netherworld stood up, her long gown shimmering like black water, cascading down her body to pool at her feet. When she moved the dress rippled, revealing her decomposed legs, the bones of a long dead corpse. "Odin, what brings you and your vampyre here?" She offered the men a beguiling smile.

Lir narrowed his eyes. He did not trust the woman. He trusted no one whose reign was over death.

Odin smiled back. "As if you didn't know. Mordred Soulis must be released. It is not his time to leave the earthly plane."

"Says who?" came the voice of Arawn, Welsh ruler of the underworld. "You don't belong down here."

"I move through both the worlds of the living and the dead, along with Lir. It is not your place to tell me where I belong." Odin paced the floor, coming to a halt in front to Arawn. He leaned toward the blond man threateningly.

Ignoring Arawn's comment, Lir spoke to the crowd. "Is there no one else here who will speak on Mordred's behalf?"

A man of greenish hue, accompanied by two, four-eyed dogs, stepped from the throng. "I'm willing to hear why you think he should be returned to the living."

Lir acknowledged the Hindu god with a nod. "Anyone else?"

A familiar voice sounded in the hall. "I'm with you, Lir. I think Mordred should be returned immediately."

Death whirled, sending his black and purple cape flying out behind him. He stepped down from the dais. "I do not recall summoning you, WinterKil."

The Valkyrie, once Odin's favorite, shot him a cool smile as she walked in his direction. Great white wings swayed with her motion. "I don't serve you. You may have determined to keep me here, but it does not mean I honor you. Now, Lir, you were saying?"

Turning in a full circle, Lir surveyed the Court of the Dead. Osiris and Anubis he could pretty much count on to release Mordred. Hades he couldn't be sure of. The Norns could be very fickle, but he returned the smiles of the Norse Fates.

He couldn't begin to predict which way Xolotl, the Aztec underworld god would go. Ah Puch, the Mayan king of the dead, was easier to guess. Perhaps, because one of the vampyre kings resided in the Mayan kingdom, the ruler would champion Mordred's release.

Emma-O, the Japanese guardian and judge of the dead sat next to Erlik, the Siberian ruler, neither giving an indication of his true feelings. Every culture, every race, every belief was represented and every one of them had a stake in the outcome.

"The very fact that all of you have seen fit to leave your realms and come here gives credence to Mordred's value among us," Lir said. "He must be returned to the living. In truth, he did not fully die . . ."

"His human side *did* die," Death said, cutting Lir off, "and that's all we care about. Without his living, human form he can't be returned to the earthly plane."

"That is true," Odin said. "But you forget, conveniently, that he is also partly immortal, and that part grants him the right to live again."

A whispered hiss filled the chamber. The crowd parted to reveal Kabil, another of the vampyre kings. "Lir is correct. Mordred is part vampyre and therefore not held to the same rules as mortals."

"But his human side has died three times already," Death whined. "By rights he should be mine now."

Standing in his primordial form, Kabil looked like a thing from a nightmare. His leathery wings rustled and his mouth foamed with copious amounts of saliva. Large black eyes took up most of his face; two tiny holes served as his nose. He cleared his throat. "He is not human and has greater cause than a mere mortal. What do you think will happen to us if mankind goes away? If they are destroyed there will be none left who believe in us, even you, Death.

Then what? Surely even you can understand why he must be released."

Balinese god Batara Kala said, "Kabil sees clearly why we must make an exception. There is one more powerful than each of us individually who is trying to destroy the human race, and as much as some of us might wish it otherwise, we are nothing without their beliefs. We must return Mordred to the earthly plane."

Several "ayes" followed.

"Then again," said Shiva, "Death has a point. How many times do we let Mordred's human side return to life? And what of our own realms? We have a balance to keep. How do we know this one incident won't suddenly cause our kingdoms to weaken?"

WinterKil glanced around. "We have no guarantees. And even death is not final, as you all well know. But we have no choice. Every minute we wait and debate the merits of bringing Mordred back to life is another moment the power to destroy us grows stronger."

Death pouted and narrowed his eyes. "I see I'm not going to get my way . . . again. Well, that's fine. I'll give him back to you, but I want something in return."

"What?" Lir and Odin boomed in unison.

Holding his hand up, Death fixed them with an icy

stare. "His human side died. That means I want the part of him that is most human. I want his heart."

There was a collective gasp from the assembled, and they began muttering amongst themselves.

"This cannot be allowed to happen," WinterKil said at length. "Mordred needs his heart to remember his human-ness."

Lir and Odin nodded. "If you take his heart," Lir said, "you take a chance that he may fail in his quest. If he turns completely, if you leave him vulnerable to the dark power seeking to destroy mortals, you will be responsible for the consequences."

Puffing out his chest, Death laughed. "What more misery can be bestowed upon me? I reign in a world of dead things. I have no care what happens elsewhere. And this is the only way I will allow Mordred to regain his life."

"Why, I . . ."

"Unbelievable!"

"The nerve."

"How could he?"

The whispers grew to a roar as everyone milled about in confusion. Some were satisfied, others uneasy.

Standing on a raised dais to view the entire court, Death held both hands high in a motion meant to silence the crowd.

In a few moments, the commotion ebbed, then subsided.

"We are all well aware of what is at stake, but on the other hand we need to continue to protect the balance set forth at the beginning of this age. There are rules, and each time we violate those rules, for whatever reason, we weaken ourselves.

"My final judgment stands. I will release Mordred Soulis to the earthly plane, as Odin and Lir demand. But *I* will keep his heart!"

AUTHOR'S NOTE

This book is first and foremost a work of fiction. Among the pages you will find historical references to real places, people, events, and organizations. However I would like to make it clear that I have used these details for the benefit of the overall fantastical story, changing, embellishing, and recreating things as needed. This book has one purpose, and that is to provide entertainment.

FOR NEWS, UPDATES, CONTESTS
AND BEHIND-THE-SCENES
INFORMATION ON
THE LORDS OF DARKNESS
SERIES, VISIT:

www.lgburbank.com

*For more information
about other great titles from
Medallion Press, visit*

www.medallionpress.com

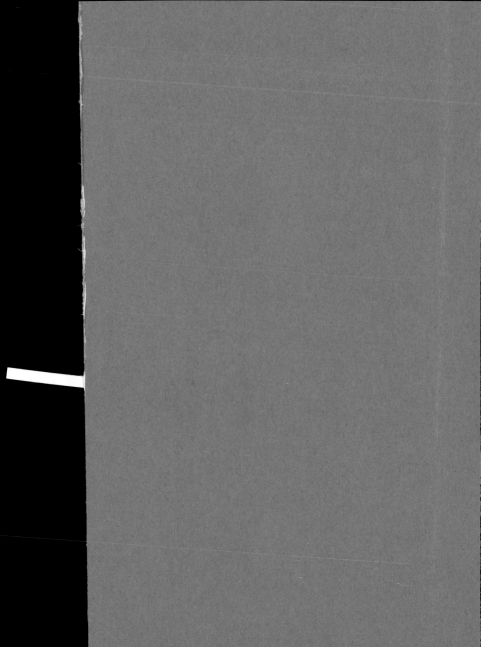